"N... it was a ghost?"

"I'm willing to admit that it's a possibility," Will allowed.

"No wonder your former boarding house manager couldn't get anyone to stay here." Nuala walked to the window and stared out at the dark night, trying to quell her fear.

Will touched her shoulder. "Nuala, you don't have to be alone tonight," he said gently. *Nothing ever turns out the way you expect it,* he hastened to remind himself, cushioning himself for the blow of her refusal.

Her eyes studied his, seeming to resolve something of importance. She said softly, "My place or yours?"

"What?" He was sure he hadn't heard her correctly.

"I don't want to sleep alone, Will," she said.

"Are you sure, Nuala?" he asked, thinking his chest would burst with his longing for her.

"I'm sure."

ABOUT THE AUTHOR

Pamela Browning is a former nonfiction writer who decided to write fiction one cold rainy day when she was touring a dump for an article about waste reclamation. She says, "As the rainwater sluiced downed my neck, I thought, *There's got to be a better way to get a story!*" Writing romance fiction was it. The warmhearted romances Pam loves to write brought this author in from the cold and into the hearts of the many readers who enjoy her books.

Books by Pamela Browning

HARLEQUIN AMERICAN ROMANCE

101—CHERISHED BEGINNINGS
116—HANDYMAN SPECIAL
123—THROUGH EYES OF LOVE
131—INTERIOR DESIGNS
140—EVER SINCE EVE
150—FOREVER IS A LONG TIME
170—TO TOUCH THE STARS

These books may be available at your local bookseller.

Don't miss any of our special offers. Write to us at the following address for information on our newest releases.

Harlequin Reader Service
901 Fuhrmann Blvd., P.O. Box 1397, Buffalo, NY 14240
Canadian address: P.O. Box 603,
Fort Erie, Ont. L2A 5X3

The Flutterby Princess
Pamela Browning

Harlequin Books

TORONTO • NEW YORK • LONDON
AMSTERDAM • PARIS • SYDNEY • HAMBURG
STOCKHOLM • ATHENS • TOKYO • MILAN

This book is for Melanie Rowe—
a hard Rowe to whoa.

Published January 1987

First printing November 1986

ISBN 0-373-16181-6

Printed in Canada

Chapter One

"Anthony Guest House," read Nuala in the light of the match. The flame flared and went out, scorching her fingertips. With a sharp exclamation, she dropped the hand-drawn map showing the way to the boarding-house. The paper landed somewhere on the floor of the hearse.

Nuala fumbled around with her foot, which encountered layers and layers of white gauze. Fabric ripped. It was those crazy pointy-toed shoes; she should never have bought them at that last flea market. Still, they were just the thing to go with the long flowing dress and the high conical hat. But they weren't so good for driving.

Nuala gave up on the slip of paper. She didn't have another match, and the map was lost in the wispy convolutions of her skirt. She'd have to find the boarding-house on her own, and it shouldn't be too hard as long as she was on the right road.

Rain slashed against the windshield, rendering visibility almost nil. A diaphanous mist glistened and swirled like smoke in the beam of the headlights. Long swaying beards of Spanish moss brushed the roof of the hearse, and Nuala shifted forward in her seat, peering

anxiously into the gloom of the surrounding woods.
What if, after she arrived at the Anthony Guest House,
there was no room for her? She hadn't been able to
reach anyone on the phone when she'd called ahead. A
droning computer voice had informed her that the
number was not in service, which was anything but reassuring.

"Nice weather we're having," intoned Cole, the mynah bird, who occupied a cage beside her on the front
seat. "Nice weather we're having. Nice weather we're
having."

"I ought to disconnect *you*," Nuala said. "Hush."

"Once upon a time, in a land far away," Cole said in
a hushed and reverent voice. "Nice weather we're having."

"You're an exasperating old buzzard," she told him
with affection.

"What a *guy*!"

Nuala pulled her old raincoat over the cage, and Cole
subsided with a peevish squawk.

"Let's see," Nuala said, slowing the hearse. "We've
gone five miles, I'm sure of it. Where *is* this place, anyway?"

And then, in a break in the woods, she saw it in the
headlights. Her heart sank.

It was a huge old house, two stories, built of sodden
gray clapboard, which, judging from the flaking paint,
had orginally been white. The house was aproned by a
wide front porch, and it was surmounted by a gabled
roof adorned with cupolas; the place would have given
Nuala the creeps if it hadn't been for the smiling pink
plastic flamingo perched smack in the middle of the
quagmire that passed for a front lawn. A swaying sign,
missing some letters, on a post beside the curving

driveway assured her that this was indeed the NTHONY
GUES HOUSE.

"'Gues house' is right," grumbled Nuala, shutting
off the engine. "Maybe I'm supposed to guess if they
take boarders." A muffled squawk came from the covered bird cage on the seat beside her.

There were no lights on in the house that she could
see. A chill wind howled outside the hearse, and Nuala
shivered. She couldn't spend the night in the hearse
again, that was for sure. It was much too cold and damp
on this inclement November night.

What to do? Honk the horn? Get out and ring the
doorbell? She sat for a moment, trying to make up her
mind.

She decided to ring the bell first and see if that got
results. She pulled the conical hat off her head and
tossed it over the back of the seat, but the long trailing
scarf caught on one of the dashboard knobs. Well, the
scarf would provide some protection from the ele-
ments; she wrapped it around her head. She would have
liked to pull on her old Rain Dears, but they were folded
in their vinyl carrying case in the back of the hearse, and
besides, she had an idea that they wouldn't fit over her
pointy-toed shoes. She hauled the raincoat off Cole's
cage, which she hated to do. Removing it would probably stir him up, and that she could do without.

The bird blinked at her but made no sound as she arranged the raincoat over her shoulders, a fact for which
she was grateful. Cole could, if he wanted to, make
enough noise to wake the dead. Which she hoped would
not be necessary in this gloomy place.

As she stepped outside into the curtain of rain, Nuala slammed the hearse door behind her and ran as fast
as she could toward the porch. Weeds sucked at the

pointy-toed shoes as if to pull them off her feet. It was
with some relief that she arrived breathlessly on the
porch, more or less in one piece.

Without stopping to catch her breath, she pounded
with her fist on the front door. She was rewarded not by
welcoming twin rectangles of light beaming through the
glass sidelights, not by the smiling, bespectacled face of
a plump housekeeper, not by the sudden flinging open
of the door as a solicitous voice insisted on taking her
wet coat. No, none of these things happened. What
happened was that a gust of wind flung the equivalent
of a pitcher of rain into her face and the NTHONY GUES
HOUSE sign blew over with a resounding *Thwap!*

Nuala wiped the water out of her eyes and stoically
rewound the scarf more tightly around her head. The
raincoat over her shoulders wasn't doing much good;
her white dress was soaked. Well, that was okay. It
would dry.

She hammered both fists on the door this time, but
again nothing happened. Cautiously she explored the
porch, its floorboards squeaking ominously. Using a
dry corner of the scarf, she wiped a clean spot on one of
the dusty windows and peered inside. Nothing. Only
blackness.

What was she to do? She had driven out of her way
on the recommendation of someone at the fair this
afternoon, and there were no motels nearby. She was
deep in the boondocks near the St. Johns River in
sparsely populated north-central Florida, where she
knew not one soul. She was almost flat broke; she
needed a cheap place to stay, and this was supposed to
be it.

Perhaps she could get in the house. It didn't look as
though she'd disturb anyone if she did, and at least

she'd have a place to dry out. She tried the handle of the door to no avail. The door was securely locked.

"It was a dark and stormy night," intoned Cole from inside the hearse. She could barely hear him over the flailing of the trees.

In spite of it all, Nuala's lips curved into a smile. Soaking wet, and she could still smile. Why, if she stood on one leg she'd look like a twin to that grinning pink flamingo out there.

She laughed. She couldn't help it. She was tired and she was cold and she didn't know where she was going to sleep tonight, and if she couldn't find a warm bed someplace she'd have to sleep in the hearse again. It was funny that Cole had come up with exactly the right phrase from his repertoire, and then there was that silly flamingo standing there with one leg uplifted in garish welcome. If she hadn't been able to see the humor in it all, she would have sat down in a puddle and cried.

Inside the house, the man looked up from his papers. He could have sworn that he heard someone laughing. But who could it be? He was alone here.

A glance out the window told him that no one with any sense would be out in this foul weather. Alarmed, he pulled off his reading glasses and set the papers aside. He listened. He didn't hear anyone laughing now.

He loped down the dark back stairs, wincing at the sudden clap of thunder. He wished he hadn't had the telephone removed. He wished he weren't alone.

He also wished that the former manager of this place hadn't told him about the ghosts that had driven away the last few boarders.

Ghosts? Of course he didn't believe in ghosts. Did he?

Laughing, however briefly, made Nuala feel better. A jagged wire of lightning sizzled the distant sky, and she cringed at the crack of thunder. She'd have to do something—she couldn't just stand there being a human lightning rod.

She ran down the steps and dodged through the numerous big live oaks, wincing as a particularly low-hanging clump of moss clutched with dripping tentacles at her scarf. She'd check the back of the house and see if she could find an open door.

Around back, she thought she spotted a glimmer of light through one of the windows, but it quickly went out. She hesitated, unsure of herself. Could someone be inside? If so, why hadn't whoever it was answered the door?

The man fumbled with the light switch and then, when the bright overhead light flared on, thought better of it and flicked the light off again. The curtains at the kitchen windows were flimsy, and there was no point in letting whoever—or whatever—was out there see him.

He felt slightly ridiculous creeping around the big old house in the dark, but he did it anyway. He made sure the windows in the study were secure, then quietly worked his way through the familiar hallway to the living room, his silent and furtive journey occasionally illuminated by a flash of lightning.

Now that was odd. Out beyond the trees, masked from view by low-hanging moss, a vehicle was parked in his driveway. He could tell that's what it was because the lightning winked off the chrome. He couldn't however, see it well enough to discern the make or the year.

Very quietly and very carefully he opened the front door. He didn't see anyone. He was about to close the door when he heard the voice.

It was a very faint voice, low like a man's. It said, "It was a dark and stormy night. It was a dark and stormy night. It was a dar—"

What else the voice might have said, the man didn't pause long enough to find out. He slammed the door and leaned against it, his heart beating wildly.

What if there was more to those ghost stories than he'd ever suspected?

Nuala tiptoed closer, watching the window where the light had appeared. She didn't see it again. Maybe it had only been the reflection of a bolt of lightning—but if so, why hadn't she heard an answering rumble of thunder?

Slowly she crept closer to the house. Her dress clung to her thighs, and once it tripped her. She yanked at the material, but there were yards and yards of it and it was most tenacious.

She barely discerned a porch in back, so she worked her way toward it, braving a mud slick overlaid with nasty brown leaves, which clung to her ankles like leeches. She considered discarding the shoes, but at least they were some protection from whatever dangers might be lurking in wait, like sharp twigs or snakes....

The man ran through the house, tripping once over a brass gargoyle that served as a doorstop. He wanted to make sure the back door was locked.

He saw it through the kitchen curtain. A trailing flash of white flitting through the trees.

It couldn't be human. Nothing human would be out on a night like this. Unless it was ... insane?

He pulled the curtain aside. The figure had a definite shape, he was relieved to see. A definitely *female* shape.

He narrowed his eyes, trying to peer through the whirling rain. The figure stopped, lifted a foot and regarded the foot intently. That's when he decided that it was a solid figure. A wet figure. And wearing a raincoat yet.

As soon as he realized that it was real, not ghostly, he knew he had nothing to fear. Now he was only curious.

What was it doing there?

A spotlight blazed suddenly, blinding her.

"Gotcha!" said a deep masculine voice.

Nuala screamed and was instantly ashamed of herself. She never screamed.

A lanky figure towered above her on the porch. All she could see was its spare outline, definitely male.

"Come on up here," he said. "I might as well get a look at what's haunting my property."

"I'm not haunting," Nuala said indignantly, fighting with the scarf. It had suddenly developed a mind of its own and was adhering to her face instead of whipping wildly in the wind. She ran up the porch steps as quickly as she could.

"In an outfit like you're wearing, I would most certainly consider what you're doing a haunting of sorts. Halloween was last week. Did you get lost trick-or-treating?"

"Look, do you mind if I come inside? I'm soaking wet and I don't want to stand out here listening to you make wisecracks. I'd like a room for the night, please."

He opened the back door and made a deep bow. "After you," he said soberly. Even though he wore a beard, she noticed the corners of his mouth twitching.

Nuala tried her best to sweep past him with dignity. She found herself in a big, cavelike kitchen with shadows encroaching from all sides. Still, it was dry.

"How do you do?" she said politely, turning to face him. "I'm Nuala Kemp."

The man's frankly startled gaze took in her long rain-saturated scarf, the clinging white dress, the pointy-toed shoes.

"Excuse me, but the last tornado for Oz left a few years ago. There isn't another one—"

"All right. It's obvious that you're not glad to have me as a guest. Why, then, do you run a boarding-house? Why didn't you answer my knock? Why do you—"

"I was concentrating on something and I didn't hear anyone knock," he said. His eyes were the shade of burnt umber and crinkled into fans at the edges. His hair was dark, including the beard. "Anyway," he went on, "I don't run a boardinghouse. That was my grandfather. He's been dead for over a year. The last boarders left six months ago. So I'm afraid you've come all this way for nothing."

This was too much. "Look," Nuala said, barely hanging on to her temper, "I need a place to stay. We'll camp out in the kitchen if we have to. I'll pay."

His eyebrows lifted. He swiveled his head toward the window and peered out the dark pane of glass where the rain rattled ever harder in its fury. He remembered the stentorian male voice intoning, "It was a dark and stormy night."

"You mean there are more of you out there?"

"Well, only one. And it's not human."

His jaw fell, and then he laughed. He couldn't stop laughing. Nuala stared at him, unsure whether to laugh

with him or not. She had laughed earlier, after all. This
was preposterous. She imagined how she must look to
him dressed in this ridiculous costume with her muddy
skirt dragging around her ankles and her long hair
plastered in wet streamers to the sides of her face and
her shoes leaking mud onto the tile floor. Nuala's
mouth curled upward in mirth, and before she knew it,
she was laughing with him.

He shook his head, subsiding into chuckles. "I never
did introduce myself," he said at last. "I'm sorry I was
rude. I'm Will Anthony."

He held out his hand and she shook it. It was warm
and the flesh was smooth and taut. His eyes smiled, and
so did his mouth above that nice beard. Nuala liked
beards on men; her father had worn a beard.

"Now, how about telling me about this *in*human
creature you've brought with you, and I'll see what I
can do to accommodate you."

"It's a bird. A mynah bird," she explained.

"I see," he said calmly. He still looked amused, but
she was beginning to get used to that. She had the feeling he was the kind of man who always looked amused.

"I need a place to stay for a week," she said. "I don't
suppose you can accommodate me for that long,
though, if you're not in the boardinghouse business
anymore."

"I'll put you up," he said. "And you won't have to
camp in the kitchen. There are several serviceable bedrooms in this house, and they're all fully equipped for
guests. Nothing fancy, but they'll do. Do you have any
luggage? I'll carry it in for you."

"I have a suitcase, and then there's the bird cage."

He ducked into a closet and produced a terry-cloth
towel, which he tossed in her direction. "Here," he

said. "You can use that to dry off with for now. Follow me."

Nuala hitched her skirts up and trailed after him up a narrow back staircase.

"These are the stairs for the help," Will called over his shoulder. "The house was built in the days when it was customary to have maids. The front stairs are quite a bit grander."

They reached the second floor, and Will nudged a door open. It creaked on its hinges. He strode to an antiquated dresser and switched on a ceramic-based lamp.

"A bed," Will explained unnecessarily, gesturing at a chipped white metal bedstead. The mattress, which looked distressingly lumpy, was covered with clean striped ticking. Will rummaged in a dresser drawer and triumphantly produced a pair of sheets. A closet shelf yielded a thick blanket and a pillow.

"There you are," he said, looking pleased with himself. "Lodging for the night. The bathroom is down the hall, and I'm warning you—the plumbing plays the *1812 Overture*. But you get used to it after a while."

"We should discuss how much I'm going to pay you," Nuala said uncomfortably. She couldn't afford much.

"Don't be silly. I'm not in the boardinghouse business, as I told you. And I never charge for rescuing damsels in distress." He grinned at her engagingly, and she discovered that she had to tilt her head back to look up at him in such close quarters. He stood well over six feet, and her mother would have said that he needed a little meat on his bones. But he was likable, and Nuala's well-honed instincts and intuition told her to trust him. He seemed, well, *wholesome*.

"All right," she said. "I accept your hospitality. I don't know why you're doing this, though."

"You appeal to my sense of humor." His warmth was contagious, and she found herself smiling back at him.

"It's nice of you."

He shrugged. "I'm a nice guy. Just to prove it, I'll go get your suitcase. And the bird."

"Oh." Nuala unclenched her fingers to reveal a set of damp car keys. "Here are the keys to the hearse."

Will stared. "You drive a hearse?"

She'd have liked to explain, but she sensed that there was no way to do it quickly. She longed to put on dry clothes, and the sooner the better. She pulled the raincoat off her shoulders. "You'll have to cover the bird cage with this or Cole will make a terrific racket."

"What next?" Will said, addressing a stain on the sprigged wallpaper.

"Oh, I can explain everything," Nuala said hastily.

Then she realized that Will wasn't looking at the stain on the wallpaper anymore, but at the outline of her figure, which was clearly revealed now that she was no longer covered by the raincoat. The white fabric was thin, too; thank goodness there was so much of it, or it would have left little to his imagination—which was probably a lively one, judging from the gleam in his eyes.

"I'll get your suitcase. And the mynah bird." He turned and strode quickly out of the room and down the stairs.

Will had returned with her suitcase by the time she'd finished toweling her face and arms dry.

"I left the bird in the kitchen," he explained. "I didn't know if you wanted it in your room or not. Should I feed it something?"

"If you'd make sure there's plenty of water in his dish, I'd appreciate it," she told him.

"Uh, okay. Does—does it bite?"

"Only if he's antagonized. You know, like if he's poked with a stick or something."

"I promise not to poke him with a stick." Will grinned at her. "What's his name again?"

"Cole."

"As in Old King Cole was a merry old soul?"

"No. As in Cole Mynah. You know, because he's so black."

"Cole Mynah. Uh, right."

"It's okay. You're supposed to laugh."

He did. She had never known anyone who laughed quite the way he did, tipping his head back and letting go in robust waves of mirth. When he stopped he said, "That's a horrible pun, you know. Cole Mynah. It's just awful."

"There is no such thing as a horrible pun. The pun requires a certain sophistication, an ability to understand double meanings and to put them into context so that—"

"All right, all right," he said. The corners of his mouth turned up again. "I don't need a dissertation on the pun. It so happens that I'm a punny sort of person myself. Now, why don't you get into dry clothes and I'll make some hot chocolate. You'd better take me up on the offer. It's not one I make lightly. Or often."

"Give me ten minutes," she said, and he signaled an okay sign with his thumb and forefinger before he went out and closed the door behind him. Nuala stood staring at the door, feeling bemused by Will Anthony. Was he always so quick of smile, so kind of eye?

She peeled the gauze dress off layer by layer and hung it over a chair to dry. She dug in her suitcase and found blue jeans and a light blue sweatshirt, both of which she pulled on without bothering with underwear. Then she tried to fluff her damp hair with a comb, but she couldn't drag the comb through its long length when it was so wet, so she plugged in her hair dryer.

To her utter dismay, this promptly blew a fuse. The sudden blackness stunned her.

"Nuala?" Will's alarmed voice echoed up the stairs in the darkness.

Nuala flung open her door and hollered down to him. "I think I just blew a fuse." She was embarrassed; by this time Will Anthony must think she was totally crazy, and a troublemaker to boot.

"Not necessarily. Our electric power in these lonely parts is provided by a company that those of us in the know like to call Florida Flash and Flicker. Sometimes the power fails during a storm. But I'll check the fuses anyway." She heard him slamming drawers and doors downstairs, and it remained pitch-black where she was. Carefully feeling her way, she edged slowly out of the room and made her way downstairs. She abandoned all thoughts of drying her hair and shoved the damp strands back behind her ears.

She reached the bottom of the stairs. The house was completely dark.

"Will?" she said. Her voice sounded very small in the cavernous kitchen.

His voice materialized startlingly close to her ear. "It *was* a fuse. The main circuit, no less. Let me get this candle going." Suddenly a flame dispelled the darkness and illuminated his bearded face. He lit a candle stuck in the neck of an empty brown beer bottle and waved the match to extinguish it. The candle burned with a steady golden glow, giving the kitchen a homey look.

"Dad blast it," he went on, "I meant to get more fuses. I think I'm out. Well, I can go to the hardware store in the morning."

"I'm sorry," she told him. "I didn't mean to cause all this trouble."

"Trouble? There's no such thing as trouble. There's an important rule of life that I subscribe to, and that is that nothing ever turns out the way we expect it to. If we'd all just accept that inalienable truth, then we'd give up our unrealistic expectations, right? And if we didn't expect things to be a certain way, why, then we'd be less often disappointed, wouldn't we?"

"I—I guess so," Nuala said, following his line of reasoning but not sure she agreed with it.

"Now, the thing to do is to make that hot chocolate. I have only one packet left, so I hope you're not very thirsty."

"But the power's off. How can you heat water to make hot chocolate?"

"It's a gas stove. Lucky, isn't it?" He jiggled a tea-kettle on a burner and fumbled with the knobs of the stove. "There. Water's heating and will be ready in a jiff. Are you hungry? I don't have much around here to eat, but I can produce something if I have to."

"No," she said hastily. "Don't go to any more fuss." For the first time Nuala saw Cole's bird cage sitting on one of the kitchen chairs. The bird cocked his head at her and winked one eye.

"Thanks for taking care of Cole," she said.

"You're welcome. Say, you look a lot better than you did before. You clean up real nice."

As she was trying to figure out if he was joking or serious, the whistle of the teakettle startled her.

"Ah," he said. "Now, if I can just—" and he poured the hot water into a mug. "Uh-oh, I think I was supposed to pour the water *over* the chocolate mix." He squinted at the small print on the mix envelope. It was hard to read in the dim light, and he wasn't wearing his reading glasses. "Hmm," he said. He tore the top off the envelope and dumped it into the cup of hot water, which promptly overflowed onto the counter. He grabbed at it, knocked it over, then yelled, "Ouch!" and waved his hand around in the air. In the meantime, the overturned cup dripped its contents onto the floor.

Nuala tossed a nearby dish towel over the mess to blot it up. "Did you burn yourself?" she asked.

"Not seriously," Will said ruefully. "But I spilled your hot chocolate, and it was the last packet. Now there's nothing for you to drink."

"Don't worry, I didn't expect—"

"Aha! That's it! You didn't expect! So you're not disappointed then, are you?" He grinned at her and tossed the towel into the sink.

"Maybe I'll just go up to bed," Nuala said uncertainly. He wasn't what she had expected, either. Did he always say such crazy things?

"Oh, don't do that, Nuala," he said, looking serious. "Sit down. I can offer you only a cup of hot water, but it would warm you, don't you think?"

Nuala sank down onto a kitchen chair and accepted the cup of hot water. She'd never drunk hot water before, but it wasn't bad. Kind of like chicken broth without the chicken. Or tea without the tea. She giggled.

"That's better," Will said, visibly relieved at this display of levity. "Do you know what I thought when I first saw you flitting around between the trees? I thought you were a ghost."

"Oh, really?" she said, her ears perking. "I love a good ghost story."

"There are reputed to be ghosts in this house. I've never seen any, of course," he added, lest she think he was eccentric. He sat across from her, his long legs straddled on either side of his chair, his arms resting across the back of it.

Nuala set her mug down on the table and sent a speculative sidelong glance into the shadows. No doubt about it, this was a spooky old place. Maybe before she left, there *would* be a ghost story. She could hope so, at least.

But Will was still talking. Fighting fatigue brought on by a long and difficult day, she forced herself to listen.

"All of this brings me to Will Anthony's theory number two: Nothing is ever what it seems. Like you, for instance. You weren't a ghost. You weren't an escapee from the state mental hospital, which I thought at first was a distinct possibility. No, with the proper explanation, you turned out to be quite normal. Interesting." Will leaned back and looked at her speculatively.

Nuala knew he'd like her to tell him what she was doing here, but she couldn't oblige. She was exhausted. She yawned. "If you don't mind," she said, "I think I'll be going to bed. I've had more excitement today than I ever bargained for."

"Here, I'll find a candle for you to light your way." Will stood up and rustled in a drawer until he produced another candle, which he lit from the first one. He dripped wax from the second candle onto a cracked saucer, then affixed the candle to it. "There. That should get you safely upstairs." He handed it to her.

"Nice weather we're having," Cole said, ruffling his feathers.

Will stared. "I've never known a mynah bird before," he said. "Does he say anything else?"

"Sure, lots of things. If you have a cloth of some kind, I can cover his cage and he'll be quiet."

"I have an old tablecloth, and I'll be glad to cover him before I go upstairs."

"Oh? You're not coming up yet?"

"No, I'll go later. First I have to have a conversation with this talkative bird of yours." He lifted his eyebrows, waiting for her to question him. Despite her exhaustion, she fell for the bait.

"Talk to Cole? What on earth will you talk to him about?"

"Why, I want to find out about Cole Mynah's daughter," he said seriously, suppressing a smile.

"I jumped right into that one," she said ruefully. "Boy, I sure did."

"Don't worry. If you're staying for a whole week, you'll have plenty of chances to get back at me, won't you?"

She could still hear him chuckling as she made her way upstairs.

Once in her room, Nuala changed into her comfortable old flannel nightgown and blew out her candle. Outside, the wind still thrashed the tangled branches of the live oak trees; rain still slashed against the windowpane. But Nuala felt cozy and warm beneath her thick blanket, and she didn't even mind the lumpy mattress.

This stranger, this Will Anthony. She didn't know much about him, but she was intrigued. He was warm and funny and not bad looking. He had a pleasant smile and eyes that laughed when his mouth did, which was not true of everyone. And he had discovered her secret weakness—a love of puns.

It was a good thing that she wasn't going to be here longer than a week, because he was the kind of man who might interest her. *If* she ever decided to get interested in anyone. Of course, that question had already been decided for her. She couldn't ever get serious about anyone again. It wouldn't be fair to the man.

But for the short period of a week, it might be fun to flirt, to react to masculine admiration. Oh, she wouldn't lead him on. She didn't approve of women who did that. But a brief flirtation . . .

Maybe I Will, and maybe I won't, she thought happily as she nestled her head deeper into her pillow. And then she fell sound asleep.

Chapter Two

Will was sitting at the kitchen table eating liverwurst spread on a piece of celery when Nuala came down for breakfast the next morning. His heart lightened perceptibly at the sight of her.

She was a beautiful woman. Last night he had thought so, but after she'd gone up to bed he'd sat in the kitchen and told himself he must have imagined it. Who would have thought that a gorgeous woman like Nuala would drop out of nowhere on a stormy night at this out-of-the-way old house in the woods outside Turkey Trot, Florida?

But she was gorgeous. This morning her hair hung loosely down her back, curving into even waves all the way to the ends. It was a fascinating color, like Cheerwine, his favorite soft drink—dark, dark brown with a hint of cherry red in the ripples. And her eyes were deep blue, an intense lavender-blue, like violets. Her skin was a pale milk-white, and its texture was so fine that he knew it would be as soft as a butterfly wing to the touch. With a pang of sudden fierce longing, he wanted to touch it very much.

He warned himself to go slowly. It was not his style to come on strong, but he was feeling an unnerving urge to rush things. After all, she'd said she was going to stay only for a week.

"Nice weather we're having," Cole said when he saw Nuala.

"Lately it's been more like whether—as in whether it will rain or whether it won't," Will observed. "Good morning, Nuala."

"Good morning," Nuala said pleasantly.

She went to Cole's bird cage and bent to look at the bird, giving Will a chance to observe her unnoticed. She wore a cotton turtleneck sweater the rich shade of garnets and a strange garment that could have been either pants or skirt, or both. Whatever it was, it reached all the way to her ankles and tied around her waist with a narrow sash. He didn't know much about fashion, but this particular garment, which upon his further inspection looked like an assortment of batik scarves fastened together in an intriguing way, put him in mind of a sari. Six or seven enameled bangles clinked their way up her arm as she lifted her hand to wiggle her fingers through the bars of the cage at Cole.

Will was still trying to figure out this unusual mode of dress when Nuala straightened and glanced briefly out the window. The sun was shining. The only visible signs of last night's storm were tree branches scattered on the leaf-strewn ground. At the edge of the woods, sweet-gum trees glowed in jewel tones of red and yellow. The sky was bright blue and purled with clouds.

Will waved his celery stick in the air. "Sorry I'm out of eggs," he said. "This is breakfast. Want some?"

Nuala considered the liverwurst. "Liverwurst for breakfast? The idea bagels my mind."

"Lox of people buy liverwurst to eat for breakfast," Will said with a straight face. "They figure it's a good

way to spend their celery. Honestly, aren't you hungry?''

She was smiling. He loved the way she smiled, pure
sunshine.

"I'm starved," she said. "And something tells me the
wurst is yet to come." She sat down at the table and
spread liverwurst on a celery stick.

"Rye would you think that?"

Nuala laughed; she had a laugh like the tinkling of
glass chimes.

"Because you're a most unconventional landlord,
that's why," she said.

As she crunched on her celery, she assessed him
thoughtfully. He looked conventional enough, that was
for sure. This morning Will wore a blue oxford-cloth
shirt with the sleeves rolled up, and he had on a pair of
faded blue jeans. His abundant hair slanted carelessly
over his forehead, and humor and appreciation glinted
from his eyes. There was something Lincolnesque about
him.

"At this point, I'm a very curious landlord," Will
said. "I can hardly stand not knowing what you're
doing here. What brings you to an out-of-the-way place
like Turkey Trot, Florida?"

"I was working at a craft fair in Jacksonville," she
began. "And yesterday afternoon, when it was over, a
lady in the booth next to mine said she knew of a decent boardinghouse not far off U.S. Highway 17, and
since I was going to Turkey Trot, I thought your
boardinghouse would be a good place to stay. I tried to
call ahead from the last truck stop, but all I got was a
recording, and since I couldn't afford a motel I came
anyway. I know Turkey Trot is a small town, but I had
no idea your place would be so far out in the country.''

"And the costume?"

"Oh, that was what I had on at the fair. I didn't bother to change because I didn't know it would take so long to get here."

"I don't see what a long white dress and shoes like a witch wears have to do with working at a craft fair. Don't you weave or paint or make baskets or something?"

"I'm a storyteller. And that's one of the costumes I wear. It makes the stories more special somehow if the storyteller dresses up, especially for the little kids." She took another bite of celery, and her earrings, which Will hadn't noticed before, swung against her cheeks. The earrings consisted of cowrie shells hanging from a piece of twine that disappeared at its top end into holes in her earlobes.

"You haven't explained the hearse yet."

"It's my car. My Storymobile. It's big enough to hold all the books and records and stuff, *and* my costumes, *and* Cole. I can unroll my sleeping bag and sleep in the back if I have to, and I've had to more than once. I bought the hearse from a friend and just can't bear to part with it."

"It does have a personality, doesn't it?" he said, smiling at her. His eyes sparkled jet black.

"I've always thought so."

"So now I know where you've been. Where are you going?"

"There's another craft fair Saturday in Turkey Trot. And then I'll go on to another town, and another."

"This is what you do? Travel from town to town?"

Nuala nodded. "I like it. It's never the same, and there are new people in each place who have never seen or heard a storyteller before."

"*I've* never seen or heard a storyteller before. What kind of stories do you tell?"

"All kinds. Folktales, fairy tales, myths. Whatever strikes my fancy at the time."

"And people pay you for doing this?"

"The fair in Turkey Trot only pays a poultry sum."

"Nuala!"

She grinned at him. "I make barely enough to get by. But it's better than being a librarian, which I used to be. This way I get to meet and mingle with all kinds of people." Talking about money—or her constant lack of it—bored her. Money had never been that important.

She polished off the last bit of celery. "Do you have anything else to eat? I'm still hungry."

He'd been so absorbed in what she was saying that he'd almost forgotten his plans for the morning.

"You *could* stalk the celery in the bottom drawer of the refrigerator," he said, "but I don't recommend it. It's definitely seen better days. I'm making a shopping list. Besides new fuses, what should I get?" He pulled a notepad from his shirt pocket.

"I don't expect you to feed me," Nuala told him. "I can handle that myself."

"I'm not the best cook in the world. How about you?" he asked hopefully.

"I'm a pretty good cook, I guess."

"You've got to be better than I am. As you saw for yourself last night, I can hardly boil water. What do you like to cook?"

"Artichokes. Eggs Benedict. Veal parmigiana. I can make a few vegetarian-type things, too. Like broccoli-stuffed whole-wheat pita bread. You know." She waved her hand, and the bracelets clanked.

He wasn't sure what kind of background was indicated by a range of food like that, but he pretended to study the blank sheet on the top of the notepad. "Hmm," he said, figuring that a comment of some sort was necessary. Then he had an inspiration. "How about a roast? I have a yen for roast beef."

"Sure. I can handle a roast. And steaks. And if you have a few yen left over, even beef teriyaki."

"Here," he said, shoving the paper and pencil toward her, "write down what you'd need to cook those things, and I'll buy the ingredients. Please?"

"All right," she said, taking the pencil he offered and writing down "bean sprouts." Her fingernails were pale ovals, neatly polished.

She scribbled down the names of a few more items. "You should wait until Thursday to shop. That's when most supermarkets have their sales."

"But this is Monday. By Thursday it will be almost time for you to go, and I can't stand to miss out on that many meals."

"It is Monday, isn't it? Don't you go to work?"

"Nope. I stay here. And work."

"Doing what?"

"I'm writing a book."

"Oh, you're a writer."

"No, I'm not really a writer. I'm a lepidopterist."

"A lepidopterist! That's even more interesting. Let me guess—you study, um, the spots on leopards?"

"Butterflies. Not just the spots on them, either. My specialty is the monarch's migration patterns. I was a professor of entomology at the University of North Carolina in Chapel Hill before I came here to write."

"And you're writing a book about monarch butterflies?"

"Actually, I'm writing a novel right now. I have written a book about butterflies, though. It's all the rage in college bookstores."

"I'm impressed," Nuala said.

"I want you to be," he said, and then it was very quiet.

Nuala looked at him steadily. He was observing her, much as she thought he might observe one of his butterflies. He was studying her and waiting for her reaction.

"Will," she began, and then didn't know how to continue.

"Well, I like you. You're the most interesting thing that's happened to me in months. Must I hide my interest?"

Nuala heaved a sigh. "Your interest in my hide?"

"Nuala—"

"Sorry," she said. "I couldn't pass that by."

"If only you'd buy the pass," he returned woefully.

They looked at each other. They began to laugh. Then they weren't laughing anymore but gazing deep into each others eyes.

"You're a woman I can laugh with. Do you know how rare that is?"

"Laughing isn't all it's cracked up to be" she said, "Sometimes you need to have a serious conversation."

"Laughing relaxes you. Some people believe that if you're sick, laughter helps you get well. Does a serious conversation do the same thing? I doubt it."

"We may never have a serious conversation."

"Maybe we're having one now."

"Do we have to?" He was grinning at her as he eased himself up from the chair across the table.

"Seriously, Will, I'll only be here a week. Then I'll move on." She refused to return his grin.

Will paused a beat, but his expression remained affable, giving her no clue to what he was thinking.

"And I'd better get a move on, too," he said. "I have to go to the store." He stuck the shopping list in his pocket and, with a brisk nod, headed for the back stairs.

When he came back a few minutes later, Nuala was returning the liverwurst to the refrigerator.

"While I'm gone, go ahead and make yourself at home," he urged. "Wander. Explore. It's a big house. And outside you can walk along the road for miles and not see anyone. It's good if you like your solitude."

"I do," she said.

"I figured you did. That's a good sign, do you know that? People who don't like being alone sometimes don't like themselves very much."

"And how about you?" she asked. "Do you like being alone?"

"I couldn't live out here if I didn't," he said. He smiled at her cheerfully and ambled outside where he disappeared in the direction of a garage in back of the house. A few minutes later she saw him driving away in a mud-spattered Jeep.

"What a *guy!*" Cole said, hopping from one perch to another.

"You can say that again," Nuala whispered.

But Cole didn't.

WILL HUMMED A TUNE as he drove toward town. Then he stopped humming the tune and wondered how long it had been since he'd been happy enough to hum.

He'd been here almost six months. He'd arrived last summer after he'd wound up things at the university. One of the things he'd wound up was a liaison with a woman who wanted to be his wife.

A wife! What did he want with a wife? At thirty-two, he considered himself a confirmed bachelor.

The woman who wanted to be his wife was named Virginia, and she, too, was a professor of entomology. Her field was coleoptera—beetles. Virginia was two years older than he, highly sexed, and not bad to look at except for two deep frown lines between her eyebrows and hair worn too short for her overlong neck. The two of them had more or less drifted together out of boredom and sexual need, keeping steady company for more than a year. For Will, one of the benefits of his relationship with Virginia was that she helped to keep the inevitable nubile coeds at bay.

But then Will had conceived the idea for his novel. Fine, Virginia said, when Will told her he was going to write a book. With the advances from a second textbook about monarchs, they could get married.

He had certainly never intended to let things go so far. It had been an open-ended relationship with no strings attached. Or so he thought. Apparently Virginia had thought otherwise.

"But it's not a textbook," he had protested. "It's a novel."

"It doesn't matter," Virginia insisted. "It's still extra money."

Will tried to explain something about the book to her, but Virginia wasn't interested in the plot or the characters of his novel. She was only interested in bringing the reluctant Will to his knees and thus to the altar.

When Will refused to be brought to his knees and had indeed been so ornery as to drag his feet, Virginia realized that their relationship had problems. With the tenacity of a true scientist—which, of course, she was—Virginia had applied the scientific method to their relationship.

First of all, she'd stated the problem. "I want to get married. You don't," Virginia said flatly one night before they climbed into bed.

"Right," Will had affirmed, wishing he wasn't part of any of this, wishing he'd followed his instincts and gone out for a beer with the guys.

"I think you don't want to get married because you have unresolved problems about your mother," Virginia said, forming her hypothesis.

His mother? His mother, like his father, was long dead, and they'd gotten along fine. His mother had nothing to do with this. What had to do with this was that he didn't love Virginia. He didn't love her because there was no joy in her. He didn't love her because she elicited no joy from him. He didn't love her because she was quite open about not wanting children. And trivial but true, he didn't love her because her hair looked as though it had been trimmed by a Weedeater. But how could he tell her any of this? Lying beside her in bed, he couldn't.

Next, ever true to the scientific method, Virginia observed and experimented. She hid the picture of his mother that he carried in his wallet. He didn't notice that the picture was missing for a month. When he wondered about it, Virginia said "Aha!" and accused him of not wanting to get married because he didn't want to be unfaithful to dear old Mom.

Will was bewildered. One day he complimented Virginia on the pickled peaches she served for dinner. "My mother used to have those," he said nostalgically, and again Virginia said "Aha!" She commenced to interpret the data she'd gathered, all of which were false, and to draw her off-the-wall conclusion, which was that the two of them ought to go for psychological counseling, premarital in nature.

At about that time, Will happened to pick up one of the magazines in Virginia's apartment and started reading the dog-eared article to which it was folded open. "Does Your Man Have a Hang-Up About Mom?" blared the headline. In disgust, Will tossed the magazine into the garbage. But at least it gave him some insight into the lengths that Virginia, in her desperation to marry him, was prepared to go.

He told her he didn't love her enough to marry her. She understood, she said, frowning understandingly. She would wait until he came to his senses.

He told her he wouldn't ever love her enough to marry her. She cried and said she would wait. Surely he would see what he was missing, she said sourly as she mopped at her cheeks with his handkerchief. Eventually.

Virginia was always so serious. So humorless. So intent. Whatever enthusiasm had ever been part of her personality had been winnowed out, probably by diligent use of the scientific method. There was no joy in her.

Will had always wanted to write this novel. The manager he had hired to take care of the Florida boardinghouse, which had been left to him by his grandfather, walked out, complaining about ghosts. The brouhaha with Virginia was running along at full speed and showed no sign of abating. Why not take time off and write the book? He left Chapel Hill one damp, foggy morning in June, with Virginia grimly waving him goodbye.

Virginia had expected him back at the beginning of the fall semester. She'd telephoned him in Florida repeatedly, demanding to know if he'd lost his senses. Didn't he know what he was giving up? His teaching job? Her? Was he crazy?

What he'd given up ultimately—and no, he wasn't crazy—was the telephone. Had it taken out. Which meant no more impassioned phone calls from Virginia. Which meant no more hassle. Which meant little communication with the outside world. Which meant almost unbearable loneliness.

And now here was Nuala. Beautiful, intelligent and unmistakably joyful. To be around her made him feel happy. To laugh with her would make him look forward to each day.

She couldn't leave in a week! That would be too soon! He was intrigued with her, was stimulated by her, was turned on to her.

He could have sworn she felt the same way about him.

AFTER NUALA WASHED her mud-spattered white gauze dress and finished unpacking and putting her clothes away, she explored.

The house sat on a bluff overlooking the St. Johns River, something Nuala hadn't been aware of last night during the storm and that she didn't find out until she ventured outside, making her way through the strand of live oaks, past a chipped sundial and a huge magnolia tree, whose red cones were beginning to spill their seeds,

until she stood watching a spindle-legged white ibis
wading pensively in the wide river's shallows. On the
riverbank was beached an aluminum canoe, bottom
side up. It must belong to Will. She turned back to the
house. She'd ask Will later if he would mind her taking
the canoe out by herself.

The Anthony Guest House was a big house; it was
huge, in fact. A stuffed five-foot-long alligator dominated the parlor from a stand in one murky corner. The
rest of the parlor was haphazardly furnished with non-
descript furniture, most of it very old. There was a dining room with a long shiny table and twelve chairs.
Silver reposed on the sideboard, and some of the pieces
might have been good ones, but they had grown such a
furry coat of gray dust that it was hard to tell.

The study across the hall from the dining room was
immense. Unlike the other rooms, it showed signs of
use. Tall bookshelves packed with books lined all the
walls except one, which was dominated by a huge
boarded-up fireplace. Here and there perched stuffed
birds, which molted both dust and feathers from their
niches among the shelves. A meager shell collection,
painstakingly labeled, occupied a glass-fronted case. An
imposing rolltop desk stood between two long windows. The rolltop was closed, but from the look of papers scattered on the top, many of them with penciled
corrections, Nuala assumed that this was where Will
worked.

She climbed the front stairs, which were indeed grand
and opened out on a wide upstairs hall. All the bedrooms she glanced into were devoid of personal ef-
fects, their mattresses bare. But then she found the
room that must be Will's.

The bed was neatly made, and his brush and comb were arranged on top of his dresser according to a sense of order. It was a double bed, with pillows piled high at the headboard as though someone was expected to flop down soon to read. In fact, six or seven books rested on the bedside table and more had spilled onto the floor, some opened facedown to preserve their place, others marked with strips of paper.

What did someone like Will Anthony read, anyway? She flicked her eyes over the titles. A zoology textbook. A paperback romance. A best-selling spy thriller. A poetry anthology.

"My, Will Anthony, you are a man of eclectic reading tastes," she said aloud.

At that point she heard his Jeep tires crunching on the driveway, and with a peculiar sense of elation, she hurried downstairs to greet him, taking the back stairs two at a time.

"Hi," Will said, breezing in carrying two grocery bags that he let fall on the kitchen table with a thump. "Come see what I bought."

Nuala reached into one of the bags. "Pickled eggs?" she said dubiously. She reached in again. "Kool-Aid?"

"I've given up on trying to cook eggs for breakfast. Sometimes I eat the pickled kind. And Kool-Aid—well, it comes already mixed with sugar and you don't have to boil the water." He looked sheepish.

"I guess you weren't kidding when you said cooking is a chore."

"You bet I wasn't. Thank goodness you've come along to rescue me from my ineptitude."

She raised an eyebrow. "When do I have to prove myself? I have a feeling I'm going to need to practice."

"I was hoping you could manage a bologna-and-cheese sandwich for lunch. What do you think?"

"I think I can handle it."

"Great. And could you also handle a walk outside? With me? To go on a picnic?" He looked as though he expected her to say no.

She looked surprised for a moment. But then she said warmly, "I'd love a picnic."

His relief escalated into loquaciousness. "I know a place nearby. We could walk there. Do you like to walk? Or are you one of those women who hates the wind blowing through her hair?" Virginia had hated the wind in her hair.

"I like to walk, and I'm one of those women who loves the wind blowing through my hair."

Will continued taking the food out of the bags and handing it to her so she could put it away, assuming that she'd know where it went, the way he'd already known that she liked walking and liked to feel the wind in her hair. He had an urge to keep talking. It was the result of his being alone so much, he knew.

"I suspect you're a person who thrives on impulse. Who likes surprises," he said as he folded up the last of the grocery sacks and stuffed them into an empty kitchen drawer.

"You're very perceptive," said Nuala, slanting a sideways glance in his direction. The cheekbones in his angular face were unexpectedly round, especially when he smiled. And he smiled a lot.

Nuala returned her attention to the task at hand and laid out four pieces of bread on the breadboard. As she did this, Will opened the bologna package with his teeth. She slapped cheese on top of the bologna on the bread.

"You're pretty good at that," he remarked, handing her a few leaves of lettuce, which he had washed.

"And that's no baloney," she shot back.

Will shook his head, awed by Nuala's ability to snap out puns—awed and amused. And, strangely, he was swept with excitement. She was his discovery. He had found her. He congratulated himself for being smart enough not to type her as a lunatic and send her back out into the storm.

He leaned against the table with his arms folded over his chest, watching her. He felt that he could go on watching her all day.

"You know," he observed carefully, "some people couldn't stand the kind of conversations we have."

"Some people don't know what they're missing," she said. Sunbeams filtering through the kitchen curtains danced in the dark red ripples of her hair as she efficiently cut the sandwiches into triangles.

"Speaking of that, do you have a steady boyfriend?"

"No. I travel too much."

"I see," he said, his voice level.

She slid the sandwiches into little plastic bags.

"Have you ever had a serious boyfriend?" he ventured.

She lifted a shoulder. "Not in a long time."

"Do you have any, uh, phobias about a serious relationship?"

"My, aren't you the direct one?" she said, handing him the sandwiches.

He dropped them into a large paper bag. "I think it's best to attack the issue head-on."

With anyone else, Nuala might have taken offense at such probing questions. But with Will, so full of kindness and goodwill—good Will?—she found that she couldn't. She already felt as though she'd known him for years. She decided that she could be frank with him.

"I don't have much of a chance to develop a serious relationship. You know, the rolling stone syndrome."

"Don't you ever act normal? Women aren't supposed to be rolling stones. It's the men who trundle into town, break a few hearts, then trundle out again."

Nuala laughed. "Sexist."

"I try."

"What?"

"I said I try."

"To be a sexist?"

"Oh, I thought you said sexiest."

"With most people, conversations follow a straight line. With you, they keep veering off course."

"We're not most people. Here, hold this bag of sandwiches for me. I'd better get some drinks out of the fridge." He plopped the paper bag containing their lunch into her hands.

"Cream soda for me," Nuala said.

"And root beer for me," Will decided, tucking the drinks into the bag.

"You're supposed to put the drinks on the bottom and the sandwiches on top. Those sandwiches I slaved over are going to be squashed by the time we get where we're going. By the way, where *are* we going?" Nuala followed Will out the back door and down the porch steps.

"Surprise, surprise," he said tantalizingly. "Since you're known to thrive on surprise, you'll love it."

She laughed and followed along.

Will stopped long enough to rummage in the garage until he found an old blanket. "Come on," he said, his eyes sparkling beneath his dark, well-shaped brows. "We're late for lunch." He held out his hand and she took it. Will felt irrepressibly happy and excited and a good deal younger than his thirty-two years.

He was also very hungry after his celery-and-liverwurst breakfast. As she walked slightly in front of him, his eyes strayed to Nuala's hips, so cleanly outlined by the peculiar but flattering garment she wore.

He was hungry in other ways, too. He was hungry to share and to care and to know. And he was hungry for the physical things. Since he'd parted company with Virginia, he'd lived like a monk.

But his hunger would have to be stifled for now. He knew instinctively that Nuala was not to be rushed. His goal with her, he openly admitted to himself, was not a few nights of casual sex. No, it was more. Much more than that.

Chapter Three

Nuala swung into step beside Will at the edge of the deserted country road. A gray squirrel, its mouth stuffed with acorns, froze in their path sniffing the air and, apparently deciding that they were no threat, dashed up a tree trunk. The cool air was fresh with a hint of moisture after last night's downpour.

"What a deserted, lonely road," she commented. "Last night when I was looking for your house, I thought I'd never get there. What's a big house like that doing way out here?"

"It's left over from the days of the steamboat captains and logging barons," Will said. "It's been in my family for generations. One of my ancestors, the first William Anthony, foresaw tourism possibilities for this area as early as the 1850s. At that time, south Florida wasn't developed, and Anthony Guest House became a mecca for Northerners who loved to fish, hunt and imbibe at the inn's well-stocked bar."

"Is William Anthony the reputed ghost?"

Will laughed. "I don't know. He was certainly a character, well known for his profanity and off-color stories. He owned a fleet of fifteen river steamers, the biggest of which was an iron steam sidewheeler. All those riverboats and the steamers belonging to other companies needed prodigious amounts of pine to burn for fuel. So Captain Anthony went into the lumber business and made his second fortune. Too bad there was none of it left when I came along.''

"What happened?"

"My ancestor was quite a spendthrift. And then one day somebody built railroads to south Florida. Soon no one wanted to come to the older hotels on the St. Johns River. The inns languished and died for lack of business. They were all wooden structures, and some of them burned. One hotel in Palatka was moved stick by stick to Daytona. Finally only Anthony House remained in this area, ending its years in ignominy as a boardinghouse.''

"Isn't there any chance of reopening it?''

"I tried to keep it open after Grandfather died, but I didn't live here then. It was impossible to get a good manager. And finally, word got around that the place was haunted. The last manager left in a fright. Said she heard things that go bump in the night. I set a squirrel trap in the attic when I arrived here six months ago, and I put screening over the louvers in the attic where the squirrels were getting in. I haven't heard many bumps since.''

"It's a great place to write a book, I suppose. The location on the river is beautiful, and so peaceful.''

"Yeah, I know,'' Will said. "I love it here. Always have, ever since my parents and I used to visit in the summers when I was a kid growing up in North Carolina. But I guess once the book is finished, I'll put the place on the market. I've already talked to a real estate broker about it, and I'm in the process of filling out the listing form. In a few weeks, he'll start showing the house.''

They walked on in silence. "What a day for a picnic," Nuala said after a while, trying to scuff up leaves so damp that they wouldn't scuff. "It'll be wet anywhere we put our blanket."

"I know the perfect place," Will said. "Trust me."

It was good to know that she didn't have to rush anywhere or do anything. And it was good to have companionship.

"What happens when you finish writing your book?" Nuala said. "Where will you go?"

"Back to being a lepidopterist," Will said.

"But where does one practice that occupation?"

"I was at the University of North Carolina. In Chapel Hill," he said. "I teach."

"And are you going back there?"

"I suppose. I'll finish the book in a couple of months, and the university will be glad to have me back, I think. Of course, if the book's a runaway bestseller..." He dangled the sentence in the air.

"Then you'd be through being a lepidopterist?"

"Maybe. I don't know. I liked it. I hope to write another book about monarchs someday—they're fascinating."

"Tell me about them."

"They're unlike most butterflies. Every year they migrate. In the early days of autumn they start drifting south in hordes, winging their way over a southward course day after day. And they winter where it's warm, in the Sierra Madre mountains in Mexico or in California."

"Migrating's not so unusual. Birds do it."

"So do several other species of insect. What intrigues me about monarchs is how they know where to go, generation after generation. Few of them live to complete the trip, yet their offspring continue back to their homes in the northern or western United States."

"How *do* they know where to go?"

"Good question. We're still trying to figure that one out. Another question is, how do they know how to get there? On the West or the East Coast of the United States, they can use the shore as a guide. But what about the Midwestern butterflies? How does a monarch unerringly find its way across mile after mile of America's heartland, eventually reaching Mexico?"

She looked up at him curiously, surprised to see him looking so intense. With all his joking and making light of things, there hadn't been a chance to see his more serious side.

"How do they?"

"That's what I was trying to find out. That and other questions—for instance, migrant monarchs choose certain trees year after year as way stations. Every successive generation, never having seen that particular tree before, unerringly finds it. Why do they go to the same trees year after year? Do the trees hold a scent that they pick up?"

"I expect some of the monarchs of the previous year put in their two scents' worth," said Nuala offhandedly.

"Scents when do you know that?"

"Since migrate grandmother told me."

"Nuala, do you know how hard it is to keep a straight face when I'm with you?"

"Well, I larva good laugh," she retorted. "Go ahead."

He looked at her, she looked at him. It wasn't clear who broke first, but then they were collapsing in each other's arms, holding each other up.

"I never knew anyone like you before," he said when they had wiped the tears from their eyes.

"And I never knew anyone like you. This may not be normal."

"This may be—perverted?"

"Subverted."

"Inverted."

"*Re*verted. As in back to age three."

They had reached a crossroads; they hadn't seen a car since they'd started out.

"There's our picnic place," Will announced. Nuala saw a broken-down old fence across the road.

"What is it, Will? It looks like the end of the world." Nuala stared at the leaning fence pickets, the unkempt undergrowth. A wild grapevine, yellow now, snaked its way up one of the fence posts.

"It's a cemetery."

"A graveyard? We're going to eat in a graveyard?" Nuala looked distinctly unsettled.

"Sure, you'll love it. There's artesian water and a place to spread out our food. Come on." He tugged resolutely at her hand so that all she could do was follow as he nudged open a creaky gate.

Nuala surveyed the scene. Huge moss-hung trees, their north sides crusted with gray lichen, shaded the cemetery from the sun, and mockingbirds flashed in and out of the trees singing songs of crystal clarity. In the center of the cemetery someone had built a cairn from which bubbled clear water trickling into a rock-lined pool below.

"No one keeps the cemetery up. I wander over here once in a while and tear out some of the weeds, but that's about it. Look, there's a marble slab over there where we can eat our food."

"On a *tombstone*?"

"No, it's not a tombstone. I think it was meant to be a bench, but the legs collapsed over the years. See, there's no engraving on it. Besides, all the tombstones are little. Here's one." He pointed to one at the foot of a giant magnolia tree.

Nuala inspected it. It was engraved with a barely recognizable name. The person had died in the 1800s. "Are there any Anthonys here?" she asked.

"No, they're all at the family burying ground overlooking the river. This was a cemetery for some of the transient loggers who lost their lives in local juke joints and sawmills. When the woods around here became part of the Ocala National Forest, the logging industry died. These people were forgotten by everyone."

"Not everyone," said Nuala, making her way through the weeds to a grave where she had glimpsed a spot of color. It was the ribbon on a garish funeral wreath fashioned of blue plastic flowers.

"Oh, how hideous," Will said with a groan. "But I know where it came from."

"Don't tell me." Nuala shuddered.

"It was just Beckman Beecker. He's an old codger who lives about a half mile down the road. He rummages in roadside dumpsters and when he finds something appropriate for the cemetery, he brings it here. That's one of his finds, I'm sure of it."

"Will I get to meet him?"

"Beckman Beecker? Sure. And you'll like him. He's a character."

"Is he your only friend here?" Nuala asked curiously as Will spread the blanket on the marble slab. Carefully she wrapped the folds of the garment she wore around her and sat down.

"Just about. It's hard to make friends in this isolated place, especially working alone all day as I do."

"Still, it seems like you could make friends if you wanted to." Nuala set about unwrapping the sandwiches. Sure enough, as she had predicted, they were squashed.

"Of course I could make friends. But so did Baron von Frankenstein. I don't go in for his methods, I assure you."

"I can't tell you how happy I am to hear that," Nuala said. Will laughed.

They sat on opposite ends of the blanket, and Nuala bit into a sandwich. She chewed thoughtfully.

"A dollar for your thoughts," Will said.

Nuala raised her eyebrows. "A whole dollar?"

"Sure. Judging from the expression on your face, I'd guess they're worth at least that."

Nuala shrugged. "I was just wondering what I'm doing with a fellow who lives all alone in a spooky house, which is reputed to be haunted, and who takes me to lunch in a graveyard."

"Oh, I can go you one better," Will allowed. "I'd like to know how I ended up with a girl who wears flowing white garments, drives an old hearse and has a mynah bird for a familiar." He grinned at her.

"Mmm," she said. "I see what you mean. Would a bit of personal history reassure you?"

"You bet." He wanted to know more about her. He wanted to know *everything* about her. He couldn't help but wonder what sort of life would produce such an exotic creature.

Nuala fortified herself with a generous swig of cream soda. She drew a deep breath. "I was born and raised in a little town in Rhode Island," she told him. "My parents were folklorists. Stanley and Marjory Kemp. Maybe you've heard of them?"

"Fill me in."

"Well, they traveled around the world gathering folktales. I went with them. They published all these books, and—"

Then Will remembered. "And they had a fabulous radio program, didn't they? I used to listen to it every Saturday morning on the public radio station. Your father had a real deep voice, and he could make you believe, really believe. For a year after I heard him tell 'The Three Billy Goats Gruff' I was utterly convinced that a troll lived under the bridge by my house and that I'd better not hang around there any more than necessary."

Nuala beamed. "Exactly. Dad could tell a story like no one else."

"It's easy to see how you came by your talent as a storyteller," Will said. He had long been an admirer of the Kemps; in fact, he owned several of their books.

"I was their only child, and Mother and Dad took me with them to Africa, to Nepal, to Finland. We traveled to so many out-of-the-way places that I've lost count. It was an education, and it left me quite fearless about traveling on my own. In spite of what happened to them."

Will caught her change in mood. "I hadn't heard that anything happened to them."

"Eight years ago—I was in my first year of college at the time—they were on another trip to Africa, journeying into parts of the continent where few explorers have ever been. They were caught in the middle of a remote tribal feud, and they were killed."

"I'm sorry, Nuala," Will said.

"It was a long time ago. And I've always taken heart in the fact that they were doing what they wanted to do—learning about faraway cultures through their folktales. They loved what they were doing right up until the day they died."

"And you? Do you love what you do?"

Nuala nodded so emphatically that the cowrie-shell earrings bounced. "Yes, I do. I take my work seriously, and I wouldn't want to live any other way."

"You like being on the move all the time? Don't you ever feel like settling in one place?"

She shook her head. "I have no desire to go out and find new stories the way Mother and Dad did. My work is to pass along the stories my parents worked so hard to collect, so more people will hear them and understand the cultures where the stories originated. It's a mission of love for me to promote the feeling of oneness among human beings."

"You see storytelling as some sort of medium for understanding among the peoples of the world?"

"The whole world loves a good story. And when we see the similarities in stories originating in different countries, we see that we're all not so different after all. And that's pretty wonderful, isn't it?" Her eyes, for once, weren't laughing. They were serious.

His expression flickered with casual affection. "Nuala Kemp, indeed it is. And you make a pretty wonderful squashed bologna sandwich; has anyone ever told you that?''

"Thank goodness, no." Nuala polished off the last of hers and licked her fingers. They had forgotten to bring napkins.

"Let's wash off in the well," Will suggested, rising slowly to his feet. He reached out his hands to pull Nuala up from where she sat; again, standing before him, she was impressed with how tall he was.

"Six feet three inches," he responded softly in answer to her unasked question.

"I was wondering," she said, suddenly self-conscious with him.

"What do you do to your hair to make it curl like that?" he asked, touching a strand of it gingerly. There was reverence in the curve of his hand.

"Nothing," she said, and her breath caught in her throat. Something tightened in her chest and twisted in her stomach, rendering her immobile.

His eyes changed, their brown depths blazing briefly. Swiftly, as though he couldn't stop himself, he bent his head and kissed her on the lips. His beard tickled and he tasted pleasantly of mayonnaise. His lips upon hers were exquisitely soft, mesmerizing her with the gentlest of pressures, the sweetest of sensations. Warmth fanned through her, starting at her lips and spreading outward to her fingertips, her toes. She had never been kissed so tenderly, nor with so much promise.

But it was only one kiss.

He stepped away from her, entirely matter-of-fact now, and he appeared to be totally in control. It was as if their kiss had never happened.

"You wanted to meet Beckman Beecker," he said. Nuala thought she detected a vibration in his voice that hadn't been there before.

She nodded, still speechless.

"How about this afternoon?"

"Now?" A blue jay jeered overhead.

"Right," Will said casually, imposing more distance between them by bending to pick up the blanket. He shook it free of crumbs and a few clinging leaves while Nuala went to the bubbling artesian well and bent over it to rinse off her hands. Her shimmering reflection stared up at her from the pool below. Something dark and wild flashed momentarily in her wide blue eyes; she seemed a stranger to herself. It was as if she had come under the influence of some strange spell since arriving here last night—a spell that turned Will into someone who was not a stranger and turned her into someone who was.

"Are you ready?" Will asked, his voice calm.

She turned around quickly, on her guard. But he was only Will: genial, bearded, tall and lanky Will, smiling that gentle smile, which put her instantly at ease.

Matching his cool, she moved over so that he could wash his hands at the fountain.

And thought, *I should leave now, before this goes too far.*

And thought again that there was nowhere else she'd rather be than with Will Anthony.

And thought some more that she loved surprises, and that Will Anthony was a nice surprise indeed.

What would it hurt to let nature follow its course, only for a week?

THE KNOCKER ON THE DOOR to Beckman Beecker's cabin was a squirrel's paw. Nuala was glad that she wasn't the one who had to touch it. Will lifted it and let it fall. For a moment, Nuala thought there was no one home. But then a little gnome of a man pulled the door open and blinked up at them.

"Come in, come in," Beckman Beecker bade them, and Nuala, with a skeptical backward look at Will, did. She found herself in a room crowded with furniture and gewgaws of every possible description. A hula girl with a lampshade for a hat decorated an old school desk used as an end table. A moth-eaten moose head with only one antler served as a hat rack. A pair of worn pink-satin toe shoes were slung carelessly over a gold plastic rococo mirror.

"Heh-heh," Beckman said, rubbing his hands together. "So you've been on a picnic."

"Yes," Will said jovially. "And we noticed your latest decoration at the cemetery."

"Well." Beckman drew up a rickety straight chair and indicated that Nuala should sit on the couch beside Will. She did, but timidly. The couch reminded her of nothing so much as a big gray elephant, collapsed on its side and subsiding into woolly wrinkles.

"That funeral wreath is one of my latest gleanings. Oh, you never know what you're going to find in one of those dumpsters out on the highway. I found a wedding gown all done up in plastic once. Never have found anyone who could use it. Hangs in the back of the closet. Just the other day I got a perfectly good set of crutches. Don't know anyone who needs those, either. Well, you never know. And there's always the flea market."

"Flea market?" Nuala said, her ears perking up.

"Sure. Big flea market at the old drive-in theater in Turkey Trot every week on Sunday. Welcome to go with me if you want."

Will had told her that Beckman was a retired postmaster and that he lived alone here in this cabin in the woods. He could have been any age; his hair was a colorless shade that might have been either yellowed white or whitish yellow, depending on how one chose to look at it. His eyes were an oddly colorless shade of gray, and his spine was so bent that he looked like a paper clip gone awry. But there was a merry glint in his colorless eyes, and Nuala couldn't help but like him.

"Well, thanks," she said, warming to him. "I'd like that. I get a lot of my story props from flea markets," she didn't say it, but she bought a lot of her clothes at flea markets, too.

"Nuala's a storyteller. She travels around the country telling stories."

"Heh-heh," Beckman said. "You don't say. Mind if I tell the librarian at the Turkey Trot Library? Maybe she'd hire you for a story hour or two."

"Beckman's a great reader," Will said, turning to Nuala. "He's a regular patron of the library in Turkey Trot and of the one in Osofkee, too."

"Yup. Sometimes people don't throw any good books into the dumpsters for months," Beckman said. "Once I got a whole set of the *Encyclopaedia Britannica*, though. It's the 1952 edition. There it is, on the bookshelf. Missing the Del-Ep volume, though. Never did find it. I don't need the Del-Ep volume very often anyhow. I just skipped that one when I got to it. I'm reading the encyclopedia all the way through. Guess I'll never find out anything about Delaware, Abner Doubleday or Epsom salts. Heh-heh!"

Nuala looked at the bookshelf. Sure enough, there was the encyclopedia. And a lot of other books, including one that looked familiar.

"You have one of my parents' books," she told Beckman. "It's *Folklore from Kenya* by Stanley and Marjory Kemp."

"You're their daughter?" Beckman looked impressed.

Nuala nodded.

"I love their work. Say, do you tell their stories?"

"Yes, of course."

"Wait till the librarian at Osofkee hears this. Just wait. She'll track you down and insist that you come to her library to do a story hour."

"See?" Will said with a look of smug satisfaction. "You may have to stay here longer than a week. If Beckman lines up a job for you, you can't possibly leave."

"So that's it," Nuala said, the light suddenly dawning.

Will's gaze was earnest. "Yes," he said softly. "That's it." He glanced at his watch.

"Sorry, Beckman, but we've got to run. Just wanted to make sure you were getting along all right. And I wanted to introduce you to Nuala."

"They've never had anyone like you, Nuala, at the Turkey Trot and Osofkee libraries. And both libraries just got some kind of grant from the arts council, so I guess they'll be able to pay you a little bit. Are you interested?"

"I—I'd like to know more about it," Nuala said, with mixed feelings. On the one hand, she could use the money. On the other hand, she shouldn't prolong her stay.

"I'll let you know what I find out," Beckman promised as they said goodbye.

Back outside in the fresh air, Will fell into a step beside Nuala, the old blanket slung over one shoulder and his thumbs hitched through the belt loops in his jeans.

"Beckman's an eccentric old fellow, but he's one of the most intelligent men I've ever met," he said. "He's extremely well read, and he has a multitude of interests."

"Like scavenging in dumpsters?"

"Oh, well, it keeps him busy. He never knows what he'll find next, and it's all free. He's furnished his whole cabin with stuff other people threw away, and he hauls lots of things to flea markets in his pickup truck and sells them. His sizable extra income is donated to a big Christmas party for underprivileged children from Turkey Trot and Osofkee every year. And by the way— Beckman will be ninety years old next April."

"I liked him."

"Good. Maybe if I can't keep you here, Beckman will." His umber eyes seemed varnished with gold in the hazy afternoon light filtering through the tree branches overhead.

Nuala sighed. "I don't know, Will. I'm accustomed to moving on, not letting myself get used to staying in one spot. I never plan ahead because I never know where I'm going to be."

"But you can't leave in a week. We hardly know each other."

She slid a glance up at him, just in time to watch disappointment washing briefly over his expression.

"Maybe we shouldn't get to know each other," she said in a low tone.

"I don't know why you're saying that," he returned. Now there was no amusement in his eyes; he sounded perplexed.

It wasn't something Nuala could tell him, not on the strength of a twenty-hour acquaintance. She lowered her head. She didn't want to look at him. They walked on in silence. In the treetops a squirrel chattered. Another chattered back. At least, Nuala thought, somebody's talking.

Finally Will said with feeling, "We deserve time to find out. And don't say, 'Find out what, Will?' You know as well as I do."

Nuala swallowed a quick retort and made herself look off into the distance. A flippant reply wouldn't work now. She struggled for words.

Will said tightly, "We need to give ourselves time to see if this is just a temporary attraction. If it's all just a game. If—"

"If we run out of funny things to say to each other?"

"It's not just that. But the things we say are a big part of it. If we weren't so perfectly in tune, we wouldn't say them."

"I suppose you're right about that. Only there's more to a relationship than trading puns."

"Of course. Don't leave in a week, Nuala. Let us discover each other without having to rush. If I know you're leaving soon, I'll want to hurry it along, and that wouldn't be fair to either of us."

They had reached the house; Will stopped to pick up the downed Anthony Guest House sign and prop it against a tree. Nuala preceded him to the front porch, brooding. She stood in the exact spot she'd stood the previous night and remembered how kind Will had been to take her in.

He joined her and produced a ring of keys from a back pocket. Suddenly he turned to face her. He dropped the blanket he carried and gripped her by the shoulders, the keys biting into her tender flesh. She stared at him, feeling her cheeks flush deep red under his scrutiny.

His warm hands slid upward from her shoulders to cup her face, making her skin come alive. The cold metal of the keys in the palm of his hand cooled her hot cheek. Her heartbeat's rhythm pulsed in her ears, louder, louder. His eyes, so close, were honest, candid and direct.

"I could kiss you now," he said very quietly. "Not the way I did before, but deeply. We're alone here, and there's no reason why we shouldn't warm each other's bed. But I want more than a bed warmer. I want us to learn and know each other, and if it's right for our relationship to become something deeper, then we'll both decide to take it further. You're already special to me, Nuala. Please think about staying."

"Let's see what Beckman finds out about those jobs at the libraries," she said. She felt dizzy, not only from what his touch was doing to her but also from the numbing impact of his words.

Will dared to look hopeful. "I'll settle for that," he said with the hint of a lilt in his deep voice.

He was so close that Nuala felt his sweet exhalation of relief on her cheek, and she was hollowed by an aching emptiness as he reluctantly removed his hands from her face. The keys in his hand jingled as he turned to open the door.

With growing uncertainty, she followed him inside. Without wanting to, she was planning ahead after all. Planning to stay here at Anthony House with Will—if she got a job.

Chapter Four

Nuala bit into the roundness of a Golden Delicious apple and turned the page of her book. She was curled up on a dusty green velvet love seat in the study, sitting quietly as Will labored over his novel. The only sound was the tapping of the keys on Will's old manual typewriter.

Suddenly he pushed his chair back and sneezed. "Atchoo!"

"At me?" Nuala looked up from her book.

Will laughed. "You're supposed to say 'gesundheit.' Or something similar. Do you have another one of those apples? It looks delicious."

Nuala tossed him an apple. "It is Delicious. Golden Delicious, in fact."

"I think I'll knock off work for a while," Will said, pulling his reading glasses off his nose and folding them carefully. "I'm not getting anywhere with it anyway." He slammed the cover of the rolltop desk over his typewriter and stretched his long legs.

Nuala contained her curiosity. She would have liked to know what kind of novel Will was writing, but he had volunteered no information about it at all.

"If I'm in your way..." Nuala began reluctantly. This evening she wore her hair gathered into a thick mass of ripples hanging over one ear. The look of her could best be described as piquant. In fact, Will scribbled the word on a scrap of paper so he wouldn't forget it. Maybe he could use it in his novel.

"No," he told her. "I like having you in the room. You're not a distraction." Will pondered for a moment how to describe the sense of peace that swept over him at the thought of Nuala sitting so quietly, her slender legs tucked up under her, as he worked. He liked being with her, no matter what the circumstances; walking, talking, eating, laughing.

In his cage in the corner, Cole sidled along his perch. "What a *guy*!" he said.

Will laughed. "That's my favorite phrase in that bird's vocabulary. But I have the feeling that he says that to all the guys."

"He already knew how to say it when I got him," said Nuala. "I haven't been able to teach him much."

"Have you tried?"

"Not lately," she admitted. "When I got him there were a few phrases I thought it would be nice for him to learn, but no matter how often I repeated them, he never caught on. He'd always bounce back with, 'Nice weather we're having,' or 'It was a dark and stormy night,' or 'What a *guy*!' Pretty soon *I* was saying, 'Nice weather we're having,' or 'It was a dark and stormy night,' or 'What a *guy*!' And then I realized that I hadn't trained Cole. He had trained me!"

Will laughed again. "You know, Nuala, I hadn't realized how dull it was working day in and day out with nothing to break the monotony but an occasional visit

from Beckman. I'm glad you came." His eyes rested on
her warmly.

"You should have a pet. A dog, maybe. Then you
wouldn't be so lonely."

His lips curved in a wistful smile, and he leaned back
into his chair. He shook his head ruefully, as though she
had missed the point.

"A dog wouldn't be quite the same, Nuala."

Quickly she lowered her eyes to her book again so
that he wouldn't see the confusion there. And yet she
knew in her heart that he wasn't fooled. He wasn't the
type to be distracted by evasions, even evasions of the
best kind.

The clock on the desk, an old hand-wound mantel
clock, ticktocked quietly, the only sound in the room.
Cole dozed in his cage, and Will leaned back in his
chair, his hands behind his head for support, staring
into space. He thought about pulling the boards off the
old fireplace. After all, it ought to be in working condition if he was going to sell the house. And soon the
weather would be colder; already there was a hint of
frost in the air some mornings. It would be so nice to sit
here with Nuala, warmed by a fire and her graceful
presence.

They might have been of one mind, the two of them.
Nuala read another chapter, turning the pages without
sound. It was pleasant, she thought. The two of them
occupying the same space, comfortably bound by the
circle of light from the lamp they shared. It was pleasant and domestic, but she couldn't let herself get used
to it. Pleasant and domestic were fine for some people.
Not for her, however.

Even if she extended her stay past a week, she would
have to leave. Sooner or later.

NUALA WATCHED WILL that night walking among the trees behind the house. She knelt at her window, gazing up at the starry sky and the moon floating above the trees. Will emerged from somewhere below, the back door probably, and strolled along, his hands in his pockets. The moon was so bright that his shape cast a long shadow before it moved away through the trees toward the river so that she couldn't see him.

Will Anthony.

He had made plain his attraction to her. He wanted to explore that attraction. And she was undone by him, by his mere presence. And yet whenever she began to feel optimistic about him—about them—she brought herself up short.

It wouldn't be fair to lead him on, to let him think that she could give more than she was able to give. And she couldn't just blurt it out, blurt out her secret. It was something that couldn't be told until she knew him better. Except that she was determined that she wasn't going to get to know him—or anyone else—that well.

She sighed and rested her cheek against the much-painted wood of the window frame. The curtains in here smelled musty; they should be washed. Maybe she'd wash them before she left. If he was really hoping to sell this place, it would certainly have to look better than it did now. Will didn't seem to have any sense at all about housekeeping. She did. She might not look like a homebody, but a homebody was what she had wanted to be once. She was pretty good at keeping house, at cooking the things she knew how to cook and at organizing things. Those were things that she could do for Will, since that was what he seemed to need most.

She could be his friend.

Friends were something she missed in this gypsy life of hers. Oh, there were people she loved—her friend Dorrie and Dorrie's husband, Ben, and her Aunt Rose, who lived in a retirement home in Arizona. But when she had embarked upon her unusual life-style, she had given up ordinary, everyday friendship. For a long time she hadn't wanted it, hadn't even missed it. She'd been running away from everything she'd known. But now, with Will, she had tasted friendship again, and she realized how empty her life had been without it.

She'd never known anyone whose sense of humor had meshed with hers. Most people acted as though they hated puns, or maybe it was that they resented her cleverness and ready wit. Whatever it was, Will was the first person who had ever been able to return her word-play volley for volley. At first he had startled her, then he had made her laugh, and how good it felt to have his ready appreciation for her own special brand of humor. Add all that to the smoldering sexual attraction, and they had something that was definitely out of the ordinary. *Extra*ordinary.

It surprised her that she wanted to touch him when they were together, to rest her hand on his arm or lean her shoulder against his chest or—well, there was more, too. She longed to tip the hairs in his beard gently with one fingertip, just to watch them bend with the pressure. She wanted to straighten his collar, because his shirts hadn't been ironed. Today, when one of his shoelaces came untied, she had wanted to bend down and tie it for him, merely for the sake of the physical contact.

Was she crazy?

No, not crazy. Those were some of the ways men and women started physical interaction—a reaching out, a tentative invasion of another's space boundaries. And if the experimental sallies met with no resistance, the relationship progressed to hand-holding, kissing et cetera. Will had already kissed her. He had made no secret of his desire to explore the et cetera. He wanted to wait until she was ready, though, and he didn't want to rush things.

She felt a flood of gratitude toward him for that. But—to stay here longer than she had planned for the sole purpose of getting to know him better? No. No! It wouldn't be fair to him.

For one rash moment she thought about tossing all of her belongings back into her suitcase, picking up Cole's bird cage and retreating in the dark of night as mysteriously as she'd arrived. Nine chances out of ten Will Anthony wouldn't come looking for her.

But then she saw him again, his lanky figure silhouetted against the silvery sky, and even though she couldn't see his face she knew how it would look: the dark eyes bright beneath the neatly arched eyebrows, the unexpectedly soft curve of his cheekbones in that angular face, the gentle lips that smiled so easily in amusement. It was a strong face, an intelligent face. It was a face she could learn to love.

But would not.

Still, she could be his friend. Somehow, that would have to be enough.

"WHAT IS THIS?" Will paused in the doorway to the big kitchen and regarded the scene before him.

"It's called breakfast. Come in and make its acquaintance."

"Could that be scrambled eggs? We're old friends. And—and, well, if that doesn't look like something I used to know—bacon!"

Will's eyes rounded at the sight of the neatly set table, of the long-forgotten bouquet of dried flowers Nuala had discovered in the depths of a kitchen cabinet. His hair flopped endearingly over his forehead, fresh from a session with the blow dryer, and he wore a clean but wrinkled cotton flannel shirt. Nuala made a mental note to look for an iron and ironing board later.

"I can't believe that a bachelor like you has managed to exist on the likes of liverwurst and pickled eggs in the morning."

"There was always a school cafeteria where I could eat," he said in his own defense. "I always lived near a nice little mom-and-pop restaurant."

"I've decided that you should start the day with a good breakfast, and I'm going to teach you to cook one."

"A reformer, are you?" Will pulled a chair up to the table.

"That's better than an *in*former."

"Or a *con*former, which you of all people most certainly are not. Say, I hope you're going to join me. I can't eat all this by myself."

Nuala sat down beside him. She caught a fresh and tantalizing whiff of Irish Spring soap; a glance at him told her that he had missed a bit of lather behind his ear. She longed to reach over and wipe it away. But instead, she quickly focused her eyes on her plate, which Will had heaped with eggs.

"Will! I can't eat that much!"

"You can certainly try."

"Nice weather we're having," Cole said. He hopped to the floor of his cage and began tearing at a piece of celery.

"I fed Cole the rest of the celery," Nuala said. "That's so you won't be tempted to lapse back into your old ways. Which reminds me—I'd like to see you downstairs at eight o'clock tomorrow morning. I'll show you how to scramble an egg."

His eyes, so full of pleasure, rested on her warmly. "It's a deal."

"No, it's a meal."

"Nuala, must you start in so early in the morning? You hardly give me a chance to get my bearings."

She laughed. "I suppose you'd like more conventional conversation in the morning."

"Mostly I just like having you here, you know that." Seeing the shadow cross her face, he said, "What's wrong? Aren't I supposed to pay you compliments? That was a compliment, you know."

"I—I guess I feel uncomfortable when the conversation gets too personal," she said.

"Oh," he said. He consumed another forkful of eggs, then carefully set his fork down on the side of the plate.

"Look, Nuala," he said patiently and kindly, "you can't blame me for wanting to keep you around. I made my intentions clear yesterday. They're honorable, and I don't think a woman could ask for more than that. Do you?"

"No, I suppose not," she whispered, refusing to look into his eyes.

"Well, then," he said, as though that took care of everything. "What are we going to do today?"

"You're going to work on your book. I'm going to look for an iron and an ironing board," Nuala said steadily. "And a dust cloth. And a vacuum cleaner."

Will picked up his fork again. "That sounds serious. I didn't know you were such an avid housekeeper."

She shrugged, unable to resist poking fun at him. "You wanted to know more about me. Well, now you know the worst. I can't stand dust or dirt or mildew in the shower. Or tarnished silver. Or streaky windows."

"You mean you even do windows?" Will's eyes danced as he finished off his last strip of bacon.

"Uh-huh," Nuala said, pushing back her chair and carrying her plate to the sink.

"The last window washer who came here took up gambling," Will said thoughtfully.

"Oh, he did? Why?"

"Because he thought he knew how to window."

It took a few moments for this to sink in, but when it did, Nuala aimed the sprayer from the sink faucet at him with surprisingly accurate results.

"What was that for?" Will sputtered, mopping at his face with a paper napkin.

"Window. Win dough. And anyway, you had soap behind your ear," Nuala replied sweetly.

"I guess," Will said, clearly enjoying this, "that I should be thankful that the sink sprayer isn't a loaded pun."

Whereupon Nuala gleefully sprayed him again.

"YOU'RE CERTAINLY a whirlwind around the house," Will observed a few days later, watching Nuala as she briskly rubbed dry flaky silver polish off an ornate silver water pitcher. "How much more of that is there?"

"Lots," she answered. "There's a silver tea set, a coffeepot, this water pitcher and several silver trays. Not to mention a lot of flatware."

Will prowled the length of the dining room. It was only ten o'clock in the morning, yet Nuala was charging full speed ahead with this passion for cleaning the house. If she was going to have a passion for something, why couldn't it be him?

"What I can't figure out is why you're doing this. In the past couple of days you've vacuumed the entire downstairs, ironed shirts of mine that have never been ironed before and taught me three pointless things to do with a can of tuna fish. Grating apple into it—ugh! And that grater! What a sadistic instrument of torture!" He held up a grated knuckle and regarded it ruefully.

"The apple takes away the strong fishy taste of canned tuna, and that's a good thing to know. Besides, nothing that you can do with a can of tuna is pointless," Nuala said. "Especially if you're hungry. Which is a condition I've noticed you attain somewhat regularly."

Will made a face. "I don't even like tuna fish."

"Well, you should have told me that before we started our cooking lesson." She poked her polishing rag diligently into the crevices on the pitcher's ornate handle, wishing he'd be more appreciative. After all, she didn't care much for tuna either.

"Won't you come canoeing on the river with me instead of drudging away at that silver?"

It sounded tempting, and he'd been trying to talk her into going canoeing for the past two days. She'd like to explore the river, which eased darkly and quietly past the house, its waters stained brown by tannin from the surrounding pines and cypresses.

"Come on," he said, sensing her wavering.

But if she was going to finish the tasks she had set out for herself she would have to persevere.

"Not until I finish this," Nuala said, ogling her distorted reflection in the side of the water pitcher. She tipped it slightly and marveled as her face grew long. Wouldn't this be a good way to illustrate a point in a story sometime? By showing kids how their images changed in a shiny convex surface? There must be a folktale or fairy tale into which this clever idea for dramatization would fit somehow.

Will was watching her expectantly.

"And anyway," she said righteously, putting aside the idea for the time being, "the reason I'm cleaning your house is that it needs cleaning. You can't deny that," she said pointedly as Will licked a finger and used it to rub a clear hole in the grimy windowpane so that he could peer out to see who was driving into the driveway at such a reckless speed, screeching brakes as he hit the curve.

"It's Beckman. Now why would he be coming to see me?" wondered Will.

He went to the door and after an animated conversation—of which Nuala only heard snatches, like "library," and "Osofkee," and "Martha," and "high chair"— Will presently escorted Beckman into the dining room, presumably to clarify such a disjointed assortment of nouns.

"He wants to see you," explained Will.

Beckman blinked at her from under his thatch of white-yellow hair and shifted from foot to foot. "It's about the library story hour, Nuala. Martha Cale at the Osofkee Library wants to talk to you. She'd like to do a week-long after-school story hour for the kids. Are you interested?''

"Of course she is," Will inserted smoothly. "When can Martha talk with Nuala?"

"She wants Nuala to telephone her today."

"There's no telephone here," Nuala said, capping the silver polish and standing up.

Will wasn't about to let her dismiss the subject so easily. "Then we'll have to drive you to a pay telephone. Or better yet, why not go to Osofkee to visit Martha? That way you can describe how you work and discuss what she has in mind."

Beckman favored them with a brisk, approving nod. "Good idea. And I'll drive her. That is, if you don't mind, Nuala. There was an old high chair tossed in a dumpster just outside of town, and I wanted to get it out and put it in the back of my truck. But I need someone to help me."

"I'll be glad to go with you to get the high chair, Beckman," said Nuala. "But I'm not sure about this story-hour job. A whole week . . ."

"A whole week," echoed Will, his look imploring her. *One more week,* he was thinking. *If only I can keep her here one more week.*

One more week and Nuala could wash every window in this big old place, and the curtains, too. One more week and she could tackle the mildew in all the bathrooms. One more week and she could nullify the disastrous tuna cooking lesson, because in the space of a week Will could learn how to make a decent chicken casserole and possibly even a pot roast.

"Okay," she said at last, trying to look nonchalant about the smile that lit up Will's face.

Because Will decided that he couldn't let Nuala be the one to lift the high chair out of the dumpster, the three of them piled into Beckman's late-model Dodge pickup truck. Beckman drove at a speed slightly below supersonic while Nuala hung on to her pocketbook and prayed a lot as they passed other cars poking along at the legal speed limit.

"Heh-heh," chuckled Beckman, sending up rooster tails of sand as he wheeled into the weedy parking place beside the highway dumpster. "The high chair's still there. Why people throw things like that away instead of giving them to someone who can use them I simply don't know." With a spry leap he ejected himself from the pickup. Will followed at a more sedate space.

Beckman supervised Will's removal of the high chair from the dumpster. When it sat on the ground, Beckman danced around it like some wacky Druidic priest performing incantations.

"Only one thing wrong with it that I can see," he said, still prancing as Will heaved the high chair into the back of the truck. "The strap between the tray and the seat is broken. I'll fix it good as new, wait and see."

The high chair retrieved, the three of them hurtled on in the direction of Osofkee, a small town on the highway to Gainesville.

The library turned out to be an old but spacious frame structure, obviously a former house, and located on a quiet side road just off the main street. When Nuala pushed through the door, she nostalgically identified the unmistakable smell of libraries—a combination of old book bindings, glue and inevitable dust. It was a smell she'd missed, she realized.

Martha Cale bustled out from behind the checkout desk as Nuala entered. Nuala introduced herself, and Martha's wide face lit up with a toothy smile.

"I could hardly believe my luck when Beckman told me that you were in the area," she said warmly as she ushered Nuala into her cozy office. She blew a shock of carrot-red hair off her forehead and plopped herself down in a comfortable chair, breezily indicating that Nuala should do the same.

"Coke? Coffee? No? Well, anyway, I'd be thrilled if you could do a whole week of story hours for us. I've wanted to present a story hour for our local children for a long time, but unfortunately it's hard to find anyone who can do anything except read to them out of a book. With kids nowadays, that's not enough to hold their attention for long. After all, they grew up with TV programs like *Sesame Street* and *Super Friends*, where something is happening all the time."

Nuala smiled. This was a problem with which she was familiar. She had, after all, worked as a librarian herself once. She had learned through trial and error how to handle fidgety kids.

"My style is a dramatic one," she explained to Martha. "I make good use of my experience as a stage actress in amateur community theater productions, and I like to use props, such as costumes and puppets, to hold the children's attention."

"It sounds wonderful. Can you start Monday?"

Nuala had taken an instant liking to Martha and her forthright personality, and she thought it would be fun to work with her. "Yes," Nuala said emphatically. "Yes, I'd like that."

They spent another half hour discussing Nuala's salary and Martha's expectations. They decided that Nuala would concentrate on stories and folklore from a different country every day for a week, thus exposing the children to the culture of five nations.

"I'll distribute flyers in the schools and day-care centers, so we're sure to have a good crowd," Martha promised as Nuala left.

"How'd it go?" Will asked eagerly as he opened the truck door for her so that she could slide in next to Beckman.

"Great. We're starting Monday," Nuala said with obvious satisfaction.

"Wonderful," Will said meaningfully, his look saying much more than that. Nuala let her thick lashes veil her downcast eyes, wondering if she was taking too much of a chance.

Once they were on the highway headed toward home, Will heaved a sigh of relief. He had been so afraid that something would go wrong. That Nuala would decide not to take the job.

They let Beckman do most of the talking. Will's arm rested along the top of the seat, behind Nuala. Whenever she turned her head, her long hair dusted his arm. That and the fresh, sweet scent of her heightened all his senses until he wanted to lift his hand from the back of the seat and smooth the deep red ripples of her hair. He wanted to, but of course he didn't. This was not the time. The time would come, though. At last there was absolutely no doubt in Will's mind about that.

"I FEEL LIKE ELAINE, the lily maid of Astolat," Nuala said later, trailing her hand languidly in the water on one side of the canoe. Will had finally convinced her to leave her dust cloth behind and to come for a canoe ride with him. She gazed up at the canopy of cypress trees overhead.

Will's paddle sliced rhythmically through the water. "Like who?" he asked.

"Elaine was the heroine of one of Tennyson's *Idylls of the King*. She pined and died for her love of Lancelot."

"And you feel like her? Pining and dying of love?"

Will was only joking, but for Nuala there was an uncomfortable moment before she brought herself to answer.

"Well, no, I guess not," she said quietly, withdrawing her hand from the water. *Not now, anyway,* she thought. She'd gotten over all that, she hoped.

Will sensed that he'd touched a sensitive nerve, and even though he didn't understand it, he knew instinctively that it was a good time to change the subject.

"Look," he said, stopping his paddling and letting the canoe glide quietly. "Cooters."

Nuala sat up and looked in the direction he was pointing. All she could see was a knobby old log at the side of the stream. She looked at him questioningly.

"Turtles," he said, and she looked again. She saw them then. What she had thought were knobs on the log were turtles sunning themselves in the last rays of the afternoon sun.

"Some people trap them," Will told her, resuming his paddling. The cooters jumped off the log at the approach of the canoe.

"To eat?"

Will nodded. "They scare the cooters off their log, set a trap beside it, then go away and let the cooters start sunning themselves on the log again. When they come back the second time, the cooters jump off the log into the trap."

"How does anybody know which side of the log the cooters will jump off?"

Will shrugged. "No matter which way, you've got a fifty-fifty chance of catching them."

Nuala smiled and leaned her head back.

"It's about time to head for the house," Will said.

He turned the canoe so that they were headed upstream.

"Want me to paddle?"

"You don't have to. But you may if you like."

Nuala fished the other paddle out of the bottom of the canoe and knelt in the bow. Their paddling was synchronized, as though they'd been doing this together for a long time.

"You're doing a good job," Will called.

She grinned back at him, but she didn't break her rhythm.

When at last they reached the house, the sky was pearled with streaks of pale pink and the sun had almost set. They jumped out of the canoe in the shallows and hauled it up on shore, turning it over so that if it rained, water wouldn't collect in the bottom.

"Thanks, Will. It was fun." Her eyes sparkled up at him.

He couldn't help slipping an arm around her shoulders, and it was then only a short distance to pulling her into his arms.

"Will, please," she murmured, her tone so low that he could barely hear her. "I need to get my big trunk out of the hearse so I can set up my props for tomorrow's story hour at the fair."

"I'll get it for you later," he promised. He would have promised her anything at that moment.

He dipped his head and captured her lips, which were soft and warm and moved enticingly in rhythm with his. Just like paddling the canoe together. Just like—

"Will," she said. A look in his eyes told her that he would not let her go so easily. He crushed her to him, forcing her body to lean into his, and his lips pressed hers with a bruising intensity. He smelled of soap and the river, and his taste was so intoxicating that she forgot about the trunk and everything else.

She felt his hands roaming her back, pressing her closer, and her arms went around his neck.

"You don't want me to stop," he said hoarsely when he came up for air. "Admit it, Nuala."

She struggled over that one.

"Well," she said, when her heart had quieted a bit, "I suppose I don't. I'm a normal healthy woman, and you're a normal healthy man."

"I hate it when you go all reasonable on me," he said, brushing her cheek with his lips.

Nuala did what she had been waiting to do ever since that first night. She tipped the hair in his beard with one finger and watched it spring back into place. While she was doing this, his stomach growled.

He groaned.

"Maybe we can discuss it over dinner," she suggested brightly.

"Oh, Nuala," he began.

"And if you tell me you're not hungry for food, I'll know you're lying." She smiled up at him, and he couldn't help but smile back.

He let her go, but reluctantly. He kept his arm curved around her shoulders all the way up the slope to the house. He dared to think about what might happen, about what he could do to make it happen, and by the time they reached the back door, visions of the two of them attached to each other in some interesting way danced hopefully through his head.

And ended when Nuala let out a strangled little "Oh!" and ran to Cole's cage, which was startlingly empty.

Chapter Five

Nuala's gaze darted around the kitchen. "Cole?" she cried in disbelief. "Cole?" She couldn't believe the sense of terror she felt at the sight of Cole's empty cage. Beyond the cage lay the open kitchen window, screenless because Nuala had taken the screen down and hosed it off early that morning.

Not only was the bird gone, but so were Will's high hopes for the evening. And there was no sign of Cole. He felt sorry for Nuala; her face stared up at him blankly with a look of blanched pallor.

"Has this ever happened before?" he asked her gently.

"No," she said, jangling her bracelets and nibbling at the outer edge of her lip as he would like to do. His gaze fell to the cage.

Nuala went on talking. Her fingers fidgeted absently with one loose end of the sash she wore. She sounded more distraught than the situation warranted.

"The cage door's been sticking on its hinges lately," she said. "I've been meaning to spray some lubricant on them but I forgot. It looks as if a hinge gave way." She jiggled the unhinged cage door with one finger, and for a moment she looked so sorrowful that Will feared she might burst into tears.

"Hey," he said softly, touching her lightly on the shoulder. "This isn't the end of the world. It's only a mynah problem."

His touch seemed to make her jitteriness ebb out of her. He was rewarded for his attempt at humor by a tentative curving of her lips.

"Will," she said helplessly. "Oh, Will." Then he was hugging her against him, sensing the fragility of the bones beneath her skin and luxuriously aware of her hair wisping against his cheek. It was almost—but not quite—enough to make him forget his earlier thwarted intentions.

"Cole's got to be around here somewhere," he told her, reluctantly releasing her when she pulled away.

"But where?" said Nuala, swallowing the lump in her throat. It was ridiculous how upset she was over losing Cole. He was only a bird. But he was all she had.

"We'll look all through the house. He might be in here somewhere. Is there any way you call him? Would he come to either of us?"

"He's never escaped from his cage before, but I don't think he'll come if I call him. He's never given any sign of knowing his name. I know he talks like a person, but he isn't really a person. He's just a dumb bird, and he doesn't know how to take care of himself, and I don't know how cold a temperature he can withstand, so if it gets cool tonight . . ." Her voice trailed off and she cast a fearful look out the window where the twilight was fading fast.

"I'll look upstairs," Will said swiftly. "You look downstairs." He thought that at the moment he would give anything to hear Cole say one of his memorable lines, if that was what it would take to wipe that bleakness from Nuala's face.

When he bounded down the stairs after unsuccessfully searching the upper story of the house, Nuala was waiting for him in the foyer.

"He's not here," Nuala told him.

"All right," Will said calmly. "We'll look outside."

Nuala drew a deep breath and exhaled slowly. Will's steadiness kept her from running in aimless circles. His humor had put Cole's escape into perspective. She was glad he was there to take charge.

She followed him out on the back porch and down the stairs. "I don't have the foggiest idea how to catch him even if we spot him," she said worriedly.

"Are his wings clipped? Can he fly?"

"His wings have never been clipped. He could be halfway to South America by now."

"Let's hope not," Will said, tipping his head back. Overhead, a flock of birds flew by, presumably on their way to their nightly roosting spot. The woods here were deep and impenetrable; if Cole had taken it into his bird brain to hide in them, there would be no finding him.

"Let's split up," Will said decisively. "You take this side of the house. I'll take the other."

They went their separate ways, intent on the task at hand. Nuala picked up a fallen hickory branch and began to thrash the jasmine bushes alongside the house. "Cole," she called, wondering if this would do any good.

When she had searched the shrubbery as thoroughly as she knew how, she peered up into the live oaks. She flailed her branch at the shaggy beards of hanging moss. She managed to frighten a squirrel, which darted up a tree and scolded her from the safety of its heights, but there was no sign of a mynah bird.

If she didn't find Cole—well, she couldn't imagine life without him. He was the only holdover from her former life, and she was ridiculously attached to him. She could understand such an attachment if Cole had been something she could hold or pet, like a dog or a cat. But he was just a bird, and he hated to be touched. He sat in his cage all day, occasionally hopping from perch to perch, watching her with beady black eyes and tossing off a phrase now and then. It might not seem like much to most people, but Nuala was used to him. He was funny. He was alive. And he was the only living thing in the whole world who depended on her for anything.

Tears stung Nuala's eyes and she tossed the branch aside. Darkness was falling fast. If they didn't find Cole before it was night, they might as well give up.

If she couldn't find Cole, she wouldn't ever get another bird. She didn't want to depend on anyone—or anything—again.

"Nuala!"

She wheeled and ran toward the woods on the other side of the house, scarcely daring to hope.

"Look!" Will was pointing at the power line strung from a pole to the roof of the house. On it hunkered Cole, dark and crowlike, his neck drawn down into his body so he looked oddly neckless. He blinked at them soundlessly.

"Don't frighten him," Nuala said softly. "Maybe I can get him to come to me. Cole? Come on down."

"Maybe some food," suggested Will.

"Get one of those bananas you bought at the store today," Nuala said. "He loves bananas."

Will edged around the side of the house and then broke into a run toward the back door. Nuala put her hands on her hips and glared at Cole.

"Do you know how worried I've been about you?" she said. "Do you?" Cole shifted from foot to foot and cocked his head at her. It was exasperating to be standing firmly on the ground, unable to do anything to retrieve him.

Will appeared and handed Nuala a piece of peeled banana. She held it out in the palm of her hand.

"Here, Cole," she crooned. "I have some nice banana for you."

The mynah bird cocked his head in the other direction, observing her. He paid no attention to the banana.

Nuala held her hand up higher. In the gathering gloom, she thought maybe Cole couldn't see that she held his favorite delicacy.

Will stood to one side. He wondered what to do. He had no idea about a mynah bird's olfactory abilities; he didn't know if Cole could smell the banana or not.

"Come on," Nuala was saying patiently, moving closer to the power line. She moved cautiously. She dared not make any sudden movements that would frighten Cole away.

Cole eyed Nuala balefully. He did not look as though he had any intention of coming to her.

"Maybe he'd prefer something else," suggested Will. The banana was already beginning to go brown around the edges.

"But he loves bananas," Nuala said a little desperately. She had no idea what to do if this didn't work.

"I think I'll bring his cage out," Will decided. "Maybe he'll see it and want to get back in it."

"Maybe," Nuala replied doubtfully. She didn't take her eyes off Cole. She was afraid that if she did, he'd disappear.

While Will was gone, Nuala indulged herself in a few choice phrases flung spitefully at Cole. She loved this bird; how could you love a bird? Especially a recalcitrant, stubborn old buzzard like this one. Why wouldn't he come down from the power line? Didn't he know that she wouldn't try to lure him down if it weren't for his own good? Why did he insist on sitting there, grumpily gazing down at her?

"Here's his cage," Will said, hurrying around the edge of the house. "I put some celery in it. And a chunk of banana, too."

Cole stared at his cage as though he'd never seen it before.

The sky was a dark shade of gray-blue now, and the tree frogs down by the river were beginning to chirp. Soon there would be no visibility.

"When it's dark, Cole sleeps," Nuala said suddenly. "When I want him to be quiet, I darken his cage. Oh, Will, after the sun goes down completely, he won't move. He'll probably stay on that power line until morning."

"That's not good, Nuala," Will said. "There are all kinds of night birds around here. Owls, for instance. They prey on small, defenseless animals who are foolish enough to be abroad at night. We have to get Cole down from there before it's dark."

"Did you hear that, Cole?" Nuala flung the words skyward. "Will, if I ever get him down here, I swear I think I'll make Cole*slaw* out of him!"

"Once upon a time, in a land far away," Cole said, breaking his stubborn silence.

"Come down here, you old crow!"

Cole settled his head down even farther on his neck. "It was a dark and stormy night," he intoned.

"I'll go get my butterfly net, just in case he flies within reach," Will said in an undertone.

"What a *guy*!"

Nuala had the distinct feeling that Cole was mocking them. Nevertheless, she continued to try to talk him down from the power line the whole time that Will was inside the house. Her efforts were to no avail.

"If we could just get him to come down here," Will said, returning with the butterfly net. The net was made of soft white mesh attached to a hoop at the end of a pole four feet long.

"Do you have a ladder?" Nuala asked, forcing herself to consider all the options.

"The ladder wouldn't reach that high," Will said.

"It was a dark and stormy night, it was a dark and stormy night, it was a dark and—"

"Oh, you!" cried Nuala, and in desperation she bent and picked up one of the hard green oranges that had fallen off a stooped old orange tree nearby. She heaved it wildly at Cole, missing him by a good two feet. But the bird was so startled that he jumped in the air, spread his wings and glided to the ground, landing not six feet from them.

"Nice weather we're hav—"

"Gotcha!" yelled Will, whipping his butterfly net through the air. It trapped Cole. The bird went "Arrgh!" and convulsed into a spastic ball of feathers.

Will carefully turned the net over, covering the opening with a magazine he'd brought from the house. A cursory inspection told Nuala that Cole was unharmed. The bird huddled at the bottom of the net, glowering at her.

Carefully, Nuala eased the net over the open cage door. She gave the petrified Cole a gentle nudge, and then he fluttered to his perch, where he took his own sweet time settling his glossy black feathers. When that was done, he sat there dolefully, tipping his head to one side as if asking what all the fuss was about.

Will fastened the cage door with a red twist tie he'd brought expressly for that purpose.

"Whew," Nuala said, crouching on the backs of her heels. She fell backward onto damp leaves, feeling enormously relieved. All that trouble for a stupid bird. *Her* stupid bird.

"I couldn't have caught him without your help, Will," she said gratefully. "Thanks."

Will grinned a lazy grin. Night had arrived in all its starful glory, but in the dim starlight Nuala noticed how straight and white his teeth were, how dark his eyes. She admired his Lincolnesque profile, which stood out against the darkness of the trees beyond.

"You're welcome," Will said. He stood and hefted the cage in one hand. With the other, he hauled her to her feet.

"Come on," he said. "It's getting cool out here. Let's get this fine feathered friend of yours inside."

"Fine feathered fiend, I think you mean." Nuala bent to pick up the butterfly net.

"Yeah, come to think of it, that's exactly what I meant," Will said ruefully, wondering if it were possible for the two of them to regain the mood of anticipation that he had engineered before Cole's untimely escape. He doubted it.

DESPITE her unnerving experience with Cole, Nuala insisted that their evening cooking lesson proceed as usual. Happy to be with her no matter what the circumstances, Will acquiesced. They met in the kitchen after Nuala had showered and changed into a white peasant blouse and a full skirt made of tie-dyed cotton. She wore sandals laced halfway to the knee. Anyone else would have looked peculiar in such clothes. Nuala looked sexy.

But she didn't give Will time to think about sexy. She handed him a knife and a head of lettuce and instructed him to make a tossed salad.

"Now, the ham," lectured Nuala, shoving the pan in the oven, "heats very quickly. It's already cooked, you see. Just make sure you read the label and buy the kind that's already cooked."

"Yes, ma'am," said Will, who was chopping cucumbers. "What should I do with these?"

"Put them in the salad," directed Nuala. "Is the water boiling?"

Will considered the pan of water on the stove. "It's got a few bubbles around the edges. Does that count?"

"No, what we're looking for is a full rolling boil. That means big bubbles churning the surface of the water. Will Anthony, I'm going to teach you how to boil water yet!" Nuala's big hoop earrings glinted in the light above the stove.

Will cut a tomato and spread it neatly across the top of the lettuce and cucumbers in the salad bowl.

"Now you're going to toss the salad," directed Nuala, handing him a pair of salad tongs.

"You mean mess it up? After I put the tomatoes on so carefully?"

"I'm afraid so. There's a reason it's called tossed salad, you know."

"I think the water's boiling," Will told her to distract her in case he inadvertently tossed the salad right out of the bowl.

"Good," Nuala said, dumping a box of noodles into the water.

"What did you do?"

"We're having noodles Romanoff. It comes out of a box. See? The directions are on the back. All you need to do is mix the cooked noodles with butter, milk and the cheese seasoning that comes in the box. We need to turn down the heat a bit so the water won't boil over." Nuala reached around Will and adjusted the burner control. Her breast inadvertently brushed his arm.

That he couldn't ignore. He stopped tossing the salad.

"Do that again," he said softly.

"Do what? Turn down the burner?"

He swiveled his head so that his eyes found hers.

"No, Nuala. Lean up against my arm like that."

Her face flushed. "It was an accident," she stated flatly.

"Remember Will Anthony's theory number two? That things aren't always what they seem?"

"You're right," she shot back. "And this is beginning to seem less and less like a cooking lesson all the time." She busied herself by rushing to the refrigerator and yanking the butter out of its compartment and the milk off the shelf.

"What I can't figure out," Will said, as if to himself, "is why you avoid the whole issue."

"Maybe for reasons you don't know," Nuala retorted, and then she could have bitten her tongue.

"I'd certainly like to know them," he said. "You know, it seems to me like you'll go only so far. Then you stop short. I keep hoping that each time you'll go a little further. Meet me halfway. I guess what I want at this point is some encouragement, Nuala."

"I'm not sure this conversation is germane to the problems at hand," mumbled Nuala, measuring the milk.

She set the measuring cup aside and promptly knocked it over on her way back to the refrigerator.

"See? You're so uptight," Will said, mopping at the spilled milk with a sponge. He glanced up to see Nuala standing and looking at him with tears in her eyes.

He finished cleaning up the milk. Then he said lightly, "There's no use in crying over spilled milk." He ached to take her into his arms and comfort whatever needed comforting, but he sensed that at the moment his comfort would be unwelcome.

Nuala shook her head. He was always trying to lighten a serious situation, and she loved him for it. She watched him resume his tossing of the salad, blinking the glaze of tears away. If only he knew that her life was a regular morass of spilled milk and that it was all she'd been able to do to keep it from bogging her down!

"I—I'm sorry, Will," she said. "I guess Cole's little excursion took its toll. I don't think I'm over it yet."

Will set the salad on the table. "I wouldn't have thought you'd get so upset over an escaped mynah bird."

Nuala dumped the cooked noodles in a colander and pulled the ham out of the oven, taking her time about commenting. By the time Will was busy slicing the ham, she said, "Cole was a gift, Will. From somebody I cared about."

"Here," he said, handing her the platter of neatly sliced ham. "This is ready to put on the table." He watched her carefully, his interest ignited. Who was this somebody she cared about? One of her parents? A girlfriend? Some guy?

They sat at the table, both of them feeling curiously constrained.

"The noodles are delicious," Will said, after a couple of bites.

"Do you think you could make them again? All by yourself?"

"Yes," he said slowly. "If I have to. I'm hoping I won't have to."

Nuala felt inadequate for this conversation. "You know this extra week I'm staying is only a week."

"Maybe it'll be longer," Will said thoughtfully.

"Maybe it won't."

"There's the other librarian to see about a job," Will reminded her. "The one from Turkey Trot."

"I haven't decided whether I'll go see her or not," Nuala said.

From his bird cage in the corner, Cole let out a long whistle.

"I should put the cover over his cage if he's going to make noises," Nuala said.

"Let him be. I like his kind of noises. And why don't you tell me about Cole? When did you get him?"

Nuala leaned against the back of her chair, feeling reckless. If she was going to leave in a week, why not tell him everything? About the pain she'd suffered, both physical and emotional. She could depend on Will for sympathy. She was sure of that.

But all he'd asked about was Cole. So that was all she'd tell him.

"I've had Cole about three years," she said. "He's traveled everywhere with me. To Michigan, to Oklahoma, to Arizona."

"Isn't he more of a hindrance than a help? I mean, I can't imagine hauling a mynah bird all over the country."

"Cole has been a big help to me in my work. There he sits in his cage when I'm ready to begin my stories, and he's a conversation piece. Sometimes Cole *is* the conversation. He makes the kids open up and be receptive to a stranger."

Will understood. He'd been fascinated, too, the first time he'd heard Cole talk. "That makes sense," he said. He didn't say any more because he wanted Nuala to do the talking. How else would he find out anything about her?

"He's the only thing in the world who needs me," Nuala said, plunging on because of the warm understanding in Will's dark eyes. "If I lost him, I'd be losing an important part of my life." She let out her breath in a quick burst; it was the first time she'd realized that she'd even held it.

"When you say that, Nuala, it makes me think you're lonelier than you let on."

"No, not lonely exactly, just—" She stopped, not wishing to reveal too much of herself. It was so easy to share her intimate feelings with Will. She'd have to hold herself in check so that she didn't tell him too much. Give him too much. She certainly didn't want Will to harbor any false hopes about her.

While she'd been talking, Will had finished his dinner. He stood up and walked to the sink with his plate.

"I guess I'll go out to the hearse and get that big trunk of yours," he said casually, as though she hadn't revealed anything untoward at all. He seemed to sense that she needed to be alone.

"The keys are on the hook by the front door," Nuala said very quietly.

"I'll put the trunk in the parlor," he said, and after he had left, she sat silently in her chair, thinking how easy it would be to fall in love with Will Anthony.

LATER THAT NIGHT, after the dinner dishes were done, Nuala didn't seem to mind if Will watched her while she sorted out the things she'd need for her appearance at the fair tomorrow. He sat on the floor at one end of the cavernous parlor as Nuala knelt beside the trunk, revealing its secrets.

"This is my storytelling banner," Nuala said, unfurling a quilted banner fashioned of snippets of calico and embellished with lace and buttons. "I hang it up whenever I happen to be telling my stories." Outlined in lace were the words Nuala Kemp, Storyteller.

"And this—what do you do with this?" Will asked, taking a tall brass candlestick from her hands.

"Oh, that's for my wishing candle. Before I start telling a story, I often stick a candle in the candlestick and light it. I tell the children that after the candle is lit, the storyteller is the only one who is allowed to speak. It helps me to keep order, you see. Then at the end of the story time, I ask the children to make wishes and blow out the candle. Having a lighted candle around helps create a special mood for my stories."

"You must know a lot of tricks of the trade," Will said. He was enjoying this. Nuala's trunk was full of treasures.

"I had to learn most of them through trial and error. Here, Will, light this candle, will you? I had a box of candles that got wet at a fair once when it rained, and I want to make sure this isn't one of them. I need to have a reliable candle ready for the craft fair tomorrow."

Obediently Will lit the candle with the book of matches Nuala provided. "Why don't I test all of the candles from that box?" he suggested.

"Okay." She handed the box over. Will set about lighting the candles and blowing them out one after the other.

"Here's my storytelling cape," she said, lifting it almost reverently from the bottom of the trunk. She brushed aside the tissue paper in which it was wrapped and shook it out. "It was my mother's. I think she wore it for a play she was in. She was an actress, you know, before she married Dad."

"I didn't know that," Will said. He left the last candle lit, both to augment the dim light from the lamp and because he enjoyed the way the tranquil candlelight illuminated Nuala's fine features.

Nuala stood up, wrapped the cape around her shoulders, and swirled experimentally. The cape flew out around her. Then she folded the cape and set it aside before settling herself on the floor next to Will.

"Mother's stage name was Marjory O'Toole. She was flamboyantly Irish and working as a dramatic actress when she met Dad. She gave up her career to follow him. She's the one who actually dragged him kicking and screaming out from behind his desk and encouraged him to tell stories as well as collect them. Between the two of them and their consuming interest in folklore combined with dramatics, I grew up with a love of the power and the strength of words."

"What was it like, being carted off to one place or another so your parents could gather tales?"

Nuala thought for a moment. "It was enlightening. I learned that all people are alike in certain basic ways.

And that differences can be forgotten when you're fascinated with a good story. When we were home, it certainly wasn't dull. Mother and Dad provided a steady stream of visitors—poets, writers, musicians. There was always some kind of amateur play going on. It wasn't exactly your average upbringing.''

"It was a lot different from mine," Will said. "Mine was red-checkered tablecloths on the table, chocolate-chip cookies after school, and a mother who stayed home all day. Just like on *Leave It to Beaver*. Or maybe *The Andy Griffith Show*. The town in North Carolina where I grew up is a lot like Mayberry."

Nuala dug a piece of jewelry out of the trunk and held it up. It was a necklace fashioned of gray coins about the size of quarters. Light glimmered softly off the metallic surfaces.

"This necklace was given to me by a young girl in Ouagadougou in Upper Volta, which is a small country at the edge of the Sahara desert. We went there when I was about fifteen." She turned the necklace this way and that, thinking that she'd have to wear it sometime.

Suddenly Nuala saw, out of the corner of her eye, another glimmer in the murky brown shadows beyond the range of the dim light bulb and the candle flame. She whirled her head just in time for the glimmer to fade. At the same moment, something crashed upstairs. She leaped to her feet. "What was that?"

"Squirrels, probably. I'll have to get those squirrel traps out again. Sit down, Nuala."

"But didn't you see it?" Nuala's eyebrows flew upward and her hands flew outward.

"See what?"

"That—" Her mind searched for the right word. She wasn't sure how to describe what she'd seen. What she'd *thought* she'd seen. "That—*reflection* in the corner. In front of the stuffed alligator. It looked like a fragment of light reflected by a mirror."

Will glanced over his shoulder into the gloom at the other end of the parlor. All he saw was the toothy grin of the alligator.

"I didn't see a thing. I heard something, though. If you're nervous about it, I'll go check it out." He unfolded himself from his spot on the floor.

"I don't know, Will," she said, attempting a laugh. "Maybe I'm still all keyed up from what happened with Cole. I think I'll go up to bed. I can finish doing this early tomorrow morning before I leave for the fair."

She did look tired. For the first time he noticed mauve shadows under her eyes.

"Well, if you must," he said reluctantly, unwilling to let her go. He had hoped to recapture the mood of the afternoon on the river when he had felt optimistic about overcoming her obvious reluctance to construct any kind of more intimate relationship with him.

"I must," she said, moving adroitly away from him and toward the stairs.

Unhappily he watched her as she went, deciding to wait until tomorrow to check out that crash, which he suspected came from the attic. It had sounded like rather a loud crash for a squirrel.

And that reflection Nuala claimed to have seen in the shadows—it was exactly the way the former manager of this place had described what some of the guests had seen, the guests who had claimed Anthony House was haunted.

For the first time, Will uneasily wondered if he had a ghost. He also wondered if he had a ghost of a chance with Nuala.

Chapter Six

A steady breeze whipped the bright flags that flew over the Addy Mae Burke Park where the town of Turkey Trot held its annual craft fair. Children who had visited the face-painting booth romped along the paths sporting stars, comets and flowers on nose, cheeks or forehead. In the booths set up at the edge of the picnic area, artists and craftsmen displayed wares ranging from hand-smocked baby clothes to oil paintings. Nuala's storytelling took place beneath a blue-striped canvas marquee donated by the local funeral home.

Will ambled toward it, eager to watch Nuala at work. He'd had a busy morning, what with poking around in the attic looking for evidence of squirrels, which he didn't find. The screen was still firmly stapled over the louvers in the eaves where the squirrels had come in before, and Will could find no signs of anyplace else where they might have gotten in. The crash that he and Nuala had heard in the attic last night remained a mystery.

One mystery had been solved, however. He'd flagged Beckman down on the highway and asked his advice about putting the fireplace in the study in working order. Together they had pulled away the boards from the opening. The problem had turned out to be no more than a damper that was stuck. They'd managed to unstick the damper, and immediately afterward Will had written down on the real estate broker's listing form, "House has working fireplace." This, Will thought, would be a good selling point. Or maybe, as he jokingly told Beckman, even a hot selling point, since the feature in question was a fireplace.

This morning the scraps of sky that were visible through the trees arched over the park path were a bright untroubled blue, and the temperature hovered at a salubrious seventy degrees. The whole town of Turkey Trot plus an assortment of tourists and visitors from Osofkee and other nearby communities had turned out for the fair. It reminded Will of some of the fairs he'd attended in his childhood, only none of those fairs had been lucky enough to attract a storyteller. From the size of the crowd around Nuala's marquee, Will guessed that her storytelling was a huge success.

"And then hibbledy hobbledy, wibbledy wobbledy, they all toddled off to dinner!" Nuala's voice rang loud and clear over the group of children gathered to hear the story. When Will pushed through the throng of parents who stood outside the tent looking as captivated as their offspring, he saw the children crowding around Nuala to blow out the wishing candle. From his cage, Cole surveyed the scene with a cocked head and an unblinking eye.

"Hibbledy hobbledy, wibbledy wobbledy, is there any chance of your toddling off with me to lunch?" asked Will, sidling up behind her. It was all he could do to restrain himself from nuzzling her ear.

Nuala laughed. The children were surging out of the tent, still under the spell of the story.

"It is time for me to have a break," she agreed, setting a sign on an easel below her storytelling banner. She arranged the cardboard hands of the clock on the sign to indicate that the next story would begin at two o'clock.

"May I?" Will said, reaching for the heavy velvet storytelling cape.

She nodded her assent, amazed at how happy she was to see him. She had felt a warm glow inside when she'd first spotted his tall lanky figure making its way toward her through the crown, and now his friendly smile made her heart quicken. She turned away quickly so he wouldn't notice how glad she was to see him.

Will hung her cape over Cole's cage. Cole squawked once or twice and then subsided.

"I checked the attic for squirrels," Will told Nuala as they walked through the crowd together. "There weren't any."

"Well, *something* certainly made that noise last night. It reminds me of the ghost stories that have circulated about the place. You don't suppose—oh, look," Nuala said when they rounded a corner and saw the face-painting booth. A tiny red-haired girl who was clearly forcing herself to hold still against the tickling of the paintbrush sat on a stool while her face was being decorated with a tiny rainbow. Nuala turned to Will in sudden inspiration. "Will, let's have our faces done!"

"Next?" said the artist as she finished painting the rainbow.

"Here, let me help you down," Will said to the little girl as he swung her carefully off the stool. The child thanked him and ran beaming to show her mother.

"Come on, Will," Nuala urged, grinning at him from the stool. "You, too."

"But what kind of design will we get?" Will asked. He hated to deny Nuala this, but he'd feel so silly walking around with his face painted.

"Butterflies," Nuala said in a sudden stroke of genius.

Will heaved a sigh and eased his tall frame onto the other stool. "All right," he conceded, bowing to Nuala's flight of fancy. "But only if our butterflies match."

Nuala sat still as the artist painted a tiny pink-and-blue butterfly on her right cheek. The artist's assistant painted an identical butterfly on Will's left cheek. He groaned after he looked in the convenient mirror hanging from one post of the booth. "I should have had her paint a hex sign instead. To keep away any ghosts that happen to be hanging around the house. Oh, Lord, Nuala, I hope I don't run into anyone I know here." He turned his head this way and that, despairing at the way he looked. He wished now that he hadn't let her talk him into this.

"You look fine," Nuala assured him as they walked on.

"With a butterfly painted on my face? I feel like a kid."

"When I was a kid of about two years old or so, I used to call butterflies flutterbies because that's what they did—they fluttered right by."

Will laughed. "Flutterby! I never head of that before. That just shows, Nuala, that you were clever enough to play with words early in life. Maybe it was the beginning of your love of puns."

"Maybe," she agreed.

"You've been having a pretty good turnout for your storytelling, haven't you?" Will asked.

"Yes, and the children love it." She fairly sparkled with excitement. When she smiled, the butterfly on her cheek infinitesimally fluttered its wings.

"You love it, too, don't you?"

"Yes. Oh, yes. Sometimes—oh, I can't explain it, but there's a certain energy that passes between me and my audience. It always revs me up."

An assortment of fragrant food smells floated in the air as they approached the food area.

"You must be hungry after working so hard all morning."

"Mmm, yes. I could eat a—a horse!"

"Would you settle for a sloppy joe?"

"Why not?" Nuala agreed with a grin that came close to being flirtatious.

They separated, Will to stand in line for the sloppy joes and Nuala to stand in line for tall Styrofoam cups of lemonade. They met at a vacant picnic table in a nook created by the fortuitous placement of three palmetto trees. They had thought their table would be private, which was why they were surprised midway through their lunch when Beckman's elfish face suddenly appeared between two palmetto fronds. He had a thin blond girl in tow.

"There you are!" Beckman exclaimed. "I've been all over the park looking for you two!"

"Oh, no," Will moaned as Beckman tramped noisily around the trees. "Beckman's going to introduce us to somebody and here I sit with this crazy-looking butterfly on my face."

Nuala smothered a laugh. Will did look slightly comical with a butterfly seemingly perched to land on his beard.

To Will's relief, Beckman didn't seem to notice his unusual face decoration. "Will, Nuala, this is Terry Schuler," he said without preliminaries. "She's the Turkey Trot librarian. She's been wanting especially to meet you, Nuala."

Nuala had to swallow a mouthful of sloppy joe before she could say hello. Terry Schuler didn't look old enough to have graduated from high school, much less to be the Turkey Trot librarian. She wore jeans, loafers and a blouse liberally printed with clocks. She possessed a thousand-watt smile, which she beamed on them like a floodlight.

Will asked Beckman and Terry to join them, and Terry sat down. While Beckman was standing in line to get them both a cold drink, Terry quickly raised the subject of Nuala's doing a storytelling presentation at her library.

"Before you say no," said Terry, "I might as well tell you that I won't take no for an answer. My library serves the poor children of the migrant workers who flock to this area to pick winter crops. This may be the only chance any of these children will have in their whole lifetime to hear a storyteller. Please say you'll do it." Terry smiled, which made her hard to resist. Her smile made it seem as though turning her down would be turning down goodness, truth and innocence. It gave her an unfair advantage.

"I'm booked every afternoon next week," Nuala said reluctantly.

"That's okay. I'd want to schedule you for three Saturday afternoons in a row. Saturday's the best day for these migrant children to come. It's the only day they can get transportation to town."

"But—" Nuala said, her head spinning. Taking this job would mean remaining here for four weeks, counting next week.

"Oh, and I'm pretty sure I can get you a job with the local school system the week after next. There's a teacher in-service day that week, and the school librarians would like to hear some hints from a real live storyteller."

"But how did they know about me?" Nuala said, bewildered.

"Oh, Beckman mentioned you, and he suggested I contact the school superintendent about having you talk to the librarians," Terry said offhandedly.

Beckman prompted by Will, thought Nuala, gauging Will's studious expression as he concentrated all too hard on eating his sloppy joe. He saw her looking at him and avoided her eyes, choosing to focus them instead on an ant crawling its crooked way across the table.

"Think of the kids, Nuala," Beckman urged. "These are some of the most disadvantaged children I've ever seen. They travel around with their parents to harvest one crop after another, hardly able to stay in one school long enough to make friends. Most of them put in long hours alongside their parents in the fields, picking beans or tomatoes. It would mean so much to them to hear a storyteller."

"It would open whole new worlds to these children, that's for sure," Terry said, flashing that brilliant smile.

"Hmm," Nuala said, weakening.

"Please, Nuala. You won't be sorry, I know it." Beckman regarded her anxiously.

Nuala didn't have a job after the storytelling assignment next week at the Osofkee Library, and since when did she ever turn down a job? The truth was that she was almost flat broke.

"Well," she said, ignoring for the moment the disturbing possibilities that would present themselves if she continued to live at Will's house, "okay, I'll do it."

"Wonderful! Terry said.

"Terrific!" Beckman said.

Only Will did not try to communicate his approval, but then, it really wasn't necessary. He went on quietly eating his sloppy joe and drinking his lemonade, and Nuala couldn't help but read his happiness in his eyes.

WHEN THE FAIR was over and Will long departed in the direction of home, Nuala gathered up her equipment and Cole in his bird cage and stowed everything away in the hearse. She was tired, but it was a pleasant tiredness. Still, she wished she hadn't planned on another cooking lesson for Will tonight. She should have planned to pick up a takeout dinner at the Bojangles chicken place.

Nuala drove her Storymobile slowly toward home. She drove slowly because now that she knew she was going to stay here for another four weeks, she needed to think about Will's presence in her life. And she needed to think about her presence in his.

Once on television she had seen a psychologist who had been holding forth on something called limerence. Limerence was the word she had coined for the state commonly known as "being in love." The psychologist had systematically studied the romantic love phenomenon, trying to distinguish among infatuation, desire, liking, fondness and affection. There was a difference, she said, between "being in love" and loving.

This had made sense to Nuala, who was desperately hoping at the time that Joe Morini loved her. If the psychologist was right, Nuala was limerent over Joe. This meant that, among other things, Nuala was obsessed by thoughts of him, that she looked for encouragement in every nuance of Joe's expression, that she was devastated if he didn't call. All in all, it was a miserable state in which to find herself.

Joe was her limerent object, or the person about whom Nuala was limerent. Eventually they had each become the other's limerent object. This was a much improved state of affairs. Of course, when it was over, Nuala had grieved almost as though it had been a person who died and not a relationship.

And now here was Will Anthony, and she had no doubt that she was Will's limerent object. When it was necessary for her to rebuff him, she felt terrible pangs of guilt. When he was kind to her, as he had been yesterday when he'd helped her find Cole, she found that she wanted to do something equally nice for him. And when he slid half-lidded glances at her—when he thought she wasn't looking—her pulse quickened and she yearned toward him.

She'd managed to hide her reactions to him, at least most of the time. How would she manage to do this if she lived with him for four more weeks?

It was certainly flattering to be the limerent object of an attractive man like Will Anthony. It made her feel good about herself. It was wonderful to feel important to somebody again—important to a real person and not just a bird. Her overreaction to Cole's disappearance yesterday had made her take a long hard look at herself. She'd come to the reluctant conclusion that she was much too attached to Cole, and the reason was that she hadn't attached herself to a person since Joe. She'd managed to turn off good feelings toward other people—men—time and time again since she'd begun her travels.

Why? Why didn't she simply succumb and enjoy the attentions of the men she met? Maybe, if she were the type to remain emotionally uninvolved, she could have. But she wasn't that type. She knew that now.

A sudden vision of Will's hands flashed into her mind's eye, a vision of hands that could be gentle when easing a piece of fruit through the bars in Cole's cage or businesslike when poising a pencil over a typed manuscript page or efficient when chopping cucumber for the salad. How would they be when touching a woman's body—oh, all right, not just any woman's body, but her body? Would they be tender? Abrupt? Feverish? Graceful? All of the above? None of the above? She broke out in gooseflesh just thinking about it.

Speaking of a woman's body, she suddenly saw one on the side of the road. Not exactly a body, but a dressmaker's form that somebody had heaved into a garbage dumpster. She was getting as bad as Beckman; every time she passed such a spot she looked to see what goodies might have been deposited there.

As tired as she was, she had to stop. Beckman could sell the dress form at the flea market, she was sure. She hopped out of her van, shushed Cole's inquiring squawk and waded through the weeds to look the thing over. It was in pretty good shape, she thought punfully to herself, so she opened the back door of the hearse and heaved it in.

The hearse ate up the miles on the dark highway, and then, rounding a curve, she saw Will's big old house lit up golden inside. The chinaberry tree at the edge of the property, right by the split-rail fence; the driveway's gray canopy of moss swinging gently in the soft breeze; the house itself, with its lapped wooden siding and two cupolas surmounting the gabled roof—all seemed so familiar to her now.

Nuala's heart lifted at the sight of that house. In a few moments she would be seeing Will. That was all it was, and yet it was everything. The prospect gave her great joy. She felt it warm within her, like a promise.

She pulled the car to a stop in the driveway just past the grinning pink flamingo, feeling as though she wanted to groan out loud in dismay at the knowledge of what this newly realized happiness meant. She should have acknowledged it sooner, before she'd agreed to stay for four more weeks. She probably would have acknowledged it sooner, but she had a sneaky suspicion that her subconscious mind had repressed her true feelings until it was safe to let them surface.

All this time, she realized belatedly, she'd been working around to the knowledge that she was limerent about Will Anthony. *In love* with Will Anthony. She didn't know whether to laugh or to cry.

Laugh now, cry later she decided as she slammed the door of the hearse and stood outside the big house. It was impossible to cry tonight, when she felt so happy.

The night was the coldest so far this autumn, with a cool breeze blowing out of the north and frost predicted overnight. Nuala ran up the front steps of the house, shivering slightly from the cold.

"Nuala!" Will, who had been watching for the hearse's headlights, met her at the door, face flushed. Only a smear of the silly pink-and-blue butterfly remained on his face. It was warm inside the house, warm and inviting. From the kitchen emanated a tantalizing mix of odors.

She closed the door behind her, sniffing the air. "What are you up to, Will?" She was so glad to see him; he had left her only a few hours ago, and yet merely setting her eyes on him again pleasured her beyond belief. What more proof of limerence did she need?

"I thought you'd be tired when you came home, so I decided to cook dinner tonight as a surprise for you. Are you surprised?" He looked like an eager child. Her heart was gladdened and she felt unbelievably happy and touched to think that he had gone to this trouble for her.

"I certainly am," she said, smiling up at him. He knew she liked surprises. She would have liked it if he had surprised her a bit further by kissing her on the cheek. For a moment she thought he might, because he seemed to hesitate. She was disappointed when he turned away a bit too abruptly, almost as though he had wanted to kiss her but thought better of it.

She followed him into the kitchen. It was a mess, with utensils scattered everywhere, but Nuala didn't care. Their clean-up sessions, of which there had been many, were always so much fun.

"I read in the cookbook how to broil a steak, and I made the salad and baked some potatoes," Will explained. "I put the steak on when I heard you roll into the driveway. It'll be ready in a few minutes." He looked justifiably proud of himself.

"Good," she said. "That gives me just enough time to run upstairs and freshen up. Unless you want me to stay and help?"

"No, no. You go ahead. I'm doing this," Will said. It occurred to him that he could have said, "I'm doing this for you," but surely she would know that, wouldn't she?

Nuala did. She beamed at him and ran up the back stairs suddenly feeling uncommonly shy.

With some regret, Nuala scrubbed off the butterfly painted on her face. Then she leafed through the dresses hanging in the closet, and suddenly none of them seemed good enough. This one was too short and would show her knobby knees. This one was too old, she must have bought it ages ago. This one was a shade of green that didn't do all that much for her. Finally she settled on an ecru Gunne Sax dress, which she had bought recently in a little thrift shop in Baton Rouge. The dress had a scooped neckline, yards of crocheted lace instead of a collar, and ruffles at the bottoms of the sleeves that draped elegantly over her wrists.

She managed a quick shower, brushed her hair before fastening it behind one ear with a beribboned clip, and slipped into the dress. She thought it looked okay, but she wished she looked better.

Will thought she looked beautiful. He greeted her at the bottom of the stairs, admiration pouring from his eyes.

"You look lovely," he said softly, sending her heart into a spasm.

He had donned a tie for the occasion, and he'd transformed the kitchen into an intimate little dining nook for two by the clever use of a brass lamp from the study and a candle on the table.

"Where'd you get the candle?" Nuala asked.

"Don't you recognize the candlestick? It's one of the silver ones you spent so much time polishing. It once belonged to old William Anthony himself. See, there's the monogram right at the base. Creates a nostalgic atmosphere, don't you think?''

"It's very nice," Nuala said.

"I got the idea from your storytelling candle. You said it creates an atmosphere. Which is why I decided I needed my own wishing candle."

"Oh?" she said. "And suppose you tell me what you're wishing for."

"At the moment, I'm wishing that I'll cook an edible dinner." But he grinned at her, and she knew he was wishing for more than that.

Will absolutely refused any help from Nuala. He seated her and then proceeded to serve the dinner. He started with the wine, a beguiling Burgundy that slid easily down her throat and warmed her from the inside out.

"What's the matter, isn't it good?" Will asked anxiously when Nuala merely picked at her food.

"Oh, no, Will, it's delicious. Everything is wonderful," she assured him quickly. She simply didn't have any appetite. Instead of eating, she wanted to look at Will, at the neat eyebrows, which rose and fell in cadence with his voice, at the springy hair of his beard, at the slash of straight hair that fell over his forehead.

She forced herself to eat. The baked potato was fine and so was the salad. The steak was only slightly overdone. But she wouldn't have criticized anything for the world.

After they had eaten, Will insisted they leave the cleaning up for tomorrow and drink the last of their wine in the study. Carrying his wishing candle, he drew her into the darkened room where a fire glowed in the fireplace.

At Nuala's questioning look, Will said, "I fixed it this morning. I thought it'd be nice to use it when the weather is cold. Also, it needed to be repaired if I'm going to sell the place. Anyway, it's getting close to flue season." He managed to say this with a straight face.

"That must be why I have such tinder feelings," Nuala shot back, her quick wit belying the nervousness she felt.

Will laughed and set the candle on a nearby table. "Help me pull this couch over to the fireplace," he said.

The couch was of horsehair, well past its prime, and had been nibbled by mice. Will hauled a fringed woolen car throw rug from a cabinet beside the fireplace and spread it in front of the hearth. He lifted the seat cushion from the green velvet love seat and leaned it against the couch's legs. They sat on the blanket and rested their backs against the cushion, cradling their wineglasses in their hands. In front of them the fire crackled and sent little golden sparks rushing up the chimney.

In the rich blend of candlelight and fire glow, Will's skin was softened to a mellow shade of bronze. They sat very close, sharing the moments quietly. Nuala lost herself in sensation: the warmth of the fire upon her face, the roughness of the blanket against her bare legs, the piney fragrance of the logs piled next to the hearth, the wine inducing a comfortable languor. She closed her eyes only to have them fly open in startled awareness when she felt Will's fingertips graze her arm.

Will gazed at her through partially closed eyelids, the firelight picking out the amber highlights in his dark eyes.

"Nuala," he said lazily. "That's a pretty name— Nuala." Her name rolled easily off his tongue and she thought she had never heard it pronounced more beautifully.

"My parents named me after the Nuala in Irish mythology," she told him as his fingers progressed up the inside of her arm, sending little tremolos spinning straight to her heart. "The original Nuala was the wife of the king of the western fairies."

"I can see her in my imagination," Will said a trifle dreamily. "She would wear filmy dresses gleaming with dewdrops. She'd fly on gossamer butterfly wings—"

"Flutterby wings," injected Nuala.

"Flutterby wings, and she would be very beautiful. But not nearly as beautiful as you. You are well named, Nuala Kemp. Because I think of fairies as joyful beings, and I find great joy in you, do you know that?" His fingers continued to stroke the inside of her arm. Then he added under his breath, "And joy is so rare between men and women."

"It is?"

"It always has been in my case," he said.

At the moment, warmed in the glow of Will's attention, Nuala was unwilling to be reminded that there might ever have been anyone else in Will's life.

His voice was urgent. "Do you mind if I tell you about it?" He felt a compulsion to speak of Virginia, almost as though doing so would dispel her from his thoughts for good.

Nuala would have drawn back, but Will sensed it and slid his hand down her arm until his fingers laced with hers.

"No," Nuala said reluctantly, taking heart from his hand clasping hers.

"There was a woman before I came here," he said in a low voice. "I saw her for about a year, but I was never in love with her. I was sorry when I had to hurt her feelings, but I broke it off when she decided she wanted to get married.''

They were silent for a long time. Finally the silence was broken by the clock on the mantel striking eleven. Then, ''What was she like?'' Nuala asked in a small voice.

''She is a professor at the university, and she is—scientific. And basically an unhappy person. You're such a happy contrast to her that—well, let's say I appreciate you, Nuala, after my experience with her. That doesn't mean that Virginia isn't a fine person. She is. But she's not for me.''

He appreciated her, Nuala. So what was she supposed to reply to this sort of revelation? *You appreciate me, I limerence you?* Will would think she was as nutty as a—

Something fell over in the attic. It sounded like the same sort of crash they'd heard last night.

''I thought you said there weren't any squirrels,'' Nuala murmured.

''They must be getting in someplace,'' Will said, not interested in squirrels or anything else but Nuala at the moment. He lifted Nuala's hand so that her palm lay against his face, and then he was moving it so that her fingers brushed his beard and finally curled around the back of his neck inside his shirt collar. He released her hand there and let his hand come to rest on a trailing lock of her hair. Then he brushed it back over her shoulder and, breathing faster, slid his hand around her back so that it pressed against her shoulder blades, pulling her slowly toward him.

She turned and allowed her free arm to slide around him, savoring the warm hard flesh beneath her palm. A sharp pang of desire pierced her, ebbing into a kind of entranced inertia. His beard brushed the side of her face, and she lifted her lips to his.

His mouth upon hers was soft and sent a quiver through her, a breathless wondering at the rightness of it. As his arms crushed her to him, she felt his body spring taut with longing for her. She strained against him, concentrating on the silken moistness of his lips, which laughed so readily, and which incited a hunger in her.

Despite the warmth of the fireplace, Nuala suddenly felt as though a cold draft had whipped through the room. The candle flame quivered momentarily but did not go out. The draft was enough to make her stiffen against him but it was not enough to make her stop what he was doing to her.

"What's wrong?" Will murmured, stroking her breast. His eyes looked sleepy, as though he had just awakened.

"I felt a chill," Nuala whispered, casting a fearful glance into the corners of the room.

"Poor baby," Will crooned, lapping the corners of the blanket over her shoulders. "I'll have to try a little harder to keep you warm."

"You're doing a pretty good job," she acknowledged, burrowing against his chest. It was so cozy, so cozy and warm, and Will's fingers drifting slowly again and again across her breast were increasingly arousing. She lost herself in his deep kisses, which were becoming more urgent and more insistent. *I limerence you, Will Anthony,* she thought, muzzily wondering if Will had ever heard of that particular theory of love and romance and what he thought of it if he had. Her lips curved upward into a tender smile just as his lips captured hers.

Her fingers locked behind his neck, drawing him down beside her, and Will marveled at how rosy her usually pale skin looked in the light of the flickering fire. He felt a sudden aching hunger for her, and he realized belatedly that sheer instinct was overruling caution. He told himself to take it easy, that he didn't want to rush, but when he felt the racing heartbeat beneath her gently rounded breast, he couldn't help moaning with the tension of holding back.

He lifted her from the blanket, pausing to press his lips once against the throbbing pulse in her neck, weaving his fingers through her long hair. He raised her until she knelt above him, an ecru-clad goddess limned in fire glow, marveling at the lovely perfection of her even features, her pale skin, her violet-blue eyes.

"Nuala the fair," he whispered. "Nuala the beautiful," and he buried his face in the hollow between her breasts.

Her dress buttoned down the front with little pearl buttons, and slowly, carefully, he began to undo them. Nuala's warm moist breath feathered the strands of hair slanting across his forehead; her chest heaved as though she couldn't catch her breath. When his warm hands touched the cool flesh in the space between the parted opening, Nuala gasped, a quick intake of breath.

Slowly he drifted his hands across the smooth skin of her rib cage, and the lacy bodice slid to her waist. He unfastened the wisp of a bra and she shrugged first one shoulder, then the other, so that it fell away. Her breasts were high and round and firm.

She let him look at her, her eyes dark with emotion. She started to unbutton his shirt, and then, without any preliminary warning, they heard it.

"What was that?" Nuala gasped, clutching her bodice.

Will sat up straight, listening intently. But there was no doubt in either of their minds exactly what they were hearing.

Heavy footsteps were plodding slowly down the creaking front stairs.

Then the candle flame shivered and died.

Chapter Seven

Will bounded to his feet and switched on the lamp. A hundred-and-fifty watts of harsh incandescent light flooded the room. They blinked at each other in frozen shock.

Will ran to the archway between the study and the hall. No one was there; the front door was securely bolted. He cast a wary look up the stairs. A single light burned on the landing; he had lit it earlier, before Nuala came home.

It was Nuala who first broke the silence.

"Unless squirrels have taken to wearing clodhoppers, that was no squirrel!"

"Then what was it?" Will, usually calm and unflappable, was not calm now.

Nuala had slipped her arms through the sleeves of her dress and was fumbling with the buttons. She jumped up, her heart pounding.

"I don't know what that was. But I didn't like it. I'm getting out of this house!"

"Nuala, be sensible. Where would you go?"

"I—don't know," she said, her breath catching in her throat. It was true; there was nowhere to go. She didn't have the money for a motel, and she knew virtually no one around here except Beckman. She could hardly imagine herself knocking on the door of his little cabin and asking for lodging for the night. Where would she sleep? On Beckman's sagging gray couch? The prospect was not inviting.

"Come with me," Will said suddenly. "I want to check the parlor, the dining room and the kitchen. The upstairs, too."

"In the dark?"

"No," Will said, striding to his desk. He yanked a drawer open and pulled out a large flashlight. He flicked on the beam.

"We'll turn on lights as we go, but this is in case they don't work. Let's go." He gripped her hand firmly in his.

Carefully they worked their way through all the downstairs rooms. Nothing was out of place; both back door and front door were locked and showed no sign of being disturbed. In his cage in the kitchen, Cole blinked at them in puzzlement. They tossed a tablecloth over his cage so that he'd sleep.

They used the back stairs, and Will shone his flashlight on the four-foot-high door that led to the attic. "Want to check up there?" he asked.

Nuala shook her head. "No."

"I left the key downstairs anyway," Will said, who had no desire to tackle the dark, cramped attic. He could do that tomorrow.

Nothing appeared amiss in any of the bedrooms. There was no sign of anyone other than themselves. In every room, they left a trail of lights.

"Let's not turn any of the lights out," Will said when they were back downstairs in the study. "Somehow the lights make the house seem more safe."

Nuala, suddenly cold, picked the blanket up from the floor and wrapped it around herself. Tears flooded her eyes. She didn't know what to think. Was she in danger? Should she be afraid? Why was this happening?

When Will saw her tears, he vaulted across the room in two steps. He pulled Nuala, blanket and all, into his arms. "I was just as frightened as you were," he said when her cheek rested against his chest. "But I think we should stick it out. Together."

Nuala nodded numbly. "Do you suppose it was the...the ghost?"

Will chuckled. "I don't believe in ghosts. But I'm not afraid. If there's a logical explanation for such an occurrence, I'll find it. Tomorrow, not tonight, when I can check out the attic. I prefer to do any further exploring in broad daylight."

"Thank goodness for that," breathed Nuala. "And Will, don't you dare leave me. I don't want to be alone. And I don't think we should turn off the lights tonight."

"I have no intention, darling, of letting you be alone. We can leave the lights on as long as you like. Come on, sit with me again in front of the fire." He sat and pulled her down beside him.

"I'm still frightened," she said, hugging her knees. The romantic mood of only minutes ago was irrevocably shattered. She felt a stab of sadness for that, but there was no helping it. In place of her frankly sexual feelings was a feeling of a common bond with Will. They had just shared a very strange experience, one that she'd find hard to explain to anyone else.

Nuala shivered. "When I first heard those footsteps on the stairs, I thought someone had broken into the house."

"So did I," Will said. "But there couldn't have been anyone. Both doors were bolted."

"That crash earlier—it was like the crash last night when we were looking through my trunk. And remember the funny reflection I saw in the parlor last night? I saw it just after the crash we heard in the attic. The footsteps tonight happened right after the crash."

"I'm afraid I have no answers," Will said, feeling frankly puzzled. His scientific mind searched for reasonable explanations, but there didn't seem to be any.

He knelt in front of the hearth and added another log to it so that the flames shot higher, banishing the chill that had plagued the room since they'd heard the ghostly footsteps. He sat down and wrapped his arms around Nuala. The bright lamplight dispelled any fears; he was beginning to feel almost normal again. Nuala's trembling subsided, and Will felt comforted by a rising contentment. This was not the evening he had planned, the evening he had fervently wished for with his now defunct wishing candle, but it wasn't bad, either.

"Think about what a good story you'll have to tell," he murmured into Nuala's neck.

"This is one story I'd rather read in a book," Nuala said sleepily. She let her head fall to his shoulder, drawing reassurance from his strength until at last she felt calm again.

They sat lulled by the flames, finally falling asleep in each other's arms, where they stayed, periodically awakening and reassuring each other, until the tender light of the morning sun slipped faintly up from the horizon.

BECKMAN STOPPED BY the next day, Sunday, on the way to the flea market to relay a message to Nuala from

Martha Cale. Nuala, who didn't like standing in the front hall at the bottom of the staircase where their unseen visitor had made his presence so loudly known the night before, went out to the front porch to talk with him.

Beckman looked jaunty in his red nylon windbreaker and his blue baseball cap. "Martha says to bring that bird of yours when you come Monday," he told Nuala.

"I'm planning on it," Nuala said distractedly.

"Did Nuala tell you what happened last night?" Will said, popping out the front door. "We had a visitor."

"I'm surprised at that. Not too many people get out this way these days."

"Oh, this wasn't your usual drop-in guest. In fact, we couldn't even see it. But it knocked something over in the attic and walked noisily down the front staircase, creating quite a breeze. What do you think it was?"

Beckman's colorless eyes sparkled with interest. A big grin spread across his face. "Oh, it was the captain. No doubt about it."

"The *captain*!" chorused Will and Nuala.

"Sure. Captain William Anthony himself. He always gets nervous when there's talk about selling this place. You're still talking to that real estate fellow, aren't you, Will?"

"Well, yes, but—"

"You've got the captain all stirred up. He never did like the idea of this house being sold out of the family. Heh-heh!" Beckman slapped his knee and danced a little jig on the front porch. "You know," he said with a glint in his eyes, "I'm kind of glad to know the captain is still around."

Will and Nuala exchanged a look.

"Beckman, do you have time for a cup of coffee?" Nuala asked unsteadily.

"Sure," he said, following them inside. Nuala was careful to give the front stairs a wide berth when she walked through the foyer, but Beckman slapped the banister heartily in passing.

"So tell me more about my illustrious ancestor, the captain," Will said when they were all seated around the kitchen table.

"Oh, your great-grandfather William was something special, that's all there is to it," Beckman said with obvious glee. "He arrived here with a riverboat and ran fishing and sight-seeing excursions for the Northerners who came south for the winter. Started a logging business later, and then he built this inn."

Beckman spared a look around the big kitchen. "Oh, this was a grand old house in its heyday. Railroad barons, financiers, steel tycoons—anybody who loved to fish or hunt came to the beautiful St. Johns River to fish for bass and hunt the wild turkeys and alligators. The men brought their wives, all dripping with diamonds. Anthony House was a sight to see in those days."

"But you weren't alive then," Nuala said. She recalled that Will had told her Beckman would soon be ninety.

"I was born in '97. I grew up right down the road in a house near the cabin where I live now. Captain Anthony was an important man in these parts, and I spent many a day listening to the rip-roaring stories he told. Now there was a storyteller, Nuala. The captain served in the Confederate navy during the Civil War, and after that he was a riverboat captain on the Mississippi, and he used to hold forth with some real tales for the benefit of guests. He liked me, the captain did. Hired me to work on one of his riverboats when I was just a kid."

"You became a riverboat captain yourself, didn't you?" Will asked.

"Sure did. I was the captain of the last riverboat to travel these parts. The *Victorine*, that was her name. We scrapped her in 1925, and I soon landed the job of postmaster in Turkey Trot. Captain Anthony died not long after that."

"Did he die here—in this house?" Nuala asked.

"Yes, and there was talk of selling the place then. There weren't many tourists—people preferred to ride the trains down to south Florida by that time. And that's when I first heard talk of ghosts."

"William Anthony's ghost?" Will asked.

Beckman nodded. "I was courting one of the maids who lived here. She saw Captain Anthony quite a few times after he died. It was when it looked as though the house was going to be sold, maybe torn down. She said he liked to hang around that stuffed alligator in your parlor. Must be 'cause the captain shot it himself."

Nuala raised her eyebrows at Will. In front of the alligator was where she'd seen the funny reflection the night before last.

Beckman continued. "Right about that time, Heyward Anthony—your grandfather, Will—came back from up north and decided to run the place as a boardinghouse."

"What happened to the ghost?"

"Oh, Captain Anthony never showed himself after his son made up his mind to keep the place in the family. Heyward saw Captain Anthony a few times himself. He said the captain made noises in the attic and tramped up and down the stairs at eleven o'clock every night. That was the time, when he was still alive, that the captain used to check all the doors at Anthony House and make sure everything was locked up tight. Now, I don't know what Captain Anthony did to convince Heyward, but there was never any talk of selling the house after the ghost made his presence known. In life, Captain Anthony always said that the house must always stay in the Anthony family. He was real stubborn about that. Had his heart set on it."

Nuala turned to Will. "Will, you've been planning to sell the house. Do you think that has anything to do with the ghost?"

Will heaved a sigh. "I'm a scientist, Nuala. I've never believed in ghosts."

"But you heard that racket last night. And I think I saw something in the corner of the parlor the night before. Oh, Will! I think it's old Captain Anthony!"

"Could be," Beckman agreed. "In fact, it probably is! You know, I'd like to check out that attic with you, Will. There's got to be some reason for the crash you hear just before the captain turns up."

"Let's do it now," Will said. He pushed his chair back.

"Not so fast, not so fast," Beckman said. "I don't have time right now. If I don't get to the flea market, I won't sell the stuff I'm taking over there to sell. That high chair cleaned up real well. I put a new strap on it, you know. But I'll go up in the attic with you later today, Will. I don't think it's squirrels you've got up there."

"If I don't have squirrels in my attic, maybe I've got bats in my belfry," Will said wryly.

Beckman crackled. "No, you're not crazy, Will. It's the captain causing all the trouble you're having. I'd bet on it."

Beckman tried to persuade both Will and Nuala to go to the flea market with him, but they declined.

"Some other time, Beckman," Nuala promised. Then she remembered the dressmaker's form she'd found last night on her way home.

"Oh, I have something for you, Beckman," she told him, leading him to the hearse. When she pulled out the form, Beckman's eyes lit up.

"It's perfect! I brought that wedding dress today— you know, the one I found in the dumpster all wrapped in plastic? It'll be perfect to display the wedding dress on."

The three of them heaved the form into the back of Beckman's loaded pickup.

"I'll come back tonight, Will," Beckman said. "We can explore that attic of yours then." With a wave out the window, he roared out of the driveway and down the highway in the direction of Turkey Trot.

"I'm finding it hard to believe Beckman's theory," Will said. "The old fellow's as bright as a button, and I'd pit his intellect against anyone's, but could it be that he's beginning to fade a bit? He acted as though he actually believed in ghosts!"

"Wait," Nuala said. "Didn't you tell me there's a family burial ground around here someplace? I'm extremely curious about Captain William Anthony. I'd like to see where he's buried."

"I can show it to you," Will said. "It's only a short walk through the woods."

Will led her to a narrow path at the edge of the woods surrounding the house. The leaves of the oak trees were a rich brown, and the fallen ones crackled underfoot.

He took Nuala's hand. "I'm glad you wore sturdy shoes," he said. "On warm, sunny days like this, the rattlesnakes come out of their burrows and sun themselves."

"Rattlesnakes?"

"Oh, they're more scared of you than you are of them. They won't strike unless cornered. Most of the time they just slither off into the woods." Nevertheless, Nuala kept a firm grip on Will's hand. The path was narrow, and encroaching branches plucked at her sweater and her long, loose hair. They stopped for a moment so that Nuala could twist her hair into a knot on top of her head and fasten it with a barrette she found in the pocket of her jeans.

"Here it is," Will said finally, after Nuala had begun to see a snake in every fallen sun-speckled twig on the path ahead. "This is the Anthony family burial ground."

An iron fence surrounded a small clearing overlooking the St. Johns. Spanish moss swooped low over the headstones, which were streaked with mildew and green with moss.

"This is my grandfather's grave," Will said, brushing fallen leaves off the headstone that read Heyward Anthony. "And here's Grandma Anthony beside him." The big double headstone reminded Will of the double headboard on the bed his grandparents had shared for forty years.

Nuala wandered among the other headstones. She didn't find the one she was searching for.

"I don't see a tombstone for Captain Anthony," she said.

Will put an arm around her shoulders. "Maybe it's over here," he suggested, leading her closer to the river. "William Anthony was a riverboat captain. Maybe he wanted to be buried in view of the St. Johns."

"Mary Frances Anthony...James Anthony... Zephyr Anthony...Ezra Anthony," Nuala read. All these headstones were grouped together.

"Mary Frances was Captain Anthony's wife," Will said, looking puzzled. "The others were his children who died in infancy. My grandfather Heyward was the captain's only surviving child."

They carefully measured out their steps again, re-checking all the names.

"I don't understand it," said Will, who was clearly surprised. "According to custom, Captain Anthony should have been buried right next to his wife, Mary Frances."

"Captain Anthony died at Anthony Guest House," Nuala said. "Beckman said so. So I'm sure he wouldn't be buried elsewhere."

Finally when there seemed to be no more point in looking, they gave up the search. They trudged back to the house, puzzling over the absence of the tombstone of Anthony House's founder. As attached as the captain was to the place, Will couldn't imagine his ancestor being buried anywhere but the family plot.

"It's odd," Will said over lunch. "I've never noticed that Captain Anthony wasn't buried in the family cemetery."

"Maybe Beckman knows why there's no headstone for him," Nuala suggested.

But by the time Beckman returned late that afternoon for what he called the Great Attic Exploration, Nuala and Will were both concentrating on what they might find there. Will didn't expect to find anything related to the "ghost," but Nuala was not so sure. She was apprehensive.

She had no intention of letting the two men go up into the attic without her. "Let me go with you," she said. "I don't want to miss out on any of this."

She looked so determined that Will's eyes softened and he curved an arm around her shoulders. "Sure. Anybody who could follow her parents through the wilds of darkest Africa and up the mountains of Tibet ought to be able to handle the Anthony House attic. Anyway, you might want to go through some of the junk up there. Maybe you'll find some story props, who knows?"

Nuala followed Will and Beckman up the back stairs. At the top, Will unlocked the squat wooden door that led to the attic staircase. The door creaked loudly on rusty hinges. Will flicked a light switch, dimly illuminating both the attic and the stairs.

Nuala peered up the cramped and dusty staircase, which was as narrow as a ladder and almost as steep. "Careful," Will said. "You'll both need to watch your step." Cautiously they picked their way up the steep stairs.

The attic ceiling was so low that Will couldn't stand up straight. Beckman, stooped as he was, seemed right at home. He scurried about, poking into crates, kicking a barrel or two. Will and Nuala had to walk in a kind of half-crouch.

"When you sell this place, Will, I hope you'll let me take this old stuff over to the flea market. It'd make a fortune for my Christmas party fund," Beckman said, looking longingly at one of the crates.

"You're welcome to it," Will assured him. "In fact, you might as well take some of it now. See what you can find." Mindful of low-hanging beams, he straightened after checking the screening around the louvers where the squirrels had entered before. The screening was intact.

Nuala brushed aside a cobweb and looked around at the array of trunks, boxes, crates and old furniture while Will took his time checking the eaves. "Just like when I looked yesterday; there are absolutely no places where squirrels or other animals might be coming in," Will told them finally.

Beckman had been busy digging in a few boxes, exclaiming all the while over the things he found. He sat amid a pile of items that he knew would sell at the flea market. Nuala helped him to sort the treasures into stacks and piles.

She was about to pry open the top of one of the barrels when, with a sharp exclamation, Beckman pulled a large bronze vase out of the crate. He peered at it for a long moment with a peculiar expression on his face. His hands shook as he held it.

"Nuala, see if you can read this," he demanded. "I don't have my glasses with me."

Nuala took the vase from him. She squinted at it in the dim light. "It's some kind of inscription," she said with a growing sense of discovery. Will, his attention caught by the tone of her voice, hurried to her side. He noticed that she paled visibly as she read the words engraved at the base of it.

Suddenly Nuala seemed to lose her hold on the vase. It crashed to the attic floor. Nuala's hands flew to her face.

"Nuala? What is it?"

"It's what I thought it was," Beckman said with a satisfied little grin.

"It's the captain," Nuala said tonelessly. "That's an urn for his ashes." Her eyes met Will's. "He's not buried in the family plot, Will. He was cremated."

The three of them looked down at the bronze urn. The metal gleamed dully in the dim light.

Beckman hopped to his feet. "Sure, that's right," he said gleefully. "The captain had it written in his will that he was to be cremated. 'Course, everybody got kind of upset about it. That wasn't one of the things people around here did in those days. But the captain had some strange idea about it. Said the Hindus did it all the time. Turned out he set his own cremation up himself before he died, so they sent him down the river to Jacksonville in his coffin and he came back in this urn. Why, people came from all over the county to pay their respects afterward, but mostly it was to see if those cremation folks really managed to put the big captain into this urn."

"It's hardly what I expected to find in my attic," Will said, looking shaken. "Aren't people who are cremated usually interred in mausoleums?"

"Sure, but, Will, you have to remember that there weren't any mausoleums here in Okeelokee County back in those days. Your grandfather probably didn't know what else to do with the captain."

Will lifted the bronze urn from the floor. He stared down at it. "What'll I do with it, for that matter?" he said in bewilderment.

"Leave it here," chorused Nuala and Beckman.

NOW THAT THE DOOR IS OPEN...
Peel off the bouquet and send it on the postpaid order card to receive:

 Harlequin American Romance

4 FREE BOOKS!
An attractive burgundy umbrella—FREE!
And a mystery gift as an EXTRA BONUS!
PLUS

MONEY-SAVING HOME DELIVERY!
Once you receive your 4 FREE books and gifts, you'll be able to open your door to more great romance reading month after month. Enjoy the convenience of previewing four brand-new books every month delivered right to your home months before they appear in stores. Each book is yours for only $2.25—25¢ less than the retail price.

SPECIAL EXTRAS—FREE!
You'll get our free monthly newsletter, *Heart to Heart*—the indispensable insider's look at our most popular writers and their upcoming novels. You'll also get additional free gifts from time to time as a token of our appreciation for being a home subscriber.

NO-RISK GUARANTEE
- There's no obligation to buy—and the free books and gifts are yours to keep forever.
- You pay the lowest price possible and receive books months before they appear in stores.
- You may end your subscription anytime—just write and let us know.

RETURN THE POSTPAID ORDER CARD TODAY AND OPEN YOUR DOOR TO THESE 4 EXCITING, LOVE-FILLED NOVELS. THEY ARE YOURS ABSOLUTELY FREE, ALONG WITH YOUR FOLDING UMBRELLA AND MYSTERY GIFT.

HARLEQUIN READER SERVICE
901 Fuhrmann Blvd.,
P.O. Box 1394,
Buffalo, NY 14240-9963.

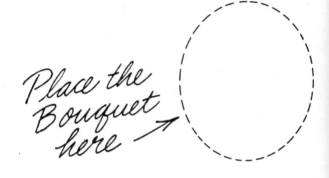

Place the Bouquet here →

Yes! I have attached the bouquet above. Please send me my four Harlequin American Romance® novels, free, along with my free folding umbrella and mystery gift. Then send me four new Harlequin American Romance® novels every month as they come off the presses, and bill me just $2.25 per book (25¢ less than retail), with no extra charges for shipping and handling. If I am not completely satisfied, I may return a shipment and cancel at any time. The free books and gifts remain mine to keep.

154 CIA NA75

Name _____

Address _____ Apt. _____

City _____ Province/State _____

Postal Code/Zip _____

Offer limited to one per household and not valid for present subscribers. Prices subject to change.

PRINTED IN U.S.A.

Take this beautiful
FOLDING UMBRELLA
with your 4 FREE BOOKS
PLUS A MYSTERY GIFT
If order card is missing, write to Harlequin Reader Service,
901 Fuhrmann Blvd., P.O. Box 1394, Buffalo, NY 14240-9963.

"It's not exactly something I want to look at every day when I'm dusting the parlor," Nuala added.

Will grinned. "All right. For now we'll leave the captain up here in the attic to play his nightly nocturne."

"Knocked urn?" said Nuala in a small voice, because she knew Will expected it.

"You got it." Will set the urn back in the crate where Beckman had found it. His hand stroked the bronze urn respectfully. "I'll bury the captain in the family plot someday," he said with a hint of reverence. "That's where he belongs, right beside Mary Frances. We'll have a short, quiet service, and I'll have a headstone made."

"I think that's best, Will," agreed Beckman. "But I think that the presence of this urn explains the crash you hear in the attic. Obviously the captain's spirit feels tied to this place and his earthly remains. Somehow, to get your attention, he makes a noise up here before he walks down the stairs. Kind of like telling you that Anthony Guest House is his territory, from top to bottom."

Will shook his head. "I suppose that theory explains the whole thing as well as anything else anybody's thought of," he said.

Without further discussion, the three of them gathered up Beckman's flea market finds and made their way silently downstairs.

"I wonder if the captain will walk down the stairs tonight," Nuala mused as they all sat in the parlor going through the memorabilia she had brought down from the attic. Some of the things she wanted to keep for her storytelling trunk.

Beckman stuffed the items he was taking home into large plastic sacks provided by Will. "Oh, I'm sure

Captain Anthony will be back. I wish I could stay to see him, but I've had a long day and I want to go home and go to sleep. Thanks for the stuff, Will.'' Beckman bade Nuala goodbye, and Will helped him stack the sacks in the back of his pickup.

When Will came back into the house, Nuala was waiting for him in the parlor.

"Look, Will," Nuala said, brushing the dust off an old picture frame. "Here's a picture of your great-grandfather's riverboat."

Will took the photograph Nuala held out.

It was faded sepia photo of a big sidewheeler river-boat tied up at a massive wooden dock. The picture had been taken from the riverside, and in the background the gabled roof of the house could be clearly seen over the tops of the moss-hung trees.

"The *Victorine*," said Will, pleased. "I'm glad you found this, Nuala. I'll hang it in the study. This is one memento I wouldn't want Beckman to sell at the flea market. What else did you find up there?"

"Oh, a wonderful lace shawl and an old children's ABC book and this lovely fan," Nuala said, sweeping a delicately wrought Chinese ivory fan open for his inspection. She peered at him through the openwork.

"Very seductive," Will said, captivated by the winsome flash of blue-violet eyes behind the fan. He reached out and touched her hair.

Nuala heaved a deep sigh. They'd have to have a talk. She'd been thinking about it all day—that is, when she wasn't thinking about the possibility of ghosts. At the moment, her memory of the supernatural events of the night before had faded. Her memory of everything else hadn't faded at all, however; in fact, with that one gentle gesture, Will had managed to call it all vividly to mind.

"About last night," she began uneasily.

"About last night," he agreed. "Maybe we could pick up where we left off before the captain interrupted us."

Nuala refused to smile. Instead, she snapped the fan shut. Then she sighed and sank down on the floor beside the couch. Will sat on the couch, and after a few moments' thought, he swung his feet up on it and put his hands behind his head. If they were in for a major discussion, he might as well be comfortable.

"About last night," Nuala said again when Will was settled.

"Second thoughts?" inquired Will. Nuala was fidgeting with a loose piece of yarn on the teal-blue sweater she wore. She always fidgeted with something when she was nervous.

She ventured a brave look at him. "Yes," she said.

"You're not going to be here for just a week, Nuala. You have jobs lined up for four weeks. And after that— who knows?"

"After that I'll be leaving," she said firmly.

"Maybe not," he said.

"I will be leaving," Nuala repeated.

"What if it turns out to be love?"

"It's limerence," Nuala said before she thought, and then she blushed.

"It's what?" He propped himself up on his elbows and looked at her.

"Limerence," she said, rapidly explaining the psychologist's theory.

"Good Lord, at first I thought that word was some kind of pun." Will lay back down on his back and folded his hands on his chest.

"Well, it is a Punday night. I can see why you'd think that." She held her breath.

Instead of replying in kind the way he usually did, Will reached out and took her hand. He squeezed it once, then threaded his fingers through hers.

"Nuala, I wish that modern men and women could fall in love and let things take their natural course without calling in a psychologist. What did people do in the days before the popular press glorified hang-ups? We're bombarded with articles like 'Six Ways to Make Your Man Stop Cheating on You,' and 'Does He Really Love you? Give Him This Test and Find Out.'"

"You don't read those articles, I hope."

"No, and I wish women wouldn't read them, either. They make mountains out of molehills. When will women get tired of being manipulated by every pop psychologist who comes along hoping to make a fast buck?" He was thinking of Virginia, who had been so far off base, and all because she had read that silly magazine article. And now here was Nuala, talking about limerence. Limerence wasn't what he wanted to hear, although there might be something to the theory. What Will wanted to hear about was love.

"It's just that what this particular psychologist says makes sense, about the way a person feels when she cares about another special person," Nuala said unhappily. "She made a systematic study of the feelings, the..." Nuala let her voice trail off in despair. Why had she shared this with him? She'd have been better off being limerent alone. And letting him be limerent alone, too.

Will sighed. "Well, if it makes you happy to think I'm limerent about you, then go ahead. From what you tell me about it, I certainly am. But there's one thing I want to know, Nuala. I suspect that it's the main reason we're having this little talk. Do limerent people go to bed together?"

Nuala couldn't help smiling at the frustrated tone of Will's voice. "Yes, Will," she said gently. "They go to bed together if they both want to. Any other questions?"

"One very blunt one. When will we?"

"We almost did last night, until your noisy ancestor interrupted us. And afterward, I thought that maybe it was for the best that we didn't. I wanted to, Will. I still do. Only if I'm going to be leaving, maybe it would be better for us to stay uninvolved."

Nuala couldn't remember ever having such a frank discussion about sleeping with a man before the fact. With Will, however, such a discussion seemed natural and right. What they were contemplating wasn't something that could be accomplished casually, with no feeling. Learning about one another sexually would affect both of them, perhaps deeply. There was no reason not to discuss it.

"Why stay uninvolved sexually when it's what we both want?" Will asked.

Nuala shrugged. "Lots of reasons. Emotions. Commitments to other things, maybe. Like you and your book. Like your girlfriend Virginia. Like me and my work."

For a minute or so, Will was very quiet. "Let's get this straight," he said finally in a voice brittle with irritation. Belatedly Nuala understood that she had angered him in some way. She lifted her eyes and stared at him blankly.

"My book is important to me because it's something I've always wanted to do, but I'm almost finished writing it, and you, Nuala, are more important to me than it. Furthermore, Virginia is not my girlfriend. She is my ex-girlfriend, a point that I've gone out of my way to make clear to her. I never did nor do I now love her, and I never will." Seeing the startled look on Nuala's face, he gentled his tone. "Actually, why would I want love with Virginia when I can have limerence with you?" He smiled at her to show that he wasn't still angry, and his eyes shone with affection.

"Now, back to what we were discussing. Why are you reluctant? I promise you that I don't have any social diseases. Fear? I can be a very considerate lover. Lack of desire? We can take care of that, I think." He was determined to smash all her objections and to do it logically, without having to resort to venting the pent-up emotion they were both feeling right now. They might talk logically, but the feeling was still there, the feeling that they wanted to lie in each others' arms.

"You've thought of it all, haven't you?" Nuala said shakily. Will still held fast to her hand, which was beginning to feel heavy in his. For the first time she was starting to feel uncomfortable. She had never seen Will's scientist's mind in action before. This was a new side of him.

"I'm not quite sure. Are you afraid you'll become pregnant, Nuala? Because I feel very strongly that people shouldn't bring new lives into the world until they're ready to provide for the child's needs. So I insist that we be protected, and I—"

With a little cry and a jingling of bracelets, Nuala plucked her hand from his. She looked as though he had laid bare her soul. Her face went a ghastly white and her eyes seemed to lose their focus for a moment before revealing an inner turmoil, which he didn't understand.

Will didn't know what he could have said wrong, but before he knew what was happening Nuala was scrambling to her feet and was off and running up the front stairs. Whatever he had said, it must have struck a nerve both sensitive and deep.

The talk had been flowing so easily between them. What had gone wrong?

Chapter Eight

He ate a solitary dinner because Nuala had run straight to her room and did not seem disposed to come out. As he heated up a can of chicken noodle soup, Will continued to ponder what had precipitated Nuala's sudden and, to his way of thinking, unnecessary flight.

He had been too blunt. And he had been angry, but, as was his way, only for a moment. He'd thought she understood.

Maybe she didn't understand. Nuala was a storyteller, perhaps caught up in a world of make-believe where genies popped out of bottles and made everything all right, where couples who were meant for each other fell into each other's arms and lived happily ever after, where all you had to do was cast a spell to right a wrong. She'd certainly had no difficulty in believing Beckman's story about William Anthony's ghost. Maybe Nuala wasn't ready to accept the harsher realities of life and love.

One of which was having unwanted babies. That was something Will was unprepared to do, and he'd always taken care that it didn't happen to him. Not that he didn't love kids. He did. He wanted several, when the time was right. For him, the time wouldn't be right unless he was married. And for so long he'd considered himself a confirmed bachelor, so having children seemed like something he might have to do without. This saddened him, but without the right woman he simply couldn't become a father. And the right woman would want children just as much as he did. This was how he knew that Virginia was not the right woman. She had told him on many occasions that she wanted no children.

But back to Nuala. Certainly he'd never had a woman blanch and run when he'd mentioned using birth control. Usually they were understanding and, yes, even grateful. He tried, but he couldn't figure out what had gone wrong. Had he blown his chances with her? Would he ever find out why she had run away? At this point, he simply didn't know. And he hated not knowing how he had caused her pain. He wouldn't have caused her pain for anything in the world.

NUALA LAY ON HER BED and stared up at the water stain on the sprigged wallpaper. She wished now that she hadn't bolted when Will had begun to talk about birth control. But it had been so unexpected!

It would have been the perfect time to explain that unwanted pregnancy wasn't a problem with her. Oh, she'd had the ultimate form of birth control done to her. She was sterile.

She rolled over onto her stomach. Why hadn't she simply continued the discussion? Why hadn't she told him she could never have children?

Because of the way Joe Morini had reacted, that's why. She was forever doomed to feel inferior and unworthy because of how Joe had behaved. She dared not tell Will that she was deficient, less of a woman. She

would never reveal her secret to any man. And that was
why it was better never to get close to a man. Never to
allow limerence to develop. Or love.

Reluctantly she got up and undressed, then pulled her
comfortable and comforting old flannel nightgown over
her head and crawled into bed. If she listened she could
hear Will puttering about in the kitchen, probably
making a mess. It didn't matter. She was planning to
give the kitchen a thorough cleaning in the morning
before she left for the Osofkee Library and her first
story hour for Martha Cale.

She couldn't imagine how she was going to explain
her running away from their discussion tonight to Will.
She was sure that he'd expect an explanation. But then,
give her time. She'd think of something.

After all, she was a very good storyteller.

SOMETHING CRASHED in the attic. For a moment, Nuala thought it was part of her dream, a dream where
Cole turned into a baby and a butterfly turned into Will.
Then Nuala's eyes popped open. The hands on her little travel clock on the bureau told her that it was eleven
o'clock, and the dream had been only a dream.

When Nuala heard the footsteps on the stairs, she
froze, and then she jumped out of bed. She fumbled for
her bathrobe. Then she had the panic-stricken thought,
Just where do I think I'm going? The footsteps continued down the front stairs, exactly as they had last night.
Her heart pounded in her chest. She didn't know
whether to remain in her room or to run.

Down the hall, Will was wide awake and pacing the
floor of his room. He was agonizing over Nuala and
yearning to hold her in his arms, despairing that he
might never get to do so. And then he heard the crash.

He raced into the hallway and reached the stairs when the footsteps began. POUND *creak*, POUND *creak*, just like last night. It was unnerving, because no one was there.

"Nuala!" he muttered under his breath, and he ran down the hallway on the other side of the staircase to her room. The door was closed and no narrow band of light beneath it signaled that Nuala was awake.

"Nuala! Nuala?" Will hammered on her bedroom door. Belatedly he realized that he wore only pajama bottoms.

Nuala threw the door open, looking scared out of her wits. She wore a bathrobe that gaped open in front, revealing a high-necked nightgown. His eyes steadied hers for one wild moment, and then before she could judge the wisdom of this, she threw herself headlong into his arms. She braced her head against his chest and held on to him as though he were salvation personified. His body was solid, strong. His heart beat steadily. The softness of her breasts pressed against his chest, and without hesitation he folded his arms around her.

Last night Will's ancestor had kept them apart. Tonight he was bringing them together.

There was justice in that, thought Will, as he buried his face in Nuala's fragrant hair.

The plodding footsteps reached the bottom of the stairs and stopped. The silence was deafening.

Will relaxed his hold on her and she allowed him to move away slightly.

"It's the same time as it was last night when it happened," he said.

"*Now* do you believe it is a ghost?" she asked shakily.

"I'm willing to admit that it's a possibility," allowed Will. "I looked down the staircase after it started, and I couldn't see a thing. That's when I ran to find you. I didn't want you to be frightened."

"Well, I was. No wonder your former boarding-house manager couldn't get anyone to stay here. If the guests had to put up with that racket every night, I can see why they'd want to leave." She walked to the window and stared out at the dark night. She reached out to grip the sturdy windowsill, trying to quell her fear.

Will touched her shoulder. "Nuala, you don't have to be alone tonight," he said gently. He wondered if she would take it the way he meant it, which was that he would stay with her in a nonsexual way if that was what she wanted. It wasn't what *he* wanted, but of course Nuala knew that. Still, he meant what he'd said in the beginning. He wouldn't push for more until she was ready.

She turned and looked him full in the face. Seconds ticked by during which his expectations hovered on the brink of her response. *Nothing ever turns out the way you expect it,* he hastened to remind himself, cushioning himself for the blow of her refusal.

Her eyes studied his, seeming to resolve something of importance. She said softly, "My place or yours?"

"What?" he said. He was sure he hadn't heard her correctly.

She smiled sweetly up at him, and he felt absurdly happy that whatever had upset her earlier in the evening, she was apparently over it now.

"I don't want to sleep alone, Will," she said. Her eyes looked soft, their pupils wide and luminous. He was stunned by the frank emotion he read in their depths.

"Are you sure, Nuala?" he said, lifting his hands to caress her shoulders. His eyes never left hers. He thought his chest would burst with this longing for her.

"I'm sure," she whispered.

"My place," he said in a trembling voice. He was profoundly moved by her unexpected acquiescence. Because he could not speak the words he longed to say, he leaned down and pressed a tender kiss upon her forehead.

They didn't stop to look for whatever was responsible for the loud footsteps on the stairs. They knew they wouldn't see anything more than they'd seen the night before. They also felt no sense of danger. What they did feel was a heightened anticipation that no eerie unexplained happenings could abate.

In his room, Will silently untied the belt of Nuala's robe and bent to kiss her lingeringly on the lips. Then he slipped the bathrobe from her shoulders and tossed it over the back of a chair.

"Will," Nuala said, uncharacteristically casting her eyes down.

He picked up her hand and kissed it. He pressed it to his cheek. "Yes, my love?"

"Will, I won't get pregnant," she said. She swallowed hard. She had prepared herself for this. She wasn't prepared to tell all, but certainly she was prepared to tell Will what she knew he needed to know.

He sensed that there was more, but he wouldn't ask her. Instead, his eyes searched her face, trying to understand the brief shadow of sadness that flitted across her features. But it was gone, and it seemed unimportant now. More important was Nuala's feather touch on his beard and the softness of the lips she lifted for his kiss.

They kissed, a series of nibbling little kisses that only whetted Nuala's appetite for more.

He took her hand and led her toward the bed. He sat down first and slid under the blankets, lifting them up so she could follow. Her nightgown was of warm flannel, the kind of flannel his grandmother had called outing, and it was by no means sexy. But to him, the way it clung to the roundness of her breasts and buttocks seemed like the sexiest thing in the world.

"Sometimes I think you're not really real," Will murmured. "That you're a figment of my imagination. That you didn't really descend on me out of nowhere on that stormy night, and that someday I'll wake up and find you gone."

"I'm real enough," Nuala said, smiling up at him, her dark hair spread out upon the snowy whiteness of his pillowcase. "See me. Feel me. Taste me."

"Only too happy to oblige," Will said, and proceeded to do all three.

They had left a small shaded lamp lit on the dresser, and Nuala was glad. She wanted to see the warm light in Will's eyes as he slowly untied the bow at the neck of her high-necked gown. She wanted him to see her fully revealed after he helped her shimmy out of it. She wanted to be aroused by Will's arousal, to glory in the sight of his body and to bask in his delight at the beauty of hers. She didn't want to miss a thing; she wanted it all.

When they lay naked beside each other, Will lifted himself on one arm and slowly stroked her neck. His eyes were lit with solemn wonder.

"I think," he said from way down in his throat, "that I have never seen anything more beautiful than you."

She lifted her arms to him, welcoming him to her. And then it began, what Nuala was to think of ever afterward as shapes upon shapes: the lean planes of his face pressing against the curve of her breasts; the length of his leg angling between her tapered thighs; the ovals of her fingernails digging into the long, smooth muscles of his back and leaving crescent-shaped imprints there. The dim light on the dresser picked out the shapes, making them shift from light to shadow and back again as Nuala and Will explored this new facet of their relationship.

It was different with Will, as Nuala had known it would be. It began with the wonderful warm light in his eyes, and it continued with his joyful appreciation of her, which he made every effort to communicate. He communicated it with his touch, so soft and insistent; he communicated it with his sweet murmuring; he communicated it with every movement of his body upon hers. For he was gentle with her, and caring, and when he filled her it was with more than himself; it was with joy.

Her heart beat rapidly, but there was a sweet, peaceful stillness swelling inside her, and there was a sense of everything being real and right. She felt a sureness about Will Anthony that she had never felt before about anyone else. It was a deep and abiding emotion that she accepted, without even questioning it, as love.

His face, lost in concentration above her, had become so very dear to her, and in such a short period of time. Those eyes, so liquid and dark, were a part of her existence now, and the beard that rested so lightly upon her cheek had become endearingly familiar. She arched up into him, pressing herself closer and closer until his harsh cry told her that it was over for him.

And then it was her turn, her turn to be the heroine in the oldest story in the world, and she clung to him throughout as though she would never let him go, and indeed, maybe she would not. Because "happily ever after" was now more than a catchy line with which to end a fairy tale, and for the first time since Joe, Nuala dared to hope that happily ever after might somehow be possible for her.

QUAIL SONG from the edge of the surrounding woods awakened Nuala in Will's arms. For a moment, she couldn't orient herself. But then she saw the floor beside the bed strewn with the many books Will read, and she saw his reading glasses on the nightstand. His blue pajama bottoms were tossed carelessly over the bedpost. Then she remembered.

Will stirred in his sleep, but he didn't awaken. She pillowed her head on her hands and watched him sleep. He looked oddly vulnerable in his sleep; not little-boyish, because Will Anthony was every bit a man. Will's vulnerability came of giving himself up to her completely. Of trusting and not being afraid to reveal all of himself to her in their most intimate moments. She, on the other hand, had not managed to trust him enough to reveal all of herself to him. There were still things about herself that she'd rather he didn't know.

She reached down and fingered a small white scar below her navel. It was so faint that she was sure that Will hadn't noticed it in those moments of passion last night. The scar was the visible sign of the trauma she endured all those years ago. She had other scars, too, but they weren't so obvious. For that, Nuala was grateful.

Will reached for her, and she slipped her arm around him, absorbing his warmth. Soon it would be time to get up and begin the day. She settled against him with a sigh, reluctant to leave the comfort of his embrace. Outside, she heard the smack of a fish as it leaped from the river and fell. The sound echoed and carried over the stillness of the water, and Nuala pictured in her mind how the silver ripples would spread out and out from the point of impact.

The stillness of the water seemed to mirror the stillness of her soul. This inside stillness of soul was new to Nuala. How peaceful she felt! And how she longed to go on feeling that way. The ripples that Will had started in her soul were widening, threatening to encompass everything about her life.

Four weeks, she thought to herself. *How will I ever give this up in four weeks?*

"So THE GHOST CAME BACK last night! Well, well!" said Beckman, helping himself from the coffeepot.

Will leaned against the doorjamb, sipping coffee from a mug. They both watched Nuala, who had just washed and waxed the kitchen floor and was now buffing it to a high shine.

"Yes," she said, vigorously wielding the rag that served as her buffer. "And he'd better not return again tonight. I do not buffer ghouls lightly."

Beckman skittered out of reach of the rag.

"Is she always like this so early in the morning?" he asked Will in a skeptical voice.

"I'm afraid so," Will said affectionately. He was growing accustomed to the way Nuala tossed out wordplay, but he would never take her for granted. She was his constant delight.

He wished Nuala wouldn't take her cleaning duties so seriously. There were other things he'd rather have done this morning, although he had to admit that standing beside Nuala at the big kitchen sink, wiping dishes while she washed, wasn't so bad. At least it offered plenty of opportunities for looking at her, which was getting to be one of his favorite pastimes. Not *the* favorite, of course, after last night.

"I think I know how to get rid of Captain Anthony's ghost," Beckman said hopefully.

Nuala sat back on her heels and stared up at him. "How?"

"Yes, how?" echoed Will. He edged around the places Nuala hadn't polished yet and treated himself to a refill from the pot.

"Take the house off the market." Beckman shrugged. "Judging from his past performance, Captain Anthony will leave if the house is no longer for sale. Simple as that."

Will took his time about replying. "It's not that simple," he said finally. "I can't afford to keep the house if it's not operated as a boardinghouse."

He shot Nuala a quick glance, measuring her reaction. Last night had been so wonderful for him, and he thought it had been the same for her. Talking about selling this place made it all too clear that soon their idyll would come to an end. Did she realize this? What would the end mean to her?

"Take the house off the market until you leave. Then list it with the real estate fellow. That way you'll be gone before old Captain Anthony can come back to haunt you. I'd be surprised if he followed you all the way back to North Carolina."

"It'll be so much easier to sell the house while I'm in it. The house looks nicer when someone is living here; it will show to prospective buyers better. No, Beckman, I can't wait to put the house on the market. It has to be done now. In fact, the real estate fellow is going to come over and put a For Sale sign up in the front yard today." Will set his lips in a stubborn line.

"Well, I thought you wanted to know how to get rid of the ghost, and I told you," Beckman said, shaking his head.

Will slapped the side of his head. "Do you realize that I've been talking about getting rid of a ghost I'm not sure I even believe in? I must be—"

"Spooked," finished Nuala, standing up and looking around at the high gloss of the newly waxed floor with an expression of satisfaction. "There, I'm all finished. I have just enough time to get ready for my story hour in Osofkee. Here, Will, wax eloquent." She tossed him her buffing cloth before running lightly up the back stairs.

Beckman rinsed his coffee cup out in the sink and then turned thoughtfully to Will.

"Is that really true, Will? That you don't believe in ghosts?" he asked.

"Well, it used to be," Will replied. He shook his head in puzzlement and raised serious eyes to Beckman. "Now I just don't know what to think anymore."

Beckman clapped him on the shoulder in passing. "Frankly, son, if I were you, I'd start believing. Otherwise, the captain might go to greater lengths to convince you that he's serious. I wouldn't want to cross him. No, sir."

And with that scarcely encouraging pronouncement, Beckman jounced away in his pickup truck, leaving Will to figure out what to do about the ghostly noises.

It seemed to Will as he went to the study to begin working on his book that he was caught in a real bind. If Beckman was correct, Will wouldn't be able to get rid of Captain Anthony's ghost because he was determined to sell the house. On the other hand, probably no one would want to buy the house because it was haunted.

Good heavens, how on earth was he going to finish this novel while he was under pressure like that?

NUALA'S STORY HOUR at the Osofkee Library went well. Afterward, she drove the Storymobile down the street to the grocery store where she had agreed to meet Will. He had insisted on riding along to Osofkee with her in order to do some errands.

Nuala hitched up her white gauze dress, ignoring the curious stares of the other shoppers, and marched into the Piggly Wiggly supermarket. She found Will pushing a basket through the produce department.

Nuala sneaked up behind him, dropped the hem of her long skirt, and clapped her hands lightly over Will's eyes.

"Guess who?" she said in a sepulchral whisper. The aproned man stacking zucchini in the produce bin lifted an eyebrow at her attire before hefting a crate and marching away down the aisle. His walk seemed to say *I've seen all kinds, lady, and now you.*

"Captain Anthony, I presume?" Will said.

Nuala dropped her hands. "Shh," she said. "The captain might hear you."

Will crooked an arm around her neck and bent her backward over the romaine. He planted a large smacking kiss on her lips.

"Lettuce begin," he said.

"Will," she protested, half laughing. "Stop it! What will people think?"

"That I'm parsley to storytellers?" said Will hopefully.

"Will!"

He only released her because he saw the produce man hurrying through the swinging doors at the end of the aisle.

Self-consciously, Nuala flicked an alfalfa sprout out of her hair.

"How do I look?"

"You look scrumptious," Will said loudly. "Good enough to—"

"Will!"

"Okay, okay. Suppose you tell me what we're going to cook tonight."

"Spaghetti sauce. Everyone should know how to make a good basic spaghetti sauce." She picked up a bag of onions and set it in the cart, then floated over to the tomatoes and selected several ripe ones.

"Bananas for Cole?" Will asked, holding up a bunch.

Nuala nodded and consulted the list she'd carried in her pocket. "Let's get some Parmesan cheese," she said.

"And wine," Will said.

It took only a few more moments for them to complete their purchases. They drove home in the gathering twilight, enjoying each other's company. When they reached the driveway, Will said, "Look, the real estate man put up the sign."

The For Sale sign stood on two sturdy posts beside the pink flamingo.

"It makes me kind of sad somehow to see it there," Will said, getting out to unload the groceries. "I didn't think it would."

"It's not wood," Nuala said. "It's clearly made of metal." Before she could get out of the hearse, Will pulled her into his arms and kissed her.

"What was that for?" Nuala murmured.

"Just because you're you," he said softly, and then he let her go.

They cooked a highly successful spaghetti dinner, after which Will and Nuala settled down at the bottom of the stairs. They were equipped with a flashlight, pillows, blankets and popcorn. Will broke out one of the last bottles of his precious private stock of Cheerwine soda to await the arrival of their nightly visitor.

This confrontation had been Nuala's idea. Under the influence of the wine they drank with dinner, she decided it would be interesting to face whatever it was that made the plodding footsteps on the front stairs. Will went along with it mostly because he was curious, and because he was sure there was no danger involved.

They were halfway through the big bowl of popcorn when the clock in the study chimed eleven. It was less than five minutes later when they heard the crash in the attic. Then the footsteps, heavy and slow, began creaking toward them.

A cold wind swept down the stairs, and Will and Nuala clung to each other. They weren't frightened; they were used to this strange phenomenon by this time. But they didn't see a thing. The staircase was apparently empty.

Still, even though they were prepared for it, the nightly visitation left them shaking. When it was over, they slowly turned their eyes toward each other in shared amazement.

The house was quiet. The only sound was the sound of their own breathing.

Nuala was the first one to speak.

"Will Anthony, this house has the best late shows of any place in town!"

Will stood up and cast an assessing look up the staircase. It was only a normal staircase. It looked no different from the way it had ever looked. How in the world would he ever manage to explain to himself—or to anyone else for that matter—what was going on here?

Nuala stood beside him, as puzzled as he was.

"Well, obviously we're not going to figure this out on the spot," he said heavily. "There's only one thing left for us to do."

"What?" Nuala asked, pausing as she screwed the lid back on the bottle of Cheerwine.

"Let's go to bed," he said, gently taking the bottle from her and setting it on the floor beside the flashlight, the popcorn and the blanket.

And taking her hand, he led her slowly up the creaking staircase to his bedroom, where they were happy to do just that.

Chapter Nine

"I'm tired of this limerence busines," complained Will, bending over the bed and rousing Nuala with a kiss.

Nuala groaned and buried her face in the pillow. "Must you start in on the heavy topics so early in the morning?" she said, her voice muffled.

The lumpy mattress caved in where he sat down on it. He slid a hand under her long hair and fanned it out over the blanket, which was pulled up around her shoulders.

"I've been thinking about it all night," he said.

"Not *all* night," Nuala said, rolling over into the caved-in place and holding her arms out to him. He allowed himself to be enfolded and buried his face in her shoulder. He inhaled deeply; he loved the way Nuala smelled when she first woke up.

"Most of the night," he amended seriously, straightening again. He looked down at Nuala, who smiled at him, her hands looped loosely around his neck. Now that he was used to being with her all the time, he couldn't imagine a time when she hadn't been there. When he thought that someday she might not be, fear clutched at his heart.

"This limerence of yours is what used to be called falling in love," Will said. He'd been worrying the problem for hours; and he had hardly been able to wait for Nuala to wake up so he could discuss it with her.

"Yes," Nuala said cautiously.

"So how long does it last? Do limerent people fall out of love?"

Nuala shifted uncomfortably amid the pillows.

"Can't you at least let me get up and wash my face?" she demanded, laughing in spite of her impatience.

"No," he said, pinning her where she was. She could see that he was entirely serious.

"All right, since you insist. The theory, as I recall, is that the limerent period, the intense falling-in-love period, lasts anywhere from a couple of weeks to a lifetime. The norm is, oh, eighteen months to three years."

"And when does it become love?"

"What the psychologist said is that if the couple form a deeper bond of affection during the period of limerence, then they stay together. If not, they part." She managed to push herself upright between his arms. "Anyway, I thought you didn't approve of all this psychology business."

Will relaxed and kissed the tip of her nose. "I approve of it now more than I did a minute ago. What I need to figure out now is how to keep you around for the three years it'll take to cement this 'bond of affection' we need if it's going to last."

"Will, I—" Her delight in him was beginning to turn to dismay. He was analyzing everything too much, and the worst part was that she had given him the tools, the theory, with which to analyze.

"We already have the bond of affection, you have to admit that, Nuala," he told her gravely.

"Yes," she said weakly, unable to argue with him.

"So we have to nurture it," he said. "And the best way to do that," he said, getting up and going to the dresser, where he had set a tray before awakening her, "is to eat breakfast together in bed."

"Will!"

"Teach me to cook, and this is what you get," he said, setting the breakfast tray across her knees. He was grinning at her irresistibly.

She looked down to see that he had placed a plate of scrambled eggs and bacon along with juice and coffee upon a crocheted place mat, and he had arranged a bouquet of red-and-yellow sweet gum leaves in a cut-glass vase. It was a remarkable tour de force for a man who only a short time ago literally could not boil water.

"It's lovely," she said helplessly, touched that he would go to this much trouble for her. "Words fail me."

"For once," Will added, and settled his mouth upon hers for a long and emphatic kiss.

A FEW HOURS LATER, they were floating down the river in the canoe. Will was sitting facing Nuala, who half reclined on a pair of orange life vests. The soles of their bare feet touched, with the toes of Will's reaching far above the toes of Nuala's smaller ones. Still, the fit of the foot to foot was comfortable, like everything else about the two of them together.

"What are we going to do for Thanksgiving?" Will asked lazily.

"Be thankful we don't have to cook a big dinner," Nuala said in a heartfelt tone followed by a little laugh. She wiggled her toes against Will's. He wiggled his toes back. They grinned at each other, completely in tune.

"But of course we have to cook Thanksgiving dinner," Will said. "I thought maybe the two of us could fix a turkey and invite Beckman."

"I think your cooking successes have gone to your head," Nuala said teasingly.

"They are—um, well—stirring events," Will said. He segued rapidly back into the main conversation before she could reply to that. "And then," he went on, watching her carefully, "on Friday after Thanksgiving, I think you and I should go to Disney World."

"Is Disney World a bribe, Will Anthony? To get me to cook Thanksgiving dinner?"

"Not exactly. There's this really neat haunted house at Disney World, and—"

"Haunted house! We could open our own haunted house. Come to think of it, maybe we should. Nightly ghost stories told by me in the parlor, with a cameo appearance just after the stroke of eleven by our very own Captain Anthony." She giggled, and the canoe wobbled on its course.

"You're avoiding the subject," Will said.

"Which is?"

"Planning ahead."

"That's not something I like to do," Nuala said, gazing thoughtfully off into the distance where a hawk circled in the sky. She watched until it landed on the gray spindly branch of an old cypress tree on the bank.

"Don't you ever get the urge to stop this rolling stone business of yours? To make a stationary kind of life for yourself?" He couldn't imagine living Nuala's life. He didn't know why she liked it so much. Surely moving around from one place to the other would pall after a while. And she mentioned once that she'd been at it for two years.

"A strolling roan gathers no Hoss," said Nuala, irrelevantly. She assiduously studied her fingernails.

"Nuala," he said, but then he decided not to pursue it. Nuala always avoided the things she didn't want to talk about by making jokes. It made it hard to achieve any kind of meaningful communication with her. If he didn't love her so much, he'd give up. As it was, for now he'd be satisfied if she'd only agree to his plans for Thanksgiving.

"All right," she said suddenly.

"All right?" he said.

"About Thanksgiving. We'll cook dinner for Beckman, and afterward, on that Friday, we'll go to Disney World."

"Whoosh," said Will. "Whoosh, whoosh, *whoosh*!"

"What's that supposed to mean?"

"It's the sound of caution being thrown to the winds. I'm not surprised that you don't recognize it. Obviously you don't do such a reckless thing very often."

Nuala laughed, and Will felt as though he had won a major victory. He would have kissed her if it wouldn't have meant upsetting the canoe. As it was, he rubbed the arch of her left foot with the big toe of his right. He had discovered that she liked this.

Inhaling the crisp fresh air, Nuala threw her head back, exposing her throat to the sun. Threads of blue sky showed through her dark hair, highlighting the red in each strand. Her skin, so white and transparent, was beginning to reveal the flush of a slight sunburn. Will loved to see her like this, so lighthearted and carefree.

"You're getting a suntan," he told her.

"It's mine for the basking," she said.

He smiled. For the time being, as he relished his success in getting her to plan with him for the Thanksgiving holiday, he felt as though neither of them had a care in the world. As though he didn't have a book to finish and a teaching job in North Carolina to which he must eventually return, as though Nuala wouldn't be leaving. Floating along in the canoe, being borne down the river by the leisurely current, he felt as though life had been reduced to a kind of slow motion.

She felt his eyes upon her and raised her head to find him gazing tenderly at her with an expression in his eyes that she had seen on actors' faces in movies but had never experienced in her own life. It was a look of passion, but also of deep fulfillment; she had never expected to be the object of such emotion.

She let her head fall back again and felt the gentle lapping of the water beneath the bow. Will loved her; she was sure of that. And she loved him, though neither of them had said the words.

For the moment, though, she didn't have to think about the future. All she had to do was enjoy being a-drift on a sea of happiness with Will.

NUALA'S DAILY AFTERNOON story hour at the Osofkee Library was an unqualified success, and Thanksgiving dinner, despite Will's overzealousness in whipping the cream for the pumpkin pie so that it miraculously transformed itself into butter instead, was delicious. Will took great pride in sitting across the huge dining room table from Nuala as she entertained Beckman with a true story of visiting the Eskimos in Alaska with her parents on one of their story-gathering excursions.

If only, Will found himself thinking, *this could be permanent.* He lost himself in this yearning reverie only to find both Nuala and Beckman staring at him and awaiting his answer to a question. He managed to answer it, even though Beckman looked at him strangely for a long while afterward.

It didn't take much talking to convince Beckman to stay for the nightly visitation of Captain William Anthony. "When does he usually get here?" asked Beckman, who insisted on waiting at the bottom of the stairs for the fun to begin.

"Oh, right about now," Will said as the clock in the study chimed eleven, and then they heard the foreshadowing crash in the attic—the "knocked urn"—followed by the now customary slow, plodding footsteps on the creaking stairs.

"Awesome," said Beckman, who had been reading another dumpster find, a teenage book about Valley girls, recently. "Totally awesome. Heh-heh!"

Beckman tried conversing with the invisible captain, much to Nuala's and Will's amusement. The captain did not answer, fortunately or unfortunately, depending on how you looked at it. Beckman thought it was unfortunate, of course, and talked about the captain's creative use of profanity. Considering that, Nuala fervently hoped that Captain William Anthony wouldn't ever get the urge to speak up.

That night Nuala and Will made love slowly and tenderly. There was no hurry and no fear, and afterward there was a lingering sense of belonging. Nuala lay in Will's arms feeling wonderful and warm and loved, and later, when they felt like talking, Will told her stories of his childhood and his hometown.

He swore that he'd gone to his high school senior prom wearing a white sport coat and, due to a science project he was completing at the time, a pink crustacean. He told her about the college biology class where he'd crossed a crocodile and an abalone and created a crocabalone. He insisted that he'd once worked at a dairy whose motto was, "You can't beat our milk, but you can whip our cream."

Nuala told him about the towns she had visited on her travels, including some of the interesting people she had met. There was Barbara Seville, the famous opera singer. And Adam Baum, the nuclear physicist. And the baby who had, no joke, been named Crystal Shanda by her parents, Mr. and Mrs. Lear.

How strange it felt, thought Nuala just before she fell asleep beside him, to be with someone who understood her wacky sense of humor. To have someone she could count on to enliven even the most mundane conversation. To have someone to care about. To feel treasured.

It was, she thought with a certain foreboding, a feeling to which she could easily become accustomed.

ON THE DAY AFTER Thanksgiving, Will and Nuala started out early in the morning for Orlando and Disney World. They left the house in Will's jeep before the chilly wisps of fog had lifted from the riverbank. A thin rime of frost coated the weeds on the sides of the road, and the sky was a piercingly clear blue. They hadn't been on the road long when the sun rose over the trees, a bright golden ball. Nuala discarded her jacket before long, and Will did, too. It was going to be a hot day for November, with only a slight breeze out of the west. They sang every song they knew along the way, Will booming out in his deep baritone and Nuala barely keeping up in her clear contralto.

When they ran out of songs, Will confided that, due to Captain Anthony's noisy objections, he was trying to consider all the options regarding the disposal of Anthony House.

"Against my will," he said.

"Against your Will?" queried Nuala, wrinkling her nose at him.

"Against my will, I've had to give up on the idea of running Anthony House as a boardinghouse," he said unhappily. "It's just too impractical, as I found out when I tried it before. I can't handle it from North Carolina."

"Maybe your best bet is to find a very large local family that wants to live in the country," she said.

"I've been thinking about dividing the place into small apartments."

"And runt them, you mean?"

"Litter-ally," he said with a groan.

"How'd we get off the track?" Nuala asked innocently.

"It's your fault."

"Is not."

"Is."

"Is not."

He kissed her, driving with one eye on the road and the other on Nuala.

"Anyway, I wish I *could* keep the place. It's a grand old house, and I can understand why the captain wanted to keep it in the family. I suppose he didn't realize that the family would dwindle to only one member. In fact, I feel responsible for its demise. If only I'd had a few kids. Then I'm sure I wouldn't want to give the place up so easily."

"Yes," Nuala said, suddenly sober.

"Anyway, the real estate man hasn't shown the place since I've listed it. I may have no choice but to keep it."

Nuala did not speak. At the moment, even puns failed her. She wasn't sure whether Will's remark about not having kids was something he'd said in genuine regret, or if it was simply a remark made in passing. Whichever, it certainly gave her pause to think.

"Look! There's a nelephant!" The tiny girl riding with her parents on the Disney World monorail pointed at the topiary "nelephant" whizzing by outside. In the distance loomed Cinderella's castle and all the delights of the Magic Kingdom.

Will and Nuala disembarked at the entrance, where Will bought their tickets. Then they were inside, strolling hand in hand along Main street. Over Nuala's objections, Will bought her a Mickey Mouse-ears hat with her name embroidered on the front. She decided she liked the way it looked perched atop her wavy hair after she saw her reflection in a store window.

Nuala bought Will a balloon, which promptly popped. They stopped to watch the Amazing Andrassys, a daring high-wire act performed high above Fantasyland, and then they headed for Tomorrowland and what Will considered the ultimate roller-coaster ride, Space Mountain. After Nuala threatened to be sick the third time they went on it, Will agreed to try the 20,000 Leagues Under the Sea ride, where he sat and mugged at the mechanical creatures that floated past the porthole as the submarine traversed the aqua-blue waters of its lagoon.

They both recoiled in mock horror at the antics of the Pirates of the Caribbean, and they agreed that none of the Tiki Birds in the Tiki Bird Revue held a candle to Cole. They stood along with many others waiting in a long line to see the haunted house.

"Ours is much better than theirs," sniffed Nuala when they emerged afterward.

"Yeah," agreed Will scornfully. "They don't even have a pink flamingo in their front yard. Say, I'm hungry. Aren't you?"

They happened to be the only people eating in the Mexican snack bar, and as they were licking their fingers after wolfing down two burritos apiece, Nuala saw a small forlorn girl crying beside a nearby trash barrel.

"I wonder where her parents are," said Nuala, looking around.

"I've been watching her," Will said. "She just wandered up. She can't be more than three years old." He stood up to toss their leftover papers and napkins in the trash and knelt beside the little girl.

"Where's your mommy?" he said gently.

The child only cried harder.

"Are you lost?"

Rubbing her fists into her eyes, the little girl nodded her head up and down.

"We can help you find your mommy," Nuala said, smiling at her encouragingly.

"Will you?" the girl asked. With great difficulty, she managed to control her sobs, and she raised her tear-stained face to theirs. She looked a bit skeptical when she saw Nuala in her Mickey Mouse ears.

"Of course we'll help you," Will assured her, taking her by the hand.

He continued to talk to the child in a gentle, soothing voice, telling her how they'd find a policeman who would call her mommy, and the child even smiled trustingly up at him. It wasn't long before they located a security guard, who managed to find the frantic mother. While they were waiting for her to arrive, Will chatted with the child, whose name was Jenny, until he had her laughing and clapping her hands at his jokes. After the mother arrived to claim her, Will bought Jenny a stuffed Mickey Mouse in a nearby booth and carried it back to her.

"Why did you do that?" Nuala asked as she slipped her hand into his.

Will shrugged and grinned down at her. "She was a cute little kid. I liked her. And I thought maybe she wouldn't have such bad memories of being lost at Disney World if I did something nice for her."

"You're a nice person," Nuala said, squeezing his hand.

He shook this off. "I just happen to like kids," he told her. "A lot."

When Nuala looked at him like that, so open and admiring, he loved her so much. He was eager to leave with her, to be alone with her in his big old house. He wanted as much of Nuala as possible, now, while they had the chance. He was all too aware of their uncertain future.

But at the same time Nuala was thinking, *He said he liked kids. A lot.* For Nuala, this statement was too clear a reminder of why she could not let this relationship with Will develop past a certain point. Soon, she told herself, it would be time to move on.

It had been a long day. Will told himself he understood why Nuala appeared pale and subdued and pleaded fatigue on the long drive back. He would have liked to talk, but companionship, he reminded himself, did not depend on nonstop chatter. Sometimes companionship thrived on quiet togetherness. He was sure that Nuala, as he did, felt their oneness after spending the whole day together. But she kept her eyes closed mile after silent mile in the dark, not even opening them when Will rested his warm hand reassuringly on her knee.

"WHOSE CAR is that?" said Nuala sleepily as they drove into the driveway of Anthony House. A small blue Chevette blocked the Jeep's way to the garage.

"I can't imagine," said Will. Then he braked sharply. The tall figure on the front porch looked all too familiar. He jumped out of the Jeep.

"Virginia!" he said in total surprise.

"Will?" Virginia called, peering through the darkness. "Is that you?"

The presence of her car should have given him a clue. But it hadn't. "It's me, all right," he said, striding toward the house. What in the world was Virginia doing here?

He bounded onto the porch and Virginia offered her cheek to be kissed. Will sidestepped her and made a great show of unlocking the front door.

"Will?" Nuala called out from somewhere in the region of the pink flamingo.

"Uh, Nuala, it's okay. It's Virginia." He watched Nuala walk hesitantly up the front walk.

"Am I interrupting something?" Nuala, colorful in her Hawaiian print slacks, ascended the porch steps wrapping her bright fuchsia jacket around her against the chill in the air. Next to Virginia's drabness, Nuala looked like a bright-plumed bird of paradise.

"Not exactly," Will hedged, at a loss as to what to do about this. Clearly Virginia expected to stay. Her overnight bag was placed in front of the door in such a way that he knew she was expecting him to carry it inside.

The two women were both looking at him. He knew he had to do something, so he did the easiest thing. He picked up Virginia's bag and carried it inside the house.

Once they were all standing awkwardly in the foyer, the two women silently took each other's measure. Will wished he could disappear and never be heard from again.

"I—I think I'll make us all a cup of tea," Nuala said uncertainly.

Will greeted this idea with a heartiness he didn't feel. "Great idea," he said, rubbing his hands together. "Great idea," he said again to Virginia when Nuala had vanished into the kitchen and there didn't seem to be anything else to say.

They stared at each other for a moment. He decided to be forthright.

"Why are you here, Virginia?" he asked her. He knew very well that he was being ungracious, but he couldn't imagine what had possessed her to show up on his doorstep at ten o'clock on a Friday night over Thanksgiving weekend.

"You have no phone," Virginia said, as though that explained everything.

He had forgotten how sharp she was. Not sharp as in clever, but sharp as in pointed. Points of cheek and chin and jaw stabbed into the air near his face; compared to Nuala, who was so soft and rounded, Virginia was like a dart. A poison dart?

"I know I have no phone," he said in exasperation. Even though he knew better, he made an attempt at humor. "We've had a pyromaniac on the loose here in Turkey Trot. He left no phone unburned."

This elicited not even a chuckle. Well, what had he expected? Virginia had never laughed at his puns. Not once.

Virginia's eyes were taking in the parlor with the stuffed alligator frozen in its toothy yawn. For the first time, Will was embarrassed at the decor, or rather, the lack of it. Then he realized that Virginia was looking at the alligator as a biology professor would—after all, it was a fine specimen.

Her inspection of the alligator lasted only a few seconds. Then, as though she couldn't remain still, she started to pace the foyer, her black low-heeled shoes clicking sharply on the wood floor.

"I had to see you, Will, just one last time," Virginia explained, walking this way and that. She'd just had her hair trimmed, and her neck seemed too long. Her neck had always seemed too long.

"Virginia, I am living my life the way I see fit," Will exploded. "If I were you, I'd turn around and walk back out that door."

"I don't think you understand, Will. I—"

"Oh, I understand, all right," he said.

Virginia heaved a sigh. She looked suspiciously near tears. He didn't think he could bear it if she started to cry.

"Now, Virginia," he said, trying to sound soothing. "Maybe we should all sit down in the parlor."

"You and your friend?" she said. He couldn't tell whether Virginia was being sarcastic or not.

At that point Nuala, carrying a tray, came into the parlor through the other door and busied herself pouring tea. Will rested his hand at the small of Virginia's bony back and propelled her into the room, where she sat down uneasily on the edge of the couch and accepted the cup of tea Nuala silently provided.

"I'm here to spend the night," Virginia said suddenly.

Holding her own cup and saucer in her hand, Nuala sat down on the arm of an overstuffed chair. Will stood beside her.

"Well, this is a boardinghouse," Virginia exclaimed when no one said anything. "I figured it wouldn't be any trouble. By the way, Will, I don't believe your friend and I have met." She set her teacup very precisely in its saucer and looked expectantly from Nuala to Will.

"Uh, please excuse my terrible manners," Will said. "Nuala, this is Virginia Abercrombie. Virginia, this is, uh, my fiancée, Nuala Kemp."

If Virginia seemed taken aback, it was nothing compared to the shock with which Nuala greeted this amazing statement. She kept waiting for the punch line.

"Your fiancée?" repeated Virginia weakly.

"Yes," Will replied firmly, pulling Nuala to him. He hoped this display of affection would be enough to send Virginia reeling. Right out the door.

"Well," Virginia said, seeming to think things over. Whatever she had been about to say, she obviously thought better of it. She cleared her throat and said rather feebly, "I've always wanted to see this area of the country, mostly because you've spoken so highly of it, Will. I'm staying, at least for tonight." Her feet were planted firmly on the floor. Will knew how intractable she was. Virginia wouldn't budge until she was ready.

"It is awfully late, Will," Nuala said, summoning up her voice.

"All right," Will heard himself say against his better judgment. "I suppose you can stay."

I can't wait to talk to Will alone and find out what's going on, thought Nuala. But what was there to do but enter into the spirit of this thing, whatever it was?

"Well, if that's settled, I'd like to take a bath," announced Virginia. She stood up and brushed off her gray flannel skirt. Nuala sent a questioning look up at Will, but he continued to ignore her with great determination.

"I'll show you to a room," offered Nuala, who was determined to make the best of a bad situation. "I'll have to get more sheets out." She admitted to herself that she was almost morbidly curious about Virginia.

"I'll help," Will decided swiftly. He knew that he couldn't possibly leave the two women alone together to compare notes. So the three of them trooped upstairs, where Will installed Virginia in a room as far away from his as possible.

"Where's the bathroom?" Virginia wanted to know. She stared at Nuala with her own unabashed curiosity. Nuala busied herself with unfurling the blanket on the bed.

"It's down the hall," Will told her.

"I'll see you both in the morning," Virginia said, yawning widely. Will wasn't sure if this was promise or a threat. He was overjoyed when Virginia dismissed them with her chin and closed her bedroom door loudly behind them. He grabbed Nuala's hand and ran with her down the front stairs.

Once they were in the study, Will indulged in a muffled howl of dismay.

"What's she doing here?" Nuala asked.

"She certainly isn't here on my invitation, if that's what you think," Will assured her.

"So why did she come?"

"I suspect that she has some misbegotten idea about getting me back," confessed Will. "What should I do?"

"Well, do you want her back?"

"No, Nuala, I don't want her back or her front or her side or her—"

"Never mind, I get the picture," Nuala said dryly. "By the way, the next time you introduce me as your fiancée, how about giving me some prior notice?"

"You're not angry about that, are you? I thought maybe she'd leave if she thought I wasn't available." Will pulled Nuala into his arms and rested his chin on the top of her head.

"I'm not sure I approve," Nuala said grudgingly. "Anyway, it makes me feel uncomfortable. I don't know how to act."

"Act? You'll act like my fiancée. Like you're madly in love with me. That ought to throw her off my track."

"We can't go mooning around the house and being lovesick," Nuala said practically.

"Why not? There's nothing I'd like better than mooning around the house and being lovesick. I've never been one to avoid expressing my tender feelings for you."

Nuala heaved a deep sigh. Will was kissing her hair and running his hands up and down her spine. "How long is Virginia staying, Will?" she managed to ask.

"Maybe she'll go home tomorrow," he said hopefully.

"What if she stays?"

Will thought for a moment. "She can't stay. She'll have to be back at the university on Monday morning, teaching. It's already Friday night. Virginia's not a threat, you know. Maybe she just wants to see for herself that there is no hope for our relationship. Once she sees it, she'll go away.''

''And in the meantime?''

''In the meantime, you and I are going up to bed. Where there will be just the two of us. And we'll take off all our clothes and make love all night, and in the morning—''

''Shh, Will, Virginia might hear you!''

''That's exactly what I was hoping,'' he said, kissing her firmly on the lips.

When the house was quiet and they were lying in bed together, Will reached for Nuala and cradled her head on his shoulder. Their opposite hands found each other; their fingers laced together.

Unexpectedly, Will chuckled.

''What's so funny, Will?''

''Virginia. Having her here, I mean. I couldn't believe it when I saw her standing on my front porch.''

''Listen, Will. Do you hear something?''

Will listened. ''Oh, it's just Virginia. She's a night person. She stays up late all the time, walking around the house, puttering in the kitchen. She's a regular Virginia creeper.''

''Will!''

''Well, I can't say I'm delighted to have her here,'' he said. ''It's not that I don't like her, it's just that she's out of my life. I'm very suspicious about her motives.''

''*I* like her,'' Nuala said, surprising herself. Despite the awkward circumstances, she sensed that Virginia was a very decent, down-to-earth sort who meant no one any harm.

"I'm glad," Will said sleepily. It had been a long day. He kissed Nuala's hair and dozed, thinking as he drifted away that their lovemaking would have to wait until the morning....

When they awoke it was to a scream of terror.

For a moment, Nuala couldn't orient herself. She cast a wild glance at the glow-in-the-dark hands of the bedside clock. It was slightly after eleven, too early to wake up. Why, they had just fallen asleep!

"What is it?" Will said, sitting bolt upright in bed.

"Someone screamed," Nuala said, jumping up and shoving her feet into her slippers. She slid her arms into her robe and ran to the door. Will was only steps behind her.

In the hall, which was blazing with light, they found Virginia standing at the head of the stairs, looking white.

"I heard footsteps!" Virginia exclaimed.

"The captain," breathed Nuala. "We didn't warn her about the captain."

"And who," said Virginia, "is the captain?"

"A ghost," said Will, preparing to explain.

But no explanation was necessary, because Virginia fainted dead away.

Chapter Ten

"What are you supposed to do for someone who faints?" Will asked. He and Nuala both knelt beside the supine Virginia, and all he could think of to do was to fan Virginia's face ineffectually with his hand.

"Chafe her wrists. Hold smelling salts under her nose." Nuala bent over Virginia anxiously.

"Do *what* to her wrists?" asked Will, picking up Virginia's limp hand.

"Oh," moaned Virginia, opening her eyes.

Nuala smoothed Virginia's forehead with a gentle hand. "It's all right," she soothed. "You had a shock. You fainted for a moment."

Virginia struggled to sit up. She was wearing a neat brown velour robe, which zipped up the front. She clutched at the collar of it.

"Are you hurt, Virginia?" Will asked gently.

"No, I'm all right," Virginia said. She wiggled her toes experimentally. "Yes," she said more definitely. "I really am all right." She looked around her uncertainly. "Did you say there was a ghost?"

Both Will and Nuala nodded solemnly.

"Help me up, Will," Virginia said.

Will assisted her to her feet. Virginia rubbed her head. "I got a seminasty bump," she said in surprise.

"I'll see you to your room," Nuala said. "I suppose you'd like to lie down."

"No, I'd rather hear about the ghost," Virginia said unexpectedly.

"It's very late," Will said. He yawned widely in order to punctuate this remark.

"I'm not sleepy. I'm curious," Virginia insisted. "Who is this ghost, anyway?"

"It's Will's great-grandfather, Captain Will Anthony," supplied Nuala. "At least that's who we think it is, don't we, Will?"

Virginia, in her typically dogged way, was not about to relinquish this interesting topic. "Well, who was he?" she wanted to know. "And why is he here? I've read some research on ghosts. I want to know about them." Will had the distinct feeling that Virginia regarded ghosts as just one more biological species, ready to be examined underneath a microscope like an amoeba or a paramecium.

"Captain Anthony isn't a harmful ghost. I'm sure he means well," Nuala began, and then she proceeded to tell what they knew about Captain William Anthony. About his years with the Confederate navy during the Civil War, about his fleet of riverboats, about his girlfriend, who was reputed to be a descendant of the Seminole hero Osceola.

"Osceola?" said Will. "How do you know that?"

"Beckman told me," Nuala said, perching on the top step and patting the space beside her, where Virginia sat entranced as Nuala spun out the tale in her own inimitable way.

Giving up on the idea of getting any sleep, Will sat down and leaned against the wall. The women were getting along splendidly, but it was all he could do to stay awake.

It was later, much later, when they all strolled downstairs and sat amicably around the kitchen table in their bathrobes and slippers while Will passed around leftover turkey and pumpkin pie. It was even later than that when they all said good-night to one another in the upper hall and dispersed.

"You and Virginia certainly got along famously," Will said grumpily when he and Nuala were at last alone in bed again.

"She has good taste in men," Nuala said, slipping her hand into his.

Whatever Will had expected, he hadn't expected this. He thought that Nuala and Virginia might hate each other. That they might at least make thinly disguised but nevertheless snide remarks to each other. Or that Nuala might have something critical to say about Virginia in private.

But no, the two women had become friends. A surprise, but a welcome one.

And I've got pretty good taste in women, too, he thought before he drifted off to sleep.

"I'M TIRED of eating in the kitchen," Nuala said the next day as they were preparing the inevitable post-Thanksgiving turkey sandwiches. They had all slept late, and lunch was the first meal of the day. "Anyway, we have a guest," Nuala continued. "And the dining room is so pleasant now."

Will had to agree, although the three of them seemed a bit lost clustered at one end of the long dining room table.

"How are things at the university, Virginia?" he asked her once they had all sat down together.

"Things are pretty much the same," Virginia said slowly. "Carl Fuhring resigned. Mel Clegg is going on a sabbatical this summer."

"Mmm," said Will. Virginia had not said one word about his returning to the university. He wondered when she would.

"How's your book going, Will?" Virginia asked.

"It's coming along well," he replied warily. He wasn't sure where this was leading; he knew Virginia had always resented the idea of his novel when he'd been in the planning stages, and she'd resented it even more when it took him, to her way of thinking, away from her.

But Virginia only smiled warmly and said, "That's good," before biting into her sandwich once more. Will detected something softer about Virginia, something more—pliable? He didn't understand it, and he certainly couldn't define it. But she was the same and yet different from the Virginia he remembered. His heart warmed to her for a moment as he thought of all the good times they had shared. The limerence that had never grown into real, lasting love.

"I'd like to meet Beckman Beecker," Virginia said after lunch. "Will has spoken about him from time to time."

"We can walk to his house," Will said, and that is what the three of them proceeded to do.

"Is this the cemetery where you come to think sometimes?" Virginia asked as they passed it.

"Yes," said Will.

"It is quiet," said Virginia. "I can see why you like to spend time here."

They went inside the picket fence and had a drink of water at the artesian well. Virginia looked around with interest. The ground was littered with fallen leaves; the water in the pool beneath the artesian well glimmered in the sunlight. Virginia looked unaccountably nostalgic for a moment.

After their short visit with Beckman, they returned, walking briskly, to Anthony House.

"About dinner tonight," Will began uncomfortably when they stood on the front porch. He had promised himself before Virginia's untimely arrival that he would take Nuala to dinner on Saturday night. Over a week ago he'd made reservations for the two of them at a fine restaurant in St. Augustine, the lovely resort city on the coast thirty or so miles away. But as nice as Virginia had been, it seemed unkind to leave her out of their plans.

Nuala was way ahead of him. "Virginia could come with us to St. Augustine," she said. "I'd like that." Will knew she meant it.

Virginia shook her head slowly. "No, I don't want to change any plans you've already made. I'd like to stay here and eat another turkey sandwich for supper and go to bed with a good book. Honestly."

"We wouldn't mind if you came to dinner with us," said Will. Amazingly enough, he meant it, too.

Again, Virginia declined and stated that she'd like to go for a quiet walk along the river. Which is what she did while Will and Nuala went to get ready for their night out.

Will took leave of Virginia feeling as puzzled as ever. Why had she come here? What had she wanted? She had made very few remarks of a personal nature, and none about their former relationship. She had confined herself to expressing interest in things he had told her about his life here before their communication had stopped altogether. And she was going home tomorrow. He simply couldn't figure her out.

Nuala decided on a leisurely bath before getting dressed, and as she was running water into the claw-footed tub, she noticed an unfamiliar hair dryer, which she assumed belonged to Virginia, on the bathroom shelf. Nuala figured she'd return it to her later, on her way back to her room. She enjoyed a long warm soak, dried herself, and had just put on her underwear when she heard the sounds through the door. She was standing in her lace bra and bikini briefs when Virginia barged in.

"Oh," Virginia said, looking startled. "I didn't know anyone was in here."

"It's all right," Nuala said. She reached for Virginia's hair dryer. "I suppose you've come for this."

"Yes," Virginia said, frankly appraising Nuala's figure.

Nuala felt distinctly uncomfortable under this inspection and reached for her robe.

"You're prettier than I am," Virginia said without a hint of envy or malice. She was stating a fact; nothing more, nothing less.

"I—"

"Oh, you don't have anything to fear from me. I didn't come down here to break you and Will up. Especially since I didn't know there were two of you."

"Why did you come here, then?" blurted Nuala. As much as she had grown to like Virginia, she couldn't imagine what had possessed this woman to drive so far and to insinuate herself into Will's life again without warning, especially since Will had told her everything was over between them months ago.

Virginia shrugged. "Will and I had a good thing going for a while. I thought I was in love with him. I— I said things that might have led him to think that we might get back together sometime. I had to set things straight before—" She hesitated, her eyes assessing Nuala, wondering if she could trust Nuala to be a confidante. Strange, expecting your old boyfriend's fiancée to be a confidante, but still...

"Set what straight?" Nuala said. She felt a little peculiar standing here in the bathroom, discussing Will with his old girlfriend and wearing nothing but her underwear and an old bathrobe.

Virginia seemed to realize suddenly how uncomfortable Nuala was.

"Come into my room, where we can talk," Virginia said swiftly. "Would you mind?"

Nuala shook her head and followed the other woman to her room. Somehow she couldn't imagine Will with this woman. They'd be a total mismatch. She thought about how she and Will looked together, he tall and bearded, she shorter and rounder. They were perfect.

In her room, Virginia sat down on the side of the bed and motioned Nuala to do likewise. Virginia managed a little laugh. "Isn't it wonderful to be in love?" she said with a lightness that Nuala certainly had not expected.

"Oh, I guess you've been in love before," Virginia rushed on before Nuala could speak. "But for me, it's all new. I thought I loved Will, but it wasn't really love. It was just—*being used* to each other. But with Roy—" Virginia laughed again. Her laugh sounded a little bit like rusty machinery, probably because she didn't use it often enough.

"Roy?" ventured Nuala.

"Roy Nelson. He's a country and Western singer. Oh, he's got his own band, and he plays at the Two Bit on the outskirts of Chapel Hill—and we're going to get married!"

"Married?"

"As soon as possible. He stopped to help me change a flat tire on my car, you see, and he asked me out, and soon we were seeing each other every night. All this time I've felt guilty, because I had a hard time letting Will go when he left for Florida. In fact, I led him to think that I'd wait for him. Will's such a nice guy; I didn't want him to come back to the university and find me married. I couldn't call him, and I'm not sure he's ever received any of the letters I sent him. So I came here to tell him in person." Virginia stopped this flow of words to furrow her forehead at the clearly bewildered Nuala.

"Nothing is wrong, is it?" Virginia demanded.

Nuala shook her head. "I'm surprised, that's all," she said. "But I am happy for you." She noticed the becoming flush of Virginia's cheek, the sparkle in her eyes. Sure signs of limerence. She wondered if Virginia, scientist that she was, would be interested in that particular theory. She wondered if she should tell her abut it.

"I'm so glad Will has you. Because if he didn't, he might be heartbroken." Virginia spoke very earnestly.

Nuala raised her eyebrows at this, because she knew heartbreak was not exactly the word to describe the emotion that Will would feel when he learned that Virginia was going to marry another man.

"I came here to say goodbye. I wanted to see all the things like the old cemetery and the St. Johns River and to meet Beckman, because they are so much a part of Will. I wanted to say goodbye to those things, too." Virginia drew a deep breath and went on. "So, I want to ask you a big favor, Nuala. Would you—would you break the news to Will for me? I'm afraid I don't have the courage." She knit her eyebrows seriously and seemed to hold her breath, waiting.

"Why, I will if you'd like," Nuala said in surprise. "But wouldn't you rather do it yourself?"

Virginia shook her head sadly. "I would have, if he hadn't had someone else. But now surely you can see that it's not necessary for me to be the one to break the news."

Nuala nodded. "Yes," she said slowly. For one weird moment she thought of breaking Virginia's news to Will if Virginia would break hers. If only Virginia could be the one to gently tell Will that Nuala was definitely planning to leave! At least Nuala could be in sympathy with this woman. She could help her with this problem.

Nuala drew a deep breath and said, "I'll be glad to do this for you, Virginia, if it will make it any easier. I'll tell him whenever you think best. After you leave, perhaps? Or tonight at dinner?"

"Oh, thank you, Nuala! I can't tell you how much this means to me! I'll leave it up to you as to when to tell him. Use your judgment. You know him better than I ever did."

For a few seconds, Nuala thought that Virginia might hug her in gratitude. But Virginia was not the hugging type. Since there didn't seem to be much more either of them could say on the subject, Nuala stood up and walked to the door.

Virginia said quickly, "I'll be leaving in the morning, very early. That way I won't see Will again. Tell him—tell him that I hope the two of you will be very happy together. Because I do."

There won't be any together for us, she longed to tell Virginia. But she only clasped Virginia's hand.

"I hope you and Roy will be happy, too," she said warmly, meaning it.

Virginia beamed. "Oh, we will. And thank you."

Back in her own room, Nuala dressed and arranged her hair, thinking all the while. How strange life was! By leaving Virginia, Will had freed her for a better relationship with someone else. Just as, perhaps, Nuala would be freeing Will for such a relationship. Sudden tears stung her eyes. She couldn't bear to think of Will with someone new.

And she wouldn't, not tonight. She dressed carefully in a flowing chiffon dress in a becoming shade of violet. It was one of the few things she owned that she hadn't bought from a flea market or a thrift shop. Her spirits rose as she thought about an evening out with Will, and before long she was humming a little tune.

She could hardly wait to hear what Will would say when she told him Virginia's news.

BEFORE THEY LEFT for the evening, Will and Nuala pointed a willing Virginia in the direction of the refrigerator and left her to her own devices.

"Is she a good cook?" Nuala asked as they pulled out of the driveway. Will didn't seem disposed to talk about his ex-girlfriend, but Nuala couldn't help asking.

"So-so," he said, eager to drop the subject. "Anyway," he said happily, "tonight is going to be ours." He headed the Jeep in the direction of St. Augustine. "Just the two of us celebrating us."

"Celebrating us," she murmured, settling into the curve his arm made.

The night was balmy, almost like a spring evening. Nuala pushed thoughts of the future out of her mind. Tonight was to celebrate the two of them. They were worth celebrating, no matter what happened later.

Will took her to a small and intimate Spanish restaurant in the heart of old St. Augustine, where he ordered a delicious paella and a good wine.

As much as he would have preferred not to mention Virginia, Will felt as though he had to say something.

"I want to thank you, Nuala. For not making a scene when Virginia dropped in." He reached across the table and covered her hand with his.

"I was as surprised as you were," she told him.

"You could have made it uncomfortable for all of us when she first showed up," he said. "Instead, you made it easy by being so hospitable. At a time when I was truly at a loss about how to act and what to say, you jumped right in and handled it."

She smiled. "None of us drank much of the tea I made," she said.

"And by the way, you play a very convincing role as my fiancée," he told her. He didn't tell her that he liked the way she acted in that role. He didn't tell her that he'd given serious thought to actually making the fantasy real; he'd thought about asking her to marry him. From the way her pupils widened in alarm, he sensed that she wasn't ready to hear a marriage proposal. Well, that was okay. There was still time.

Fortunately, at that point the waiter brought their food, and he was pleased at Nuala's delighted exclamations over the seafood. The atmosphere changed as they both relaxed again, and Will marveled at the way Nuala looked tonight. She was sparkling, and her eyes glowed with pleasure as she talked. Dressed up in her violet chiffon dress, she seemed sophisticated, stimulating and extremely sensual. He caught himself concentrating on the sweetness of her smile, the genuineness of her interest. If he were to meet her tonight for the first time, he would still be utterly fascinated. Neither time nor the knowing of each other intimately had dimmed that first wonderful attraction.

He was so busy admiring her that he paid little attention to the substance of her conversation until Nuala told him about Virginia and Roy. She didn't need to embellish the story to make it interesting. Will stopped eating, an astounded slow grin spreading across his face at the telling of it.

When she had finished, Will let out a whoop that could be heard all over the restaurant. He managed to regain his composure as the faces of the other patrons turned toward them in startled curiosity.

"Is everything all right?" asked a waiter who appeared out of nowhere instantly and anxiously.

"Fine," Will said, treating himself to a gulp of wine. He leaned over the table.

"Virginia is marrying a country-Western singer?" he said incredulously. "Are you putting me on?"

"She's mad about him," confirmed Nuala.

"A country-Western singer? Why, I can't even imagine Virginia going into a rowdy place like the Two Bit, much less marrying someone who sings there with a band."

"Who can explain the mysterious glimmerings of limerence?" Nuala said, smiling at him over the rim of her wineglass.

Will laughed. "Well, I'm glad she's happy. Virginia's a good person and a nice person, and maybe the guy will bring some laughter into her life. She sure needs it."

"She won't be seeing you again, Will. She's going to make like a tree in the morning."

"Like a tree?"

"And leave."

This time they both laughed. Will raised his glass. "To Virginia and Roy," he said. "May their limerence grow into love. Like ours." With only a temporary pang, Nuala lifted her wineglass to her lips.

After dinner, they meandered hand in hand through the narrow streets of the town and strolled out on the Bridge of Lions for a moonlight view of the old fort built by the Spaniards on Matanzas Bay.

On a sudden whim, Will suggested a ride over to the ocean to walk on the beach. He drove the Jeep right down on the hardpacked white sand and they jumped out, shoes in hand. Not far away, the black-and-white spiral-striped lighthouse on Anastasia Island flashed its beam out to sea, intermittently lighting their faces.

"I have a favor to ask of you, Nuala," Will said as they walked.

"Oh?"

"It's about my book. Will you read it when I've finished it?"

He had kept so quiet about his manuscript, so quiet that Nuala had wondered if she'd ever get a chance to read it. She was touched that he wanted her to read it now.

"Of course, Will," she said. She would grant him anything, anything he wanted, anything that she could give. She wanted Will to be happy, the same way Virginia wanted him to be happy.

"I figure that you know what makes a good story, since you've worked with stories so much."

"I don't know if I'm qualified to perform a literary critique," Nuala said doubtfully.

"Just read it from the point of view of the reader who picks the book up in a bookstore and carries it home for a good read," he suggested. "I'd like to know what disappoints you about the book, or what you like."

Nuala smiled up at him. "I guess I can handle that," she said.

They stopped and kissed, and Nuala shivered at his touch.

"I have a couple of blankets in the Jeep," Will said. "Let's spread one out on the sand. We can wrap ourselves up in the other one."

Will laid the blankets where the high sand dunes sheltered them from the stiff breeze from the ocean. They sat down and Will gathered her in his arms. They pulled the other blanket over them for warmth.

It was a romantic evening, one Nuala would always remember. The moon lay a broad silvery path on the undulating water, and overhead, the Milky Way swept its hazy incandescence across the sky. The gentle rhythmic swish of the waves ebbing and flowing on the shore provided background music, and the air was heavy with the scent of the sea. It was the kind of night she'd want to remember always.

"Make love to me," Nuala said unsteadily against Will's cheek.

"Gladly," he said. His soft and tender kiss was quickly warmed by their mutual passion. He lay back on the blanket and pulled her along with him, exulting in their togetherness. He began to move his hands over her body, and she touched him, too; when he opened his eyes once he saw her eyes were closed, concentrating on the sensations.

As always, the two of them were exquisite together, alternately tantalizing and fulfilling. Will made love to her elegantly, considerately, and with great joy. *If only,* thought Nuala, *we could be like this forever.* No promises, no dreams, no plans. If only they could live for this moment.

And then Nuala didn't think anymore. Later she would want to remember this night and the way they had loved each other. It would be a warm memory to hold close on other longer and lonelier nights.

Chapter Eleven

"What do you think of this?" Nuala asked, holding the length of cotton print fabric up to her face.

"I think you're beautiful," Will said.

"No, I mean, does the color look all right on me?"

"It's very nice."

"I usually don't wear yellow," she said doubtfully, crushing the material in her hand. It didn't wrinkle much, which was a point in its favor; it would be ideal to wrap around her in a sari for telling stories from India.

"Go ahead and buy it," urged Beckman from behind the long portable table where he was displaying his scavenged flea-market wares. "The money goes to a good cause. Besides, it's getting close to Christmas. All the money I make here today goes toward buying refreshments for my annual Christmas party."

"You talked me into it," Nuala said. She counted the money out into Beckman's small outstretched hand.

"When do you want me to stop by and help you fix those old toys, Beckman?" Will asked.

"How about this afternoon?" Beckman suggested. "I'll be leaving here in an hour or so."

"I'll be there," Will said.

He tucked Nuala's length of fabric under one arm and slid his other arm around her waist. They were at the regular Sunday flea market at the old drive-in theater, which was almost all there was to do on a Sunday afternoon in the town of Turkey Trot. People milled around lines of long tables set up to display everything from clothing to old paperbacks to baked goods. A child entrepreneur sold iced Kool-Aid to thirsty shoppers; a sign tacked with masking tape to the side of a green van offered Free Kittens.

Unable to resist old storybooks, Nuala became entranced enough to buy a collector's edition of a Beatrix Potter book from an elderly lady who said it had belonged to her daughter.

"What are you going to do with it?" Will asked.

"Stack it with the other books in the back of the Storymobile," she said wryly.

"If you load many more books into that hearse of yours, the back of it will drag on the ground."

"In that case I'll have to rename it the Draggin' Wagon," Nuala retorted.

Will laughed. "Maybe you should find a permanent place of residence," he suggested. "One with lots of bookshelves."

She shot a startled look up at him. "Is that a hint?"

"Anthony House has lots of bookshelves," he observed with an air of diffidence.

"But you're going to sell it," she reminded him.

"Who knows how long it will take?" Will said philosophically. "Why, it could take years."

"Are you prepared to stay there that long? Can you *afford* to stay there that long?"

"Where there's a Will, there's always a way."

"Seriously, Will."

He did get serious. "Nuala, I don't know how long I'll stay. I assume that I'll go back to my teaching job, but seeing Virginia again made me realize that I've left that life behind. Maybe I'm ready for a change."

"What kind of change?"

"Any kind. Also, it's begun to occur to me that maybe I'm not such a confirmed bachelor after all." He looked down at her expectantly, as though he would like her to infer from this statement that she was the one he wanted to alter his bachelor state.

"Why are we talking about this?" she asked. "Why are we having a serious discussion in the middle of a flea market?"

"Seize the moment, I always say." He managed to make his voice light.

"Oh, Will, this is neither the time nor the place." She stopped to finger a stack of white T-shirts printed with a gaudy pink flamingo and emblazoned with the touristy slogan, Stop in Osofkee, Fla. Her hair fell forward over her face so that he couldn't read her expression.

"Two T-shirts, please," Will said to the chubby kid behind the table.

"You're buying these T-shirts?" Nuala asked.

"Sure. One for you and one for me. They remind me of the flamingo in the front yard." He dug his wallet out of his pocket and paid the boy, and then they strolled on.

"Resuming our previous conversation—" Will said.

"Must we?" despaired Nuala.

"Resuming our previous conversation, I hope you know that you are welcome at Anthony House as long as you choose to stay."

"You know I never stop in one spot for long," Nuala said quietly. The crowd was thinning out now, and many dealers were packing up their trucks and campers and heading out the gate.

"I know, but now you don't have to move on. You have a place to stay. Free of charge, as long as you like."

"I don't know what to say." They had almost reached Will's Jeep; he took her hand and swung it between them.

"Dear Nuala, all you have to say is that you'll stay."

"For a while," she hedged.

"Until after Christmas?"

"I hate to be pinned down."

"I only pin down butterfly specimens, never flutterbies. Anyhow, you wouldn't want to miss Beckman's big party for the underprivileged children. It's fabulous."

"I suppose I wouldn't," she said.

Will tossed her fabric into the Jeep and climbed in after it. Nuala sat straight in her seat, hands clenched on top of the old Beatrix Potter book. He noticed her white knuckles and wondered why it was such a big decision for her to stay with him until after Christmas. Wasn't she happy? Didn't they get along well?

He reached over and unclenched her hands. He held one of them in his and stared at her until she finally turned her head and looked him in the eye.

"Until after Christmas?" he urged gently.

Her eyes were dark with emotion, and she nodded her head yes.

"Good," he said, knowing he had won a major victory, and it was with a sense of victorious jubilation that he drove home to Anthony House.

"YOU'RE DOING a good job with that doll, Nuala," Beckman said.

Nuala twisted the doll's long blond braid on top of its little head and pinned it. "I used to love to play with my dolls when I was a kid," she said, holding the doll at arm's length to observe the effect. It looked pretty good for a doll that had been in pieces just an hour ago. Beckman had refitted its head to its body while Will, working on a broken wagon, sang "I Ain't Got Nobody" at the top of his lungs. Then Beckman had replaced one lost arm from a seemingly inexhaustible supply of doll limbs, which he kept in a large cardboard box over his workbench. Nuala had found clothes in another box and had appointed herself doll hairdresser for the day. The results pleased them all.

"There," Will said, experimentally twisting the wagon's handle this way and that. "I think this'll stay fixed. The wagon's in fine condition, Beckman. I can't imagine where you found it."

"In a dumpster, of course," he said. He was gluing the leg back on a table that would eventually furnish a Barbie's dream house.

Nuala attacked the coiffure of another doll with her own brush. This one took considerably more doing. The doll's short red hair looked as though someone had styled it by sticking the doll's finger into an electric socket.

"Did your friend finally leave, Will?"

"Virginia? Oh, yeah. In fact, she sent me a note thanking me for my hospitality and inviting me to her wedding."

Nuala, who had read the note, continued to brush the doll's hair.

"You going?" Beckman asked.

"Nah. It's in Chapel Hill. I'm planning to stay here through Christmas."

"That's good. I can use all the help I can get getting ready for this party I'm throwing. You gonna be here, Nuala?"

She nodded.

"Can I count on you to tell Christmas stories for the kids?"

"Of course," she assured him.

"Hot *dog*." Beckman grinned. "It'll be the best party yet." He fastened the tiny table leg on with a clamp and stood back. "We've accomplished a lot today. Thanks to both of you for stopping by."

Will stood up and stretched. "It was fun," he said. "I just keep thinking of the happiness shining from those kids' eyes when they see the gifts you give them."

Beckman chuckled. "I do, too. It kind of makes up for having no children of my own."

"Tell me, Beckman," said Will thoughtfully. "Do you ever regret not having kids?"

Beckman smiled wistfully. "I used to. But my Gracie and me, we had a good marriage. A long marriage. We took care of other people's kids when they needed it, and I started this Christmas party for kids who wouldn't have many presents without it, and I kind of feel like I've done what I was supposed to be doing, if you know what I mean. How about you, Will? Do you regret it?"

"Sometimes," said Will.

"Well, you've got lots of time left," Beckman said kindly. "Lots and lots of time."

Nuala set the doll on the pile with the others and turned away to put her brush and comb back in her purse. All the while she was thinking, *I shouldn't have told Will I'd stay until after Christmas.*

It was too late now. She'd given her word, and Beckman was depending on her for his party. There was nothing she could do but stay, no matter how much harder it made it to leave later.

NUALA AT WORK was something to see, thought Will as he watched her cast a spell over the forty or so children who had come to her Saturday story hour at the Turkey Trot Library. In performance she exposed her vulnerability, her values and her deepest feelings. Because she cared so obviously about the African stories she was relating today, her audience listened with open minds and open hearts.

Will looked around at the spellbound listeners. Most of them were the children of migrant workers, but there were others, too. After Nuala's success at the Osofkee Library, her fame had spread. Today several parents had lingered to watch her work, and they were as caught up in Nuala's tale of "Why the Sky Is Far Away" as their children were. Nuala, wearing a kind of burnoose made of hand-woven cloth from Zimbabwe along with her Ouagadougou necklace, fairly glowed.

Will would like to think that she glowed because of her love—although she persisted in calling it limerence—for him. Yet he couldn't think that, because he sensed that with him, she still did not dare to do what she did in front of an audience. With him, she didn't expose her vulnerability, and he intuited that he hadn't really plumbed her deepest feelings. Whether that were true or not, certainly today he felt that he could have watched Nuala's expressive face forever as she wove her magic web of words.

The children stirred, and Nuala called a birthday boy to the front of the room to blow out the wishing candle. The story hour was officially over.

Will stretched and looked at his watch. Time always flew at one of Nuala's story hours. He didn't realize that in stretching, his foot had blocked the aisle for a boy who appeared to be about four years old. The boy clutched a big storybook under his arm, and he wasn't looking where he was going. Expelling a sharp *oof!* as the wind was knocked out of him, the child fell headlong on his stomach in front of Will.

"Hey!" Will said, instantly sorry he hadn't pulled in his feet in time. "Are you okay, fella?" Gently he lifted the boy up and sat him in his lap.

As soon as he could draw air into his lungs, the boy began to wail.

Terry Schuler was there in an instant. Nuala shot Will a worried look from across the room, but there were so many children crowding around her to look at her necklace and other African items she'd brought that Nuala could do no more than telegraph her concern with raised eyebrows.

"That's little Tommy Phillips," Terry said. "His mother left him at story hour while she went to the store. Shh, Tommy, you're all right." Terry checked carefully to make sure that Tommy hadn't skinned his knees or elbows.

"Hush, Tommy," Will said, patting Tommy comfortingly on the back.

But Tommy wailed even more.

"Oh, dear," Terry said with a worried look toward the front desk. "The kids all want to check out books after story hour, and there's no one to help."

"Go ahead," Will urged her. "Tommy's okay, and I can handle this." He had to speak loudly to be heard over Tommy's sobs.

Terry gave Tommy a final pat. "There, there," she said distractedly. "You're in good hands, Tommy." She hurried away to tend to business.

"Now, Tom," Will said in a sensible man-to-man tone. "It's not all that bad. Your mom will be here in a minute, you know."

Confronted by this manly and matter-of-fact attitude instead of the fluttery solicitousness he'd expected, Tommy drew one long shuddering breath and stared at Will, clearly fascinated by his beard.

"You like my beard, do you? Well, go ahead and touch it."

Tommy, wide-eyed and teary-cheeked, reached up a tentative finger and barely touched Will's beard.

"You'll have one someday, too," Will said, a statement that elicited a skeptical giggle from Tommy.

Bolder now, Tommy stroked Will's beard and poked a forefinger into it, hard.

Will winced. "Watch it, Tom," he cautioned. "You'll be giving me a dimple."

"I got a blue lion," Tommy said loudly. "He likes to eat golf clubs."

"Is that so?" Will said. "If you go around telling tall tales like that, they'll be hiring you to do the library story hour before you know it. Did you hear that, Nuala?" Will asked.

"What, is this guy trying to take my job?" Nuala knelt on the floor beside them and winked at Tommy.

Tommy laughed with glee at the thought. At that moment his harried mother arrived with one drooling baby draped over her shoulder and with a fussy two-year-old in tow.

"I falled down and I want to check out a book, Mommy," her eldest son told her loudly.

"He's all right," Will assured the mother. "At least his fall didn't hurt anything that a new library book won't cure."

Tommy's mother raised exhausted eyes to the ceiling as she tried to calm her whimpering young daughter. "And me with only two hands. Show me the book you want, Tommy."

"I'll help him check it out," Will volunteered.

"Oh, would you?" His mother spared Will a grateful smile.

"Sure," Will said, scooping the delighted Tommy up in his arms and settling him on his shoulders, a high vantage point from which Tommy obviously enjoyed lording it over the children below.

Nuala watched wistfully as Will efficiently completed the book-checking-out process. He was so natural with Tommy; he knew exactly how to talk with him, how to handle him. Just as he had known how to handle that little lost girl at Disney World. No doubt about it, Will was a born natural with kids.

"It went beautifully, Nuala," Will enthused after Tommy had gone and the crowd in the library had thinned out. He picked up the box of story props to carry out to the hearse for her.

"Did you think so?" she said, forcing a tired smile.

"You had them hanging on every word."

They walked down the steps and Will heaved the box into the back of the hearse. Will sneaked a kiss because no one was looking.

But Nuala was too tired and too dispirited to find comfort in familiar banter. Try as she might, she couldn't come up with any clever witticisms. Will smiled affectionately as he slammed the door of her Storymobile after her and walked around to the passenger's side.

He didn't understand her reticence of mood, but he made up his mind to adjust to it. She seemed to have a lot on her mind lately, and it dated back to just after Virginia left. He attributed her mood to her story-hour schedule at the library and the in-service training she was to conduct for the local school librarians next week.

On the way back to Anthony House, Nuala drove abstractedly, glad that Will didn't insist on talking. She needed to do some serious thinking. In fact, she'd been doing some serious thinking ever since she had promised to stay through Christmas.

She rolled down the window on her side of the hearse and let the breeze whip through her hair. The countryside along the highway to Turkey Trot was familiar to her now, almost as familiar as Anthony House. Almost as familiar as Will.

She braked behind a school bus that was letting children off at a school-bus stop and watched dispassionately as they scuffled with each other, giggled together and ran toward home. One girl with two ponytails tied with yellow ribbon waved shyly at them from her seat in the back of the bus. Will waved back.

"Cute kid, isn't she?" Will said.

"Mm-hmm," Nuala agreed.

"I've always wanted a couple of kids," Will said thoughtfully. His unexpected words, which tied in so closely with the very insecurities that threatened to overwhelm her, hit Nuala right in the stomach, pinning her to her seat.

The school bus started up again, and Nuala automatically pushed on the gas pedal, feeling Will's statement like a bruised bone deep inside of her.

Joe Morini, her former fiancé, had looked forward to having kids, too. Joe had been one to toss a softball around a vacant lot with the neighborhood children for hours. He had been an active member of Big Brothers. He'd always wanted, from the time he could remember, children of his own.

And he had wanted Nuala until he found out that she couldn't give them to him.

With an all-too-familiar wretchedness, Nuala admitted to herself that she would never be right for Will Anthony. She could no longer ignore the signs, especially now that Will had put his desire for children into words. *I've always wanted a couple of kids.* He couldn't have put it any plainer. And he'd been thinking about kids more and more lately. She inferred this not only from Will himself, but from the conversations they'd had. A case in point was Will's asking Beckman if Beckman had ever regretted not having children.

The handwriting on the wall was all too plain. If Nuala allowed her heart to overrule her head, it would be the same way all over again. The same way it had been with Joe.

Chapter Twelve

"Deck the halls with boughs of holly, fa-la-la-la-la-la-la-la-la," sang Will, carting in a clear plastic bag so packed full of holly that leaves were falling out of the top.

"Where'd you get that?" Nuala asked, closing the front door and then trailing after him, picking up fallen leaves and berries in his wake.

"Off the holly trolley," he said.

"This may be a holly folly," Nuala said skeptically. "What are you going to do with it all?"

"Decorate for the holly daze. Say, do you think Cole will ever learn to sing 'Jingle Bells'?" For the past week Will had been trying to teach the recalcitrant bird that particular song.

"No, lately his record seems stuck on 'Nice weather we're having,'" Nuala said.

"Come on, Nuala, help me arrange this holly on the mantel. I'm no good at such things." Will pulled two chairs over to the fireplace for them to stand on, and Nuala climbed up on one.

"You know," Will said as they worked, "at this time of year people in North Carolina are flocking to the malls to buy their Christmas presents."

"Is that so?" Nuala said, concentrating on arranging the holly as artistically as possible.

"Yes," Will said, his serious tone belying his dancing eyes. "And at this particular shopping mall in Raleigh, there's an egg factory right in back of it. Well, one cold December day the heating system failed in the chicken coops. The temperature fell and fell until it was below freezing that night. The poor chickens would have died if the mall owners hadn't taken pity on the chickens and told the people at the egg factory that the chickens were welcome to stay in the mall overnight. In fact, the owners of that particular mall enlisted the help of all the other malls in the city. The employees at the egg factory worked for hours to transport chickens to the shopping centers, and they built big wire enclosures for them right in the middle of the malls. Unfortunately, the wire enclosures weren't very stable. And the chickens were so excited that they ran around all night, finally breaking out of these hastily constructed pens. So do you know what happened?" He had stopped arranging holly and stood on his chair regarding Nuala with a diabolical grin.

Nuala sighed. Knowing Will, she had a pretty good idea what to expect. "No, Will," she said. "What happened?"

"They wrecked the malls with fowls of Raleigh."

He had obviously worked hard and long on that one. In spite of the fact that her nerves were balanced on a thin edge these days, Nuala had to laugh. Then she felt better. She had an idea that Will was trying to cheer her up. "Ho ho ho," she said, just to show him that he had.

He laughed. "I've been scheming on that story for days," he admitted.

They poked and nudged and rearranged the holly until the mantel was artfully decorated. Finally Will jumped down from his chair and regarded the mantel critically.

"It needs a touch of red," Nuala said from her perch on the chair. "A bow or something."

"Aha," Will said, striding to his desk and producing a roll of red velvet ribbon. "Do you think you could do the honors?"

"I guess," Nuala said. She looped the ribbon around her hand and fashioned it into a big puffy bow, which she attached to the mantel with a proffered piece of tape.

"That looks great," Will said enthusiastically. "Let's put another one on the other side."

Nuala climbed down from her chair and up on the one on the other side of the mantel. She caught a glimpse of herself in the mirror over the mantel. She looked drawn, and her lips were compressed into a thin line. Self-consciously she tried to relax them, but it wasn't easy. Despite her laugh over Will's joke, she still felt wound tight; she couldn't help feeling tense over their uncertain future.

"I think we need a couple of candles on the mantel to really set it off," Will said, producing the monogrammed silver candlesticks and two tall white tapers. He set them carefully on each end of the mantel and pulled Nuala down off the chair and into his arms. He kissed her resoundingly.

"Doesn't that look wonderful?" he said with a sense of awe, and Nuala realized that Will wasn't talking about the newly decorated mantel. He was talking about their reflection in the big mirror above it. They wore their matching T-shirts, the ones with the gaudy flamingos and the slogan Stop in Osofkee, Fla.

She pulled away from him. "Lovely," she said.

"I've invited Beckman to come over on Christmas Day for our little get-together. Did you get a chance to mention it to Martha and Terry?"

"Yes, and Terry is going to bring her boyfriend if that's all right."

"Sure," Will said easily. "I think I'm going to like having so many people around." He was enjoying decorating this big old house. He had found mistletoe growing in the woods, had gathered great armloads of holly and was fashioning fragrant pine branches into a garland for the banister on the front stairs. He couldn't remember ever looking forward so much to Christmas.

"What about your book?" Nuala asked. "Isn't it going to suffer from neglect?" What with all the preparations for the holidays, he hadn't been working on it much.

"The book is fine," he said. "It'll be ready for you to read soon. By the way, I had a letter today from a magazine editor who has heard of my textbook about the monarch butterfly. He wanted to know if I'd be interested in writing an article about them for his magazine."

"Are you going to do it?"

"I don't know. He said to call him."

"You should do it, Will," Nuala said with conviction.

"Why?"

"In order to—to keep up with your field," she said haltingly, although that wasn't the real reason she thought Will should write the article. It would have been more honest if she had said, "So you'll have something to do after I've left."

"I thought about how good it would be to keep a hand in with a few scientific pieces," Will said seriously. "It'd be good to have a published magazine article under my belt when—or if—I go back to the university." He waited for her to ask him if he really was going back to teaching.

But she didn't. All she did was mumble something about checking on the clothes in the dryer before running out of the room.

Will sank down on the chair in front of his desk, wishing he knew what to do about her. She loved him. He knew she loved him, despite all her talk about the theory of limerence. They slept together every night, delighting in each other's body and exploring each other's mind, never tiring of their new discoveries. He felt as though Nuala were an extension of himself, and he thought at times that she felt the same way about him. But then, quite unexpectedly, she would clamp down on her feelings, make an attempt at avoiding him, or withdraw from the conversation as she had just done now. Something was wrong, something serious, and he couldn't quite put his finger on it.

Oh, well, he thought optimistically, remembering one of his pet theories. *Nothing is ever what it seems.* Probably things were better than he thought. It was a cheery idea, just what he needed to tide him over the holidays.

ON THE SATURDAY before Christmas, Nuala and Will helped Beckman load all his refurbished toys into his pickup truck. Then they drove to the Addy Mae Burke park where Beckman, heh-hehing and capering about like an undernourished Santa, distributed the toys to a large group of needy children.

Nuala recognized many of the children as migrants who had attended her story hours at the Turkey Trot Library, and many of them gathered around the massive oak tree where Nuala had tacked up her quilted storytelling banner and proceeded to charm them all with an assortment of Christmas stories.

"Isn't this a fantastic day?" said Will, in his element as the center of a group of worshiping children. He had appointed himself unofficial troubleshooter for the day, administering minor first aid where needed, putting together toys that needed assembly and producing required toy batteries like rabbits out of a hat, much to the glee of the children.

"It's wonderful, Nuala agreed, thinking that the Christmas spirit was nowhere more alive than here at the park where one bent little man with an affinity for other people's junk was making dreams come true for children who otherwise would have had a meager Christmas.

Beckman, a beatific grin on his face, rushed by. He wore a Santa Claus suit and was passing out what appeared to be an endless supply of candy canes.

"Beckman, I think you're the true spirit of Christmas," Nuala said, bending over to bestow an impulsive kiss on his withered cheek. "Thanks for letting me be a part of it."

Beckman actually blushed. "If you promise to kiss me again, I'll do all this again next year," he said impishly before hurrying on his way.

Will slid an arm around Nuala's waist. "That's a good idea," Will said in a low tone so that only she could hear him. "Let's come back next year and watch

Beckman do his thing." He was hoping that she'd give him some sign of acquiescence.

But Nuala only bit her lip and arranged her head against Will's shoulder so that he couldn't see her eyes. Surely Will knew by this time that by Christmas next year, Nuala would be long gone. Surely he must know, but didn't want to admit it. Didn't he?

ON CHRISTMAS EVE Will and Nuala put up the Christmas tree in the parlor. It was a short-needle pine Will had cut in the woods. Beckman helped decorate. With his annual children's Christmas party over, he was able to concentrate on making decorations for their tree. A thorough search of the house had failed to turn up any ornaments, so Will decreed that everything that went on their tree must be homemade. It would make a very old-fashioned Christmas tree and one that would complement the fine old house. Will did make one concession to modernity, however. He went out and bought a few strings of tiny lights.

Nuala spent hours cutting out construction paper and stringing together paper loops for chains. Beckman gathered pinecones in the woods and frosted them with glitter. Will saved the metal lids from every can he opened for two weeks and punched holes in them and glued macaroni on in what he said were snowflake shapes, although privately Nuala and Beckman agreed that they looked like nothing more than tin-can lids with macaroni glued on. Will was delighted with the tree, though, once they got it decorated. His happiness tore at Nuala's heart.

It seemed as though she were spending the last few days before Christmas storing up images to take with her, images to pull out when she needed them: the river, shrouded by lavender mist in the early morning; the shadows of the hanging moss swaying on the lapped boards of Anthony house; the fragrant cooking smells produced so proudly by Will, who was turning out to be a wonderful cook; even their peripatetic nightly visitor, Captain Anthony. And Will—his tenderness and his good humor, his attentiveness, his intelligence, his wit. She had learned to live with the dull ache around her heart and the tightness behind her eyes. But how would she learn to live without Will?

She knew that there were things he'd like to discuss, but she avoided discussing them. Maybe someday, after the initial shock of her leaving was over, he would think of her kindly and remember the good times. She didn't know yet when she would leave—she only knew it would be soon after Christmas, probably after New Year's.

There would be no harsh scenes. She would never have to explain why she was leaving, she hoped. She had a vision of herself stealing away in the dark of night as Will slept, which seemed a bit impractical. The two of them slept in the middle of Will's bed, touching. That was where the sagging mattress dumped them. He always felt it when she got out of bed at night and reacted with a sleepy, "Nuala?" and a groping about until she spoke a word of reassurance.

If she couldn't sneak out in the dead of night, she'd have to leave some other way. She only knew that she had to get away. Better to be the one to go than the one who was left. It had been her philosophy for a long time now.

WILL COULD HARDLY WAIT for Christmas. He had bought Cole a shiny new brass bird cage, one that didn't have to be held closed with a twist tie. And he had bought Nuala a tape recorder so that she could record her stories. He'd like to have some of her tales on hand so he could listen to them anytime. He was thinking of compiling an anthology of them, maybe in a book for storytellers.

He had also bought Nuala an engagement ring.

Well, why not? He'd been entranced with the idea ever since she'd role-played being his fiancée for Virginia's benefit. He loved Nuala and he wanted to marry her. She loved him. There was no mistaking it. He couldn't wait until the two of them could scrap all the silly business about limerence and call their emotion what it really was—love. If you were in love, you got married. As simple—and as complicated—as that.

He wasn't quite sure when he'd ask her. She'd been acting unhappy lately; perhaps it was because she was unsure of their future. He had been uncertain about it himself until he'd thought of the solution. Ask her to marry him, that's what he'd do. It was kind of like the hunters who hunted turtles on a log out in the river. Will figured he had at least a fifty-fifty chance that Nuala would jump toward the engagement ring. Given the way they felt about one another, how could Nuala say no? He'd bide his time and ask her when the time was right. She loved surprises. Surely she'd love this one, too.

On Christmas Eve he made a hurried trip to Osofkee, where a student on break from the nearby University of Florida in Gainesville listened to his instructions and agreed to type the manuscript of his novel before the end of the first week in January when classes resumed.

"I'm eager for you to read it," Will told Nuala when he returned.

Nuala turned away before he could see the expression on her face. She might be gone before the first week in January. In fact, she was planning on it. Her guilt was enormous. Planning to walk out, with no explanation, on the man she loved, seemed like a very cruel thing to do. It was all she could do to make it through dinner, for which she and Will collaborated on a fine Caesar salad and roast beef rare all the way through, just the way they both liked it. Nuala offered to clean up the kitchen herself that night as a Christmas present to Will, but he would have none of it.

"Working beside you is fun for me, Nuala," he said, touching her briefly on the tip of her nose with a fingertip, and so there was to be no escape to her room to cry silent and lonely tears for the pain she was soon to cause both of them.

The wind that night rose alarmingly throughout the evening, and after the nightly sound of footsteps on the front staircase had died away, Will went outside and checked to make sure that all the shutters were firmly fastened away from the windows. It had started to rain, and the wind blew crashing tides of rain against the windowpanes with the force and energy and rhythm of deep-crested waves.

"Well, it's a real bad one, all right," Will said of the storm as he stomped water from his feet in the kitchen and divested himself of his raincoat. "If Santa is out there in that kind of weather, he's going to get waterlogged."

"Nice weather we're having," Cole said chattily.

"Oh, Cole, hush," scolded Nuala. She hung Will's wet raincoat on one of the wooden pegs behind the door.

"I remember," Will reminisced, "the last storm we had like this. You fluttered into my life wearing a white gauze dress and a funny-looking pair of shoes. All storms should bring such good fortune."

Nuala clung to the wet folds of the raincoat for a second, dreading to face him. A little more than a week, and she'd be free. Free of having to pretend that everything was all right when it wasn't, free of having to extricate herself from plans that Will wanted to make and that she couldn't.

Will's hands went around her from the back, and he pulled her to him. She could feel his hipbones pressing against her, and he was kissing her tenderly on the cheek.

"Let's take advantage of this weather," he said slowly and seductively. "The power will probably go off and we'll be left standing here in the dark. Why wait for it to happen? Let's go up to bed. Now." His hips moved against her insistently, and she felt a quick shudder of desire for him.

It occurred to Nuala in that moment that love and sorrow are similar, that each could be expressed in passion. Suddenly she wanted Will more than she ever had. She wanted him fiercely, angrily and out of desperate need. In their passion she knew she could lose herself for a short while, and she needed to blot out realities.

"Yes," she said, the word bursting from her in anguish, but she did not want to wait until they got upstairs. Feverishly she led him into the cold, damp study, and there she turned to him quickly with a little cry and pressed herself to the angular contours of his body.

Her touch burned into him and made his breath quicken against her hair. Hungrily he clutched at her, losing himself in her deep kisses. Somehow they fell onto the uncomfortable horsehair couch, both of them too impatient to undress completely, and there the tension built until it exploded in both of them. Nuala cried out because he was tender and gentle and because he did not hurt her. And she desperately wanted to be hurt, because she hurt so much inside.

The rain rattled the windowpanes and she sobbed helplessly in his arms, and Will didn't know what to make of it, and so he only held her and smoothed her hair until the sobs became quieter and finally died away. Then she lay passively in his arms while he kissed her face and brushed away her tears with gentle fingertips.

Once Will had dried her tears and quieted her sobs, she lay in his arms scarcely breathing and wondering at the desperation with which she had completed this act of love.

"Am I too heavy for you?" murmured Will, whose body still covered hers.

"No," she whispered.

"Let's go up to bed," he said.

He still didn't understand why Nuala had been so impatient for love, nor did he know why she had cried afterward. He only hoped dimly that the ring he was going to give her at an appropriate moment sometime during the next week would make everything all right.

IT WAS MIDNIGHT when the pounding on the door awakened them.

"Will?" Nuala said, pulling the bedclothes up around her chin.

"'S the ghost," he mumbled. He had fallen asleep with difficulty after lying awake beside the passion-spent Nuala for over an hour. He was reluctant to give up his sleep.

"No, Will, something is knocking on the door." She sounded alarmed.

He was awake in an instant. He pulled her to him, listening to her rapidly beating heart. He still didn't know what had provoked her unusual passion and her tearful outburst when they had made love, but he knew he had to comfort her now the best he could. He listened. The pounding was regular and didn't stop. The storm still raged, and he couldn't imagine how anyone could be out in it.

"I think we should go downstairs and see who it is," Nuala said resolutely. She got up and pulled on her bathrobe.

Will sighed, but he knew Nuala was right. She tossed him his robe and he put it on.

Will flicked on the hall light and Nuala took his hand. If she was leery of walking down the front stairs, which they jokingly referred to as "the captain's territory," she gave no sign.

When they reached the bottom, Nuala pulled aside the curtain to look out on the porch. She said in surprise, "Why, there are a man and a woman out there! Open the door, Will!"

Will unlatched the door and threw it open. In tumbled a couple who looked as though they were in their late sixties. Both appeared soaked to the skin.

"Thank goodness you came!" exclaimed the man.

The woman shook drops of water off the plastic rain hat she pulled off her bouffant hairstyle. "Where shall I hang this, dear?" she said briskly to Nuala, who was standing to the side, one hand pulling her robe tight against the dampness and the cold, which had gusted in through the open door.

"Well, I . . ." said Nuala uncertainly, looking to Will for guidance.

Will had locked the door behind them. He took in the haze of fatigue on the woman's face and the utter exhaustion on the man's.

"We've been driving all day, you know. You'd better show us to our room," prompted the man. He started to remove his raincoat.

"I'm afraid there must be some mistake," Will said slowly.

"Oh, no. There can be no mistake," the man said with a worried frown. "We're the Thorpes. Mr. and Mrs. Amos Thorpe. From Columbus, Ohio?"

"You have our reservations," added Mrs. Thorpe. "We made them last year."

"We've stayed at Anthony House every Christmas for the last twenty-five years," said Mr. Thorpe. "This year we'll be staying until New Year's Day."

Will and Nuala exchanged a flabbergasted look.

Mr. Thorpe cleared his throat impatiently. He thrust his wet raincoat at Will. "Now," he said pointedly, "we're both very tired. If you don't mind, our room . . . ?"

"We have no choice," Nuala whispered during a hurriedly arranged conference in the parlor with Will. "We can't send them back out in this weather." At the moment she was feeling inordinately pleased that she had finally managed to clean the last of the stubborn mildew out of the bathrooms this week.

"I don't have a room prepared," Will said. "And then there's the matter of feeding them in the morning."

"I can manage—*we* can manage," she said, correcting herself as she thought of Will's newly gained expertise in the kitchen.

"For an out-of-the-way place, people certainly don't seem to have any trouble finding it. First Virginia, now the Thorpes. Ye gods!"

"Poor Mrs. Thorpe—she's so exhausted her lips were quivering. There's no place else for them to go, Will."

"They can't stay all week," Will protested.

"Let's just get them settled for tonight," insisted Nuala.

"Does it seem to you that every time it rains, people drop in out of nowhere?"

"These are just nice folks from Ohio, with no place to stay. You can't turn them away any more than you turned me away. Or Virginia."

Will heaved a deep sigh. "You're right," he said. He hesitated for a second, and as if to emphasize the seriousness of the storm, the wind flung a barrage of hailstones against the windows.

Will cleared his throat and marched back into the foyer.

"I'll get your bag, Mr. Thorpe," he said.

"Call me Amos," said Mr. Thorpe.

"Come with me," Nuala said, touching Mrs. Thorpe's sleeve. "I'll show you to your room. It's not made up, I'm afraid." She led the way up the stairs and Mrs. Thorpe followed.

"Old Mr. Anthony, he used to have our beds turned down for us when we got here," the plump Mrs. Thorpe said, puffing along after Nuala. "Oh, dear, I suppose that sounds critical, and it wasn't meant to be. I'm just so tired, that's all." Mrs. Thorpe shot Nuala a tentative smile, which Nuala returned.

Together she and Mrs. Thorpe, who insisted on being called Lorraine, made up the beds. Soon afterward, Will and Amos Thorpe arrived with the Thorpes' luggage.

"What time will you serve breakfast?" asked Mrs. Thorpe brightly as the four of them stood blinking awkwardly at each other in the light from the overhead light fixture.

"Uh—is eight o'clock okay?" ventured Nuala.

"Lovely, dear. Now go back to bed and get some sleep, won't you? And Merry Christmas," she said, glancing at her watch. "Since it is already Christmas," she pointed out.

"Merry Christmas," said Will, backing out of their room and pulling Nuala with him.

Once outside, the two of them stood staring at each other in the hallway.

A smile stretched across Will's face. "Well, this isn't how I intended to say it, but Merry Christmas, Nuala." He bent his head and captured her lips in a kiss.

"Merry Christmas," she whispered and would have kissed him again if the door to the Thorpes' room hadn't opened.

"Oh, excuse me," said an obviously startled Amos Thorpe, closing the door just as quickly as he opened it.

Will and Nuala exchanged an embarrassed look. Then Will pulled her down the hall to his room.

"Maybe I'd better go back to my own room," Nuala said doubtfully when Will had locked his door behind them.

"Not on your life," he objected, swinging her up in his arms and bearing her to the bed, where he tossed her unceremoniously upon it and climbed in beside her.

"We'll have to get up and cook breakfast," warned Nuala as Will made it clear that he wasn't ready to go back to sleep.

"I hate mornings," he agreed. "They're so early," and then she didn't care what time they had to get up. She gave herself up to his lovemaking, and soon the only sound in the room was the murmuring of their voices as they spoke the sweet words of love over and over, and after a while the sound of his voice and the urgent response of her body to his chased everything else out of her head.

Chapter Thirteen

"Check the English muffins, will you, please, Will?" said Nuala, who was sitrring the Hollandaise sauce.

"They're fine," said Will, shoving the pan of muffins back under the broiler to brown a bit more. He straightened up and stole a kiss.

She spared him a quick smile. "Such behavior is ill advised when I'm stirring Hollandaise," she cautioned. "It can curdle without a moment's notice."

"It's Christmas. Aren't I entitled to happy Hollandaise?"

"Only if kissing is part of your prime merry process. I have an idea that we'll all be a lot happier if this breakfast turns out all right. Have the Thorpes come downstairs yet?"

"They're sitting patiently in the dining room. I guess I'll wait until after breakfast to tell them they can't stay all week."

Nuala poured the sauce into a small pitcher and turned off the burner under the double boiler. She allowed herself a sigh of relief because the sauce had turned out well. Quickly she began to assemble muffins, Canadian bacon and poached eggs. Then she poured the sauce over all.

"I don't know, Will," she said thoughtfully. "I don't know if you should ask the Thorpes to leave after all." It had occurred to her that the Thorpes might be a convenient foil during the next week. With them around, it wouldn't get too sticky with Will. The distraction they provided might make it easier to leave when the time came.

Will balanced the two plates of eggs Benedict in his hands and stared. "You can't be thinking that they should stay!"

Nuala shrugged. She looked him directly in the eye. "Why not? It wouldn't be that much trouble. The only problem would be cooking the meals, and you and I like doing that together."

"But—" Then Will thought about how much fun it was working side by side with Nuala. She had a point.

"We can discuss this after breakfast," he decided, smiling fondly. Then he marched through the kitchen door to serve breakfast.

Nuala heard the delighted exclamations of the Thorpes when they tasted her eggs Benedict.

"They love it," Will said triumphantly, returning to the kitchen. He picked up their plates. "Come on, they want us to eat with them. You don't mind, do you?"

Nuala shook her head. No, she didn't mind. In fact, she welcomed it. It was getting harder and harder to act natural around Will, now that she knew how much she was going to have to disappoint him in the end.

Breakfast turned out to be great fun. The Thorpes were a lively couple, grandparents whose only son and daughter-in-law were working in Saudi Arabia. Getting the family together at Christmas was too difficult, considering the miles involved; the Thorpes didn't enjoy traveling in the Middle East, and their son pre-

ferred to save his month-long leave from the
construction company for which he worked so that he
and his family could spend a month with the Thorpes
in the summer. Amos and Lorraine had been coming to
Anthony House since their son was a boy. They loved
the peace and quiet.

"I am sad to think that you're going to close this
lovely old house," said Lorraine, looking around at the
dining room, which gleamed since Nuala's recent min-
istrations. "We've had such good times here."

Will shot Nuala a look. It would have been a perfect
time to tell the Thorpes that they would have to find
another place to stay for the rest of their vacation. But
something in Nuala's expression told him to hold off. In
a moment the opportunity had passed, and the Thorpes
were talking of going for a walk after breakfast.

Later, as he and Nuala washed the dishes, Will again
broached the subject of their staying.

"For one thing," he said, "I don't know how Amos
and Lorraine are going to react to Captain Anthony's
nightly ramblings."

"They seem like the type of people who have both
feet planted firmly on the ground," Nuala said.

"Unlike my ancestor, who insists on marching *his* feet
repeatedly down the stairs," Will said with a wry quirk
to his mouth.

"The Thorpes' room and board would be additional
income," Nuala pointed out. As one who was always
down to her last dollar, this did not seem like a minor
factor.

"I don't know anything about running a boardinghouse," Will said.

"Neither do I, but we can do it. What's so hard?
We'd prepare their meals all week, but we have to do it

for ourselves, anyway. And Lorraine said that she doesn't mind fixing the two of them a sandwich for lunch every day, so you and I would be responsible for breakfasts and dinners.''

Will dried the last dish and flicked the dish towel at a spot on the counter. Then he tossed the towel over a chair back and swooped close to Nuala for a kiss.

"You've talked me into it," he said, holding her loosely in his arms. Today, for Christmas, she wore a shell-pink angora sweater with a U-shaped neckline. It topped a wool shirt in a pastel print reminiscent of Navajo designs. A silver-and-turquoise necklace circled her neck, and from her earlobes swung matching earrings.

"Good," Nuala said. "We'll make the Thorpes happy." *And me too,* she thought with a certain amount of surprise. This was one Christmas when she wouldn't be lonely. Without realizing it, she had been lonely during other winter holidays, often spending Christmas Day itself en route to some other place where she would only meet more strangers, who would go on to become nothing more than fond memories. She seldom kept in touch with any of the people she met on her travels. How could she? She didn't even have a permanent post office box. And here she had Beckman and her two librarian friends and Will. She had settled into a meaningful life without even realizing she was doing it. The idea of leaving it saddened her immeasurably.

"When Amos and Lorraine come in for lunch, I'll explain about Captain Anthony," Will told her, unaware of Nuala's inner sadness. "Otherwise, his nightly visit is likely to take them by surprise."

Nuala said something, she didn't know what, and busied herself with looking after the comfort of their guests. There were clean towels to be carried upstairs to the bathroom; there were dirty ones to be tossed in the decrepit old washing machine. Never mind; it was busywork. Busywork that she and Will did together, but that kept them apart in other important ways.

If Will and Nuala had expected the nocturnal visitations of Captain Anthony to be a problem for the Thorpes, they were wrong.

"Oh, you didn't need to tell me about *that*," Lorraine said. "I've seen the captain many a time."

"You *have*?" chorused Nuala and Will.

"Oh, my, yes. He likes to stand in a corner of the parlor in front of the stuffed alligator and watch whatever is going on."

"But—but that's where I thought I saw that funny reflection on the night we were pulling things out of my trunk," Nuala said.

"Of course, that's him. That's Captain William Anthony. He always looks like he's made out of a kind of silvery light. The captain was probably interested in what you were taking out of the trunk. He's always been perfectly quiet. I'll be interested to hear him walking down the stairs tonight."

After the Thorpes went upstairs to take a nap, Will plugged in the Christmas tree lights, and that evening as they were waiting for their invited guests to arrive, he and Nuala sat on the floor under the tree and opened their gifts together. Nuala exclaimed over the brass bird cage Will had bought for Cole. With a great deal of commotion, Cole was transferred to the new cage. Looking pleased, Cole oversaw the opening of their other gifts.

"A tape recorder!" Nuala exclaimed as she opened Will's present for her.

"So I can record you telling your stories," Will said with a grin.

Will's gifts ranged from a tie with a hand-painted monarch butterfly on it ("I'll never wear it," he groaned), which he suspected had been sent only as a gag from his colleagues in the Department of Biology at the University of North Carolina, to a collector's edition of folktales autographed by Nuala's parents.

"Thank you, Nuala," he said. "I'll always treasure this." From the reverent way he ran his hands over the embossed leather cover, Nuala knew he meant it.

"Well," Nuala said when they had both opened assorted packages from faraway relatives and friends, "I guess we'd better gather up these bows and wrapping papers before our guests arrive."

They'd no sooner put everything away when the doorbell rang. They heard voices on the front porch, accompanied by Beckman's distinctive laugh.

"Nuala, our guests are here," Will said, proudly offering her his arm. She took it, and together they advanced to the door.

Will watched Nuala greeting their guests with satisfaction. With her wonderful warmth, she was a natural hostess. He had had a chance to observe Nuala in many situations, and she was never less than perfectly poised. She would be a standout at faculty parties, if that was to be his future; she would do him proud as his wife no matter what the situation. He momentarily caught her eye and communicated his pleasure, and she smiled back. He thought about the ring in its velvet-lined box upstairs and anticipated the thrill of slipping it on her finger.

The party lasted until after Captain Anthony had made his breezy trek down the front stairs, to the delight of Martha and Terry and to the total incredulity of Terry's boyfriend, Sam.

"You know, you two are missing out on something," Sam said. "I've heard of inns and resorts that stage murder mysteries over the weekend for the benefit of their guests. They hire actors to play the parts and all the guests have a role in solving the mystery. Of course, there's no murder. It's all pretend. Well, you could do something like that. You could have ghost stories, followed by the appearance of a real ghost. Honestly, you should look into it."

Will and Nuala exchanged glances.

"We have discussed something like it," Nuala said a bit uneasily. "But only in a joking way."

"No joking about it, you'd be a huge success. Some people don't want to be part of a murder mystery, no matter how staged it is. But everyone loves a good ghost story."

When their guests had finally left and the Thorpes had retired to their room, Nuala and Will worked together to pick up the empty glasses and plates. A sense of sadness settled over Nuala. It was hard to accept the fact that, like her role as his fiancée, this would be the only time she would be able to play the role of his hostess.

As careful as she was to hide it, Will began to sense a strain in the air. "Hey," he said, passing her on the way into the kitchen. He tipped up her chin with one finger. "Nothing is wrong, is it? You aren't thinking about what Terry's boyfriend said? About telling ghost stories right here at Anthony House?"

Nuala looked deep into his dark eyes, so moist and deep and loving. She managed to shake her head no.

"Well, I have," Will said to her utter and complete surprise. "More and more, I've been thinking about it. We'll talk about it, okay?"

She was about to say, "It would never work," but something made her bite the words back. She did not want to do or say anything to ruin this perfect Christmas, the happiest in her memory since before her parents died. She scarcely paid attention when Will disappeared upstairs as she lingered in the parlor for a moment before returning to sweep the kitchen floor. She looked around. The kitchen was so neat and clean; there was no reason to stay there. "I guess that about does it," she said reluctantly to Will, who had returned.

"Jingle all the way," Cole said suddenly and loudly from his cage in the corner. "Jingle all the way."

"He said it!" said Will. He went to the cage and waggled his fingers through the cage bars. "You said it, old fellow."

"You said it," Cole said.

"I don't believe it," Nuala said in utter disbelief. "Cole's learned two new phrases. That's more than he's learned the whole time I've owned him!"

"That's Cole's Christmas present to us," said Will. He peeled a banana and dropped it through the bars. Cole hopped to the bottom of the cage and began tearing at the fruit with his beak.

"Don't cover the cage," Will said. To the bird he said, "That's it, you merry old Cole. Go ahead and eat your Christmas feast." This seemed to agree with Cole, who went on gulping huge chunks of banana, interrupting his meal only briefly to look up at Will and say, "What a *guy*!"

"Before we go upstairs," Will said with an air of nonchalance, "let's go into the parlor for a minute."

"The parlor?

"Yes. There's another present for you."

"From you?"

"From me."

"But you already gave me a present," Nuala said in confusion.

"And I'm going to give you another one. You'll have to find it yourself, though." His eyes danced at the mystified look on her face, and he took her hand and pulled her along with him into the parlor.

"Where is it?" She couldn't understand the eager expression on Will's face. It was almost as though he was the one getting the gift.

"On the tree."

"*On* the tree?"

"That's right." He laughed out loud at her dumbfounded expression and reached over and cupped her face between his two hands. He brushed his lips briefly against hers, then let her go.

She began to feel the spirit of this game; her eyes lit up with excitement. She ran her eyes over the tree. "Is it bigger than a bread box?" she asked.

Will laughed. "No."

The tree's tiny lights winked among the pine needles, no bigger than stars. Will's macaroni-snowflake ornaments twisted slowly, and her own paper chains and Beckman's popcorn chains swooped from branch to branch. The big tree was so heavily decorated that she didn't know how she was going to find anything on it.

She walked around the tree and tentatively pushed a few ornaments aside. She ran her fingers along one of the popcorn chains.

"I don't know how I'm going to find it," she complained.

"You'll find it," he assured her.

Nuala remembered how she'd played various games that required searching when she was a child. "Am I hot or cold?" she asked.

"Cold," replied Will, watching her circle the tree. The pretty sweater she wore outlined her curves, and her skirt showed more leg than most of her skirts.

"Hot?" she asked, moving to the other side of the tree.

"Warm," conceded Will.

"Warmer?"

"Cooler."

"Warmer?"

"Warm."

"How about now?"

"Hot. Oh, very hot." He followed her as she stared up at the loop of a paper chain. If she'd look a few more inches to the right, she'd have it. He couldn't wait to see the expression on her face when she saw it.

Her eyes scanned the branches, sparkling in anticipation.

"Hot?"

"Still hot," he agreed, enjoying the suspense.

And then her eyes traveled the length of one particular branch. They grew wide. Her mouth drew into an O.

He reached up and plucked the diamond ring from the branch.

"Will," she breathed.

"Yes, Nuala," he said. She turned to face him. Her face was illuminated by the glow of the Christmas tree lights. Her eyes were large, their pupils dark.

"I want to get married, Nuala."

"You bought me a ring," she stammered. She looked very surprised.

He lifted her hand and slipped the diamond solitaire on her finger. It winked and flashed in the light.

"It looks very nice there," he said, kissing each of her fingertips in turn.

She stared at the ring, transfixed. It was exactly the kind of ring she would have wanted if they were going to be engaged. But they weren't going to be engaged. She was going to leave.

"But," she said, and then stopped. Tears filled her eyes.

"Why, Nuala," he said tenderly, raising her face to his. He was smiling at her with happiness. "You must know I love you. I never want to lose you. I want us to get married, to settle down together, to have children."

Tears streamed down Nuala's face.

"Will," was all she managed to say. For a moment his dear face changed shape and swam before her. She fought to get a grip on her emotions. She felt physically sick.

In the euphoria of the moment, Will didn't notice her anguish, or else he mistook it for something else. He kissed away her tears. For a brief moment he pulled her to his chest. His beard tickled her temple, and then he drew back. He kept his arm around her, though.

Nuala lifted her hand and looked at the diamond sparkling so brightly on her third finger. And wondered how in the world she was going to tell Will that she could not wear his ring. She could not wear his ring, she would never have his children and she could not marry him.

She wrenched away from him and ran blindly toward the stairs.

"Nuala!" Will was after her like a shot out of a cannon. Her feet clattered on the bare wood; his clattered after her. As they reached the top, Amos Thorpe opened the bathroom door and strolled out. He was several yards down the hall, but he waved and called cheerily, "G'night. See you in the morning." He went in his room and closed the door.

Will and Nuala stood for an indecisive moment, listening to the plumbing play its inevitable *1812 Overture.*

"Come into my room," urged Will. He noticed that she had pulled the ring from her finger and was holding it in her trembling hand.

When she didn't answer, he opened the door of his room and pulled her inside.

"Now, suppose you let me tell you what I have in mind," he said. Nuala still held the ring in her hand, but she had stopped trembling. He wanted nothing more than to reassure her about the kind of life they would lead together.

"What I've been thinking about," Will said, leading her to the bed and easing her down beside him, "is what Sam said. You know, about entertaining people with our ghost stories and providing a real ghost as the climax to the evening. What better way could there be to turn this house's biggest liability into an out-and-out asset?"

"Oh, Will," she said.

He wrapped his long arms around her and leaned back against the pillows. His dark eyes were only inches from hers, and they were earnest and bright with new ideas.

"Think, Nuala," he said. "There's lots of river lore surrounding the St. Johns and its environs. Lots of stories about loggers and love gone wrong and juke joints where men and women fell in love. Riverboat stories, and stories about the rich people who came here to fish and hunt along the picturesque St. Johns River."

"Will, can't you understand that—" She didn't know exactly where all this was leading. She only knew that she couldn't be a part of it.

"Wait a minute, let me finish. Why, Beckman knows scores of tales, tales he heard when he was a riverboat captain himself. He even knows the stories Captain William Anthony told, and from what I've heard, there's nothing to match them for sheer excitement. And no place in Florida is anything like this area, with its deep freshwater springs and its hanging Spanish moss and its abundance of wildlife. There's still solitude here, and people aren't crowding each other like they are in the southern part of the state."

She was captivated by his earnestness; when he looked at her for approval, she nodded slightly. He seemed to take heart from this and plunged on.

"I've got this old boardinghouse, which my ancestor refuses to have sold out of the family, and you're a storyteller of great renown, and together we're becoming sensational cooks. Now what does it all add up to?" Will fairly glowed with excitement.

"Life savoring?" ventured Nuala.

He sat up and stared at her as though she were a genius.

"Exactly. A place to savor life. As Captain William Anthony and his guests savored it so long ago. A new concept for Anthony House, one that I think would meet with my great-grandfather's approval."

By this time, Nuala was feeling as though this whole concept was getting away from her. Will had somehow made all these plans—and he had mistakenly included her.

"We'd reopen the boardinghouse, only this time we advertise it as a place with a gimmick. A little refurbishing here and there—I'm pretty handy with paint and tools, you know—and we'd advertise in upscale magazines, like *Town & Country, Southern Living.*"

"You don't mean you're really thinking of what Sam was talking about—some kind of campaign for people to spend a weekend in the country with a ghost!"

"I think Sam is right—some people would travel anywhere to be part of a real ghost story. There's a place in the North Carolina mountains—an old inn, as I recall—that stages a fake murder mystery every so often and charges each guest five hundred dollars for the three days! We could easily accommodate thirty guests here, with room to spare."

"You'd want to accommodate thirty guests every weekend? Will, that's a lot of eggs Benedict!" Despite herself, she was drawn into his plans. His enthusiasm was contagious.

"No, we could have guests, oh, say, only one or two weekends a month and still produce a tidy income. You'd tell the ghost stories, stories about the surrounding area, stories with a basis in fact. We'd add Beckman for a little local color—he'd love it, especially if he could dress up in his old riverboat captain's uniform. The climax of the evening would be Captain William Anthony's nocturnal ramble down the stairs. At midnight, we'd offer a sumptuous buffet, and after a day of long walks in the woods, guided canoe trips down the St. Johns, delicious gourmet-style meals prepared by you and me and our handpicked staff, our guests would wander off to their bedchambers for a good night's sleep. Hopefully undisturbed," he added thoughtfully.

"That's just it. How do we know Captain Anthony would cooperate by continuing his walk down the stairs every night at eleven or so? And how do we know that he won't try running all over the house at odd hours?"

"He's embarked on his late-night ramblings every time the house has been put up for sale, and the way Beckman tells it, it's always been at eleven o'clock at night. My guess is that as long as the For Sale sign is in the front yard, the captain will stick around, and probably at the same time every night. And since according to Beckman, the captain always loved a good story, don't you think he'll approve of what we want to do with this house?" Will grinned at her.

"But what about your plans to go back to Chapel Hill and the university?"

"I'm so interested in writing this magazine article about monarch butterflies that I'd rather try my hand at doing that first. And maybe I'd like to tackle another textbook about them—this one with a broader appeal than the last. The academic life has begun to pall, anyway. I'm ready for a new beginning, Nuala. I can't think of a better place to write another book than Anthony House."

"What about your novel?"

"I want you to read it as soon as I get it back from the typist. I hope you'll think it's as good as I think it is. But my writing career has to have variety, Nuala. I expect to keep up with my scientific writing, too. This new article I'm doing about monarchs is a good opportunity to ease back into it."

"When there weren't any guests in residence, you'd be writing?"

"When there aren't any guests, the two of us will be living here together, free to do whatever else we choose. You could take in a few craft fairs now and then and tell your stories to the children who love them so well. And yes, I could work on my writing."

"I see," Nuala said, beguiled by the charm that such a life would offer. Her stories, Will's writing, their friends, this spacious old house by the peaceful St. Johns—it would all be too perfect.

"You see, my darling, how wonderful it could be. Just the two of us—and Cole, of course—and later, plenty of room for children. *Our* children, Nuala. Oh, Nuala, can't you see? It's meant to be. Let's get married, Nuala. Let's get married and live happily ever after."

She rolled across the bed, away from him.

"Nuala?" He was stunned to see the mixture of emotions flitting across her face—denial, despair and, unbelievable to him when he knew how much she loved him, anger.

Inwardly he cursed himself for not handling this with more aplomb. He should have embellished this proposal of marriage with the words a woman would want to hear. But he wasn't that type of guy. "We love each other, Nuala," he said softly.

"Limerence," she corrected with a nervous laugh. "It's only limerence."

"Love," he insisted. "I love you."

Will was talking, running on in a reasoning tone. She wanted to stop him from saying all the things he was saying. She wanted to stop him because all the things he was saying were true.

"I know you love me, Nuala. It's in the way you look at me, in the way you talk to me, in the way you respond to me, both in bed and out. Look at me, Nuala," he said, putting his hand to the side of her face when she would have turned her head way. Her skin was rose-petal soft; her eyes looked as though they held her very soul.

"You love me, Nuala," he said. "I won't let you deny it."

His hard warm palm cupped her face, and his fingers splayed to caress her earlobe. She realized in that instant that she couldn't deny her love for him; it was emotionally impossible for her to do so. How barren her life had become in terms of human relationships! And it was barren no more. She might have to leave, she might never marry him—but she had to tell him she loved him. If only this once.

"Yes, Will," she said, her heart aching. "I do love you. I love you very much."

Slowly he eased himself closer to her and enfolded her in his arms. He pressed his face to hers and held her as one would hold something precious and dear. He listened to her heart beating in time with his. She seemed to melt in his arms; he could feel all the stiffness and strain flowing out of her. Just when he thought it was going to be all right, she jumped up and ran to the window, where she stood with her head bowed. The dark red ripples of hair spilled over her shoulders, beautiful hair. Beautiful shoulders. Beautiful Nuala.

"I—I can't marry you, Will." She was balanced on a keen edge of despair. He wanted promises she couldn't give, promises she couldn't keep.

How could she tell him the real reason she didn't want to settle down? That she could never bear his children?

She couldn't stand it if the light in his eyes were to turn to rejection. No, better to keep her own counsel. Better to move on, to be the one to leave. Not the one who was left.

"We're part of each other's life now, Nuala," he said tenderly, close behind her. "You can't deny that."

"No," she said, not even wanting to. They were part of each other's life. She had let it happen, even though she shouldn't have, but at least she knew that they were part of each other's life only for now. It could not and would not go on.

He stood and went to her, hesitating only briefly. Then he put his arms around her from behind and rested his chin on top of her head. Their reflection stared back at them from the dark window, and to look at it broke Nuala's heart. There had never been anyone more right for her than Will Anthony—never. Certainly not Joe Morini. What they had shared didn't even come close to what she had with Will.

Will turned Nuala around to face him. "If it's time you want, you can have time," he said carefully.

She buried her face in his chest, inhaling what she had grown to know as the scent of him, loving him so much that she'd rather die than leave him.

"I'm sorry, Will," she said in a low tone. "Time won't help. I can't marry you. I told you in the beginning I would never stay."

She reached for his hand, opened it, and put the beautiful engagement ring in it. Then she carefully closed his fingers over it.

She lifted her head to see Will's face go completely white.

"You can't be saying this," he said, unclenching his fist and staring at the ring. She could tell from the expression on his face that he was tied in knots, and she longed to soften the blow. Unfortunately, she knew from experience there was no way to soften such a crippling blow. She had suffered such a blow once herself. She had hoped to spare Will. Her cheeks ached with dammed-up tears.

He dragged in a long breath. "I thought we meant something to each other," Will said desperately.

She could not reply to this. Forever afterward, she knew, she would awaken on various lonely nights in strange towns and lie awake immobilized by guilt. Guilt for letting Will think she might change her mind and settle down with him. Guilt for letting him know she loved him.

She sighed heavily. "I'll stay to help you with the Thorpes until they leave," she told him calmly. "Then I'll be going, too, Will."

"What is it, some inborn wanderlust?" His words shot at her, sharp as bullets. Will looked completely distraught, as though he might tear out of the room and out of the house. She almost wished he would so that she wouldn't have to see the raw, uncomprehending pain on his face.

"Call it that if you like," she said softly. Inside, she was shaken deeply. She felt as though her heart—and yes, her soul, too—were being slowly torn asunder.

"We get along so well. If there were ever any two people who were more perfect for one another, I don't know who they could be." His dark eyes had dulled, and he seemed to be extending a great effort to keep them focused on her face. He was hurting inside.

She forced herself to look into his eyes as a painful object lesson for herself, something to remember if she were ever tempted again to fall in love with a man. *As*

if there could ever be anyone like Will Anthony again,
she thought blindly. She knew that in giving him up, she
was giving up all hope of finding the ideal man for her.
Will Anthony was that ideal man, the other half of what
could have been a perfect whole.

And then he lashed out at her, totally unexpectedly,
his face twisting in fury.

"You're the original flutterby, you know it, Nuala?
You're just like a damned butterfly, fluttering about
with no discernible pattern. Just light here, light there,
then pick up and flutter blithely away, not caring what
you've started. A flutterby princess, that's what you
are!"

His words stunned her, because Will so seldom
showed anger. And to have it directed starkly at her, and
rightly so, made her feel as though she had been stabbed
through the heart. For one long terrible moment, Will
stood before her, white-faced and accusing, and then he
flung himself from the room, slamming the door behind him.

Chapter Fourteen

She heard him running down the front stairs, heard the front door open and slam. It was Christmas night, and Will was going out alone in the dark, and she couldn't let him do that. She had no idea what he would do to himself. She couldn't imagine where he would go.

The relentless fury of his accusations echoed inside her brain, and before she knew it she was running after him. On the front porch she saw no sign of him, and she stood for a moment hugging herself against the biting cold. Frost was expected that night; neither one of them wore any protection against it. They could not stay out here long in this weather.

Then she saw him halfway across the front yard, futilely trying to stick the fallen pink plastic flamingo back into the boggy ground. She walked toward him, brushing aside the damp trailing tentacles of moss hanging from the trees, not knowing what they would say to each other, only knowing that something must be said.

"I don't know who put this stupid flamingo up here in the first place," complained Will, giving up on it and tossing it down on the ground. He sounded dejected, but he was no longer angry. Seldom angry, Will didn't know how to hold on to anger when he felt it. Now he

only felt foolish for his outburst. Still hurt, of course—
hurt forever and always because Nuala did not love him
enough to stay with him. Because she didn't love him
enough to be his wife.

Nuala looked down at the flamingo, to her a symbol
of Anthony House since that first night when she had
approached the house in the storm. She couldn't stand
to see it fallen in the mud. To Nuala, the grinning pink
flamingo was part of Anthony House. Yes, it was tacky;
yes, it was dumb; but it belonged here. She couldn't
imagine the house without it. Just as she couldn't imagine the house without the ghost. Or without her.

She picked the ugly plastic bird up from the muddy
ground, getting her hands and skirt soiled in the process. "You can't get rid of the flamingo," she said simply and matter-of-factly. She stuck its one leg down into
the ground, and miraculously, it stayed. She brushed a
bit of dirt off its flouncy pink plastic tail. "There," she
said. "It belongs here." She looked down at her hands.
The palms were caked with mud.

Will took her both hands in his, ignoring the mud.
"So do you belong here, Nuala," Will said. "If I could
pick you up as easily as you picked up that flamingo, if
I could push one of your legs down into my front yard
and expect you to stay, that's what I'd do."

"Flutterbies don't act like flamingos," she said.

"That's true," he replied. "But I've spent most of my
life studying the migration patterns of monarchs. Do
you think there's a chance I might be able to catch on
to the migration patterns of flutterby princesses?"

She loved him. She loved him so much that she could
not stand it. She loved him so much that she would not
want to go on living if she couldn't spend the rest of her

life with him. She loved him so much that she was willing to face the rejection.

Once the decision was made, it was made with lightning swiftness. She would tell him the thing she thought she would never tell any other man. Because with Will Anthony, it would be different.

Nuala shrugged her shoulders and smiled up at him. The dirt gritted between their palms, but she squeezed his hands anyway. She supposed gritty palms weren't very romantic when one was about to accept a marriage proposal, but then nothing had gone the way it was supposed to go between the two of them from the very beginning.

"I'd like to talk about it," she said, looking up at his dear bearded face, all angles and smiles. "But I don't want to freeze my tail off while we're having our little discussion."

"Won't you step into my parlor?" Will said, making a deep bow in the direction of the open front door. The lights of the Christmas tree winked inside.

"Said the spider to the fly?" answered Nuala, heading for the house and its warmth at a speed approaching a gallop.

Will had to run to keep up with her. He would run to keep up with her for the rest of their lives if he had to.

"Said the spider to the flutterby," he said, as he held the front door open for her. "To my dear, darling flutterby princess."

They headed instinctively for the kitchen, which for them had always been the center of the house. They stood together and washed their gritty hands at the kitchen sink.

"This time *I'll* make the hot chocolate," Nuala said, putting on the kettle.

"Once upon a time," said Cole, who seemed to be enjoying the luxury of his uncovered new brass cage, "in a land far away."

"Do you want me to cover his cage?" Will asked.

"No," said Nuala, sitting down at the kitchen table. "Because the story I have to tell you happened once upon a time, in a land far away. And Cole was part of it—he was a gift from my fiancé."

"Would you mind waiting a minute?" Will said, jumping to his feet. "I seem to have forgotten something."

"I'm about to unburden my soul and you are going to run out of the room?" Nuala said in disbelief.

"I wouldn't if it wasn't important," Will apologized over his shoulder, jogging up the back stairs. He dug around in his top dresser drawer until he found it, the little velvet box, and he put the ring that Nuala had refused back inside it. He spared a look at the closed door of the Thorpes' room. Thank goodness all seemed to be quiet on that front. At least he would not have Amos and Lorraine wandering in on this version of his marriage proposal, which was a good thing, because this time he was determined to get it right.

He raced downstairs again. Nuala looked distinctly unsettled when he returned.

"All right, my darling," he said, pulling her to her feet. He kissed her, the kind of kiss you see in the movies. A fervent, heartfelt kiss. There was an unfamiliar bulge in his shirt pocket. Nuala had a pretty good idea what it was.

They sat back down at the kitchen table. Will's kitchen table was not a romantic spot, but then, it had its memories. The first night, when Will had served Nuala hot water because he had spilled the last packet of hot chocolate. That memorable breakfast the next morning, when they had eaten liverwurst on celery. Considering all this, the kitchen table was as romantic a spot as they needed.

"I was engaged," Nuala said, by way of preliminaries.

Will shrugged. "I wasn't," he said. He grinned at her, glad he'd told her about Virginia and that Nuala understood that whatever he and Virginia had together, it wasn't the real thing. So now Nuala was going to tell him about her past. He'd wondered about it often enough. This was all well and good. Whatever it was, it couldn't be all that bad. He wouldn't let it be all that bad.

"Will, this is serious," she said, and from the quiver of her bottom lip, he knew she meant it.

"I love you, Nuala," he told her, wiping the grin off his face.

"That is irrelevant."

"Maybe not. Because whatever you are going to tell me, I love you. I will love you no matter what. I will love you for all time. So go ahead and tell me whatever it is that will unburden your soul, and then let's go make love."

"Will! I am *serious*!"

"All right, all right. Tell me."

"I was engaged to a man named Joe Morini. It was three years ago, when I still lived in Rhode Island, working as a librarian. Joe was from a big Sicilian family. He wanted a big family. He loved kids. So do I. We were going to get married and have lots of little Morinis. All his Sicilian pride was wrapped up in having the tangible proof of his manhood that our children would be." She faltered for a moment, remembering. She'd always seen them as stair steps, those future children, a line of eight or ten curly, dark-haired kids with button eyes like Pinocchio. Well, maybe one little girl who had long dark hair with a hint of red in the ripples and with wide blue-violet eyes.

"Go on," said Will, his eyes taking on a steely glitter, almost as though he could guess what had happened.

"So—so I was going to give him children. Many children. I learned to cook Sicilian food and I was studying his religion, and I had chosen my china pattern and my silver pattern and my crystal. I was starry-eyed and romantic over Joe and our anticipated life together as only one who has been reared on fairy tales can be, and the wedding was only a few months away and—"

"And what, Nuala?"

"And I had been having abdominal pains, Will, for most of my adult life, but it seemed connected with my time of the month, and I saw no real reason to be concerned. But the pains got worse, and I went to the doctor for my premarital checkup, and when he examined me he wanted to do a laparoscopy. It's just a simple diagnostic procedure, the doctor said, done through a tiny incision in the abdomen. And so I had the laparoscopy, thinking that everything would be all right, and the doctor diagnosed advanced endometriosis."

"Endometriosis? What's that?"

"It's a growth of the endometrium, the lining of the uterus, which builds up and sheds each month, only in endometriosis, for some reason, the endometrium develops outside the uterus. No one knows why—it's a very puzzling disease. The growths can cause pain, infertility and other problems. In my case, the endometriosis was so widespread on my reproductive organs that the usual treatments, such as removal of the growths and hormonal treatment, were of no help.''

''You mean there's no cure for endometriosis?''

''The only definitive cure is removal of the uterus and the ovaries. And that is what had to be done to me.'' Her eyes, deep blue shadowed pools of pain, met his levelly.

''You can't have children,'' Will said. ''Is that what you're telling me?''

She had dreaded this moment. She had never dreamed that she could ever tell another man about this particular shortcoming of hers again. But she was.

''Yes,'' she whispered. ''I can never have children. Never, Will.''

''And Morini? What did he say about this?'' The words stabbed out in sharp staccato syllables, and Will leaned forward in his chair, his eyebrows drawn together. A muscle she had never noticed before twitched in his eyelid.

''He said one word. 'Goodbye.' '' The tears hung on her lower lashes before trickling down her cheeks.

Will was out of his chair like a shot, was kneeling beside her, was gathering her tenderly into his arms before she knew what was happening.

''The stupid fool,'' he muttered against her hair.

She was crying openly now, clinging to him. ''He wanted children, you see,'' she sobbed. ''I couldn't give them to him. I thought everything would be all right. He was a very modern Sicilian; I thought he had left all the old ways behind him and that he'd get over wanting to have babies of his own. He was nice to me while I was in the hospital. He took very good care of me while I recuperated from my hysterectomy.''

"Nuala, if you're uncomfortable—" Will whispered.

"No, I haven't ever talked about it, and I want to, oh, I want to so much. After Joe broke our engagement, I was in a state of shock for months. I sold everything I owned and bought the hearse from an ex-hippie friend and left Rhode Island and never looked back, but I can talk about it now, with you," she said.

"What I was getting at is that you're about to fall out of that chair and maybe we could find a more comfortable place to conduct this conversation," said Will, kissing away a tear that was headed toward her chin.

She laughed through her tears, then cried some more, then slid gracefully out of the chair until she was draped across Will's lap on the floor.

"Better?" she said.

"Better," he affirmed, leaning back against the sturdy leg of the kitchen table and cradling her in his arms.

"And so this Morini took very good care of you while you recuperated from your hysterectomy," prompted Will.

"Yes, and after my six-weeks checkup, when the doctor said everything was fine and we could go ahead with the wedding whenever we were ready, Joe took me out to dinner at a fancy restaurant with a menu in French and waiters all dressed in those tuxedos they wear. Joe ordered all the right wines and everything, and I thought we were celebrating my return to health, and then he told me that he wouldn't marry me. Couldn't marry me, because I couldn't give him children. Having children was so tied up with his own macho image of himself, his family's image of him as a

real man, that he couldn't imagine going through life
without having his own children.''

"Joe Morini, the moron,'' said Will in disgust.

"Oh, I was devastated. He was my life. I loved him.
I had to give up my dreams not only of the family we
had hoped to have but also of being Joe's wife. I almost went out of my mind, Will.''

He held her even closer, unable to comprehend how
a man could shut Nuala out of his life for any reason,
especially that one.

"I felt like less of a woman. I felt completely unde-
sirable. I couldn't let myself love any man again, because I couldn't bear to see that look on a man's face
again when I told him I couldn't bear his children.''

Will edged away from her slightly. "Look at *my* face,
Nuala. Do you see that look? Do you honestly think
that having children is more important to me than having you for my very own, forever and ever?''

She saw the same love on Will's face that had always
been there, the same lips that curved so easily in
amusement, the same loving expression in his beautiful
dark eyes.

"My love for you, Nuala, is real and warm and for
you, just the way you are. Of course, I'm sad for you
when I think of all you've been through. My heart aches
when I think of how unhappy you must have been when
you knew you could never have children. But marry me,
Nuala. If we can't have our kids, lepidopt.''

She stared. "How can you make jokes, Will Anthony, about something as serious as this!''

"Because I want you to know that having our own
kids is not that important to me. Sure, I would have
liked to, but we'll adopt children if we really want them.
I'd love to do that. And anyway, you've been too seri-

ous about this for too long. Our love is leavened by a sense of humor. And don't you ever forget it!'' He kissed her gently on the lips.

''I guess your Will Anthony theory number one is again proved right,'' Nuala said. ''Nothing ever turns out the way you expect.''

''You're a smart girl, Nuala, although it took you an awfully long time to catch on. Oh, and while we're at it,'' he said, fumbling in his pocket and pulling out the little velvet box. He snapped it open and the ring fell on the floor.

''This isn't exactly your average ordinary proposal,'' he said. ''Would you mind reaching over there and picking up your engagement ring? With you on my lap, I just can't seem to manage it.''

She reached out and plucked the diamond solitaire off the floor. ''Am I supposed to put it on your finger, or are you supposed to put it on mine?'' she teased.

''I had rather pictured it on yours, but since you're the one holding it . . .'' he said, extending his pinkie finger.

Nuala slipped the ring on Will's finger. ''It's a perfect fit,'' she said, regarding it critically. ''And it's a lovely ring, too.''

''You don't think it's too conventional?'' he said anxiously, looking at the way the diamond twinkled below his hairy knuckle.

''No,'' she said. ''I'm going to start living a more conventional life anyway. I wonder if Beckman still has that wedding dress he found in the dumpster.''

Will laughed at that. She loved the way he laughed, the way he always put his whole heart into it. ''Somehow, getting married in a wedding dress found in a dumpster and settling down in an old haunted house with a lepidopterist who wants to operate a distinctly unconventional boardinghouse does not sound conventional to me,'' he told her.

Nuala allowed him to nuzzle the soft spot below her right ear. ''If we want to have the wedding at eleven o'clock at night,'' she said, ''I bet we could get Captain William Anthony to walk me down the stairs.''

''If you don't mind, I'd rather not have him horning in on our wedding. I'm sure Beckman would be delighted to do the honors.''

''Mmm,'' agreed Nuala dreamily. ''I'd like to get married in view of the river. Just beyond the magnolia tree and the sundial. On a very sunny afternoon. Next week.''

''That's extremely agreeable to me, darling, and then there's the matter of our honeymoon,'' he added. ''Since you love surprises.''

She groaned. ''I'm not sure I can stand any more surprises tonight,'' she said.

''You know that magazine editor who wants me to write the article about monarchs? Well, he's so eager for me to accept the assignment that he's thrown in a trip to the Sierra Madres in Mexico. This is the time of year when the monarchs are wintering there, and I've always wanted to see them. They blanket acres of trees on the mountainside. They must be beautiful, Nuala, and they'll be so much more beautiful for me if we can see them together. It'll be our honeymoon, our flutterby honeymoon.'' Clumsily, because his arms were still wrapped around her, he removed the diamond solitaire from his little finger.

When he transferred it to Nuala's ring finger, there were tears in her eyes.

"This makes it an official engagement," he warned, warming her with his smile. "But you haven't officially agreed to marry me. All I've heard so far is just a bunch of speculation. Marry me, Nuala. Please say you will."

She brushed the tears from her eyes. There would be no more sad tears from now on. The only tears to fall from her eyes would be the happy kind.

"Will I or won't I?" she said playfully, captivated by sparkle of the diamond on her third finger, left hand.

"*I* Will. You Nuala. And I Nuala time that you would."

She laughed, all her barriers tumbled by this sweet and gentle man. No longer was she a flutterby, lighting here, lighting there, afraid to stay in one place too long. Now Nuala was a butterfly, and with Will Anthony's love, she was ready to soar.

"What a *guy*!" said Cole, hopping to his perch and regarding the kissing couple with bright eyes.

"What a *guy*!" echoed Nuala, settling herself as comfortably as she could in the arms of a man who was propped against the leg of a kitchen table and seemed disinclined to move until he had kissed her very, very thoroughly.

Epilogue

One Year Later

"Our guests are ready, Nuala," Will said, peering around the corner of their bedroom door.

Nuala was standing in front of the dresser fluffing her long dark hair with a brush. The dresser was one of the pieces of furniture that Will had refinished with Beckman's help.

She smoothed the high lacy collar at her throat and pinned on a cameo brooch that had belonged to Will's mother.

"You look wonderfully ethereal," Will said, closing the door behind him and taking her in his arms. "And you feel wonderfully solid and real."

She lifted her face to be kissed and slid her arms around his neck, where they rested lightly at the nape. They had been married a year, but whenever he took her in his arms it was as though everything was fresh and new again.

"Have you lit the candles in the parlor?"

"Yes, and Beckman is posted at the doorway in his riverboat captain's uniform. I keep telling him that he's going to make a terrific honorary grandfather."

"It may be years before he gets the chance," cautioned Nuala. "You know what the social worker from the adoption agency said."

"Yes, but I have no doubt that Beckman will be around for quite a while. He'll dote on our new little son or daughter, you wait and see."

"Son or daughter—which do you think it'll be?" asked Nuala.

"Maybe one of each, if we luck out and get twins."

Nuala laughed. "I can hardly wait."

Will kissed her lightly on the cheek. "Neither can our guests. One lady keeps asking me questions about the ghost. 'Will Captain Anthony talk to us, do you think?' she says. 'Does he ever wander around other parts of the house?' I told her that some of the guests claim to have seen him standing by the stuffed alligator, and that seemed to satisfy her."

"Are the refreshments ready?" Nuala asked.

"An assortment of sandwiches is waiting under a tea towel in the refrigerator, three salads are arranged artfully on the dining room table and four lavish desserts decorate the sideboard. Next time we do this, let's get more of that good roast beef you found in the new butcher shop in Osofkee. It makes wonderful sandwiches, and they'll go fast."

"Okay," Nuala said.

"By the way, I repaired the leaky faucet in the downstairs bathroom, but water mess it made!"

"Well, well, what a deep subject," murmured Nuala.

"In fact, I pail at the thought of going on with it," said Will. "Come on, Nuala."

With a swish of her long silk skirt, Nuala smilingly swept out the door ahead of him, and hand in hand they went to greet their guests.

They'd been running Anthony House in its present incarnation since last fall, at the start of the tourist season. Months had been spent peeling off old wallpaper and replacing it with new, repainting, replacing the old furniture and hanging new curtains. The big advance from Will's novel, which was to be published next year, had gone a long way to help with expenses.

Now Anthony Guest House shone anew, again dominating the bluff on the St. Johns River as it had in days of old. The pink flamingo still stood sentinel in the front yard, and a discreet For Sale sign was tacked to the front porch, just to ensure the continued presence of Captain William Anthony's ghost. Will had had the telephone reinstalled, and following their advertisements in various magazines and newspapers, it began to ring with regularity.

"What exactly *is* a Ghost Weekend?" their prospective guests wanted to know, and so Will or Nuala would explain, taking care to elaborate on the peace and serenity of the setting, the careful refurbishing of the old inn. And when they mentioned Nuala's storytelling skills, the prospective guests would invariably make reservations.

Will and Nuala hosted one Ghost Weekend a month, which gave Will plenty of time to work on the scientific articles he was writing now. Nuala still worked craft fairs as long as they didn't conflict with the Ghost Weekends.

So far, Captain William Anthony had never disappointed them. He continued his plodding walk downstairs every night at eleven o'clock, as if on cue.

Tonight Nuala paused in the doorway of the parlor and counted their guests. There were nineteen of them, young and old, rich and not-so-rich, all of them eyeing her expectantly as she made her way carefully to the big armchair where she liked to sit when entertaining them with one of her favorite ghost stories.

"The story I am going to tell you tonight," she said in her lovely musical voice, "is the story of Lily Ann. It's a tale that our present ghost, Captain William Anthony himself, used to tell his guests years and years ago, right here at Anthony House.

"One night in 1918, the captain was driving in his car to Osofkee to play cards with a group of friends. It was a dark and moonless night; the wind swayed the Spanish moss in the live oak trees. Out in the middle of nowhere on the long and lonely country road, the captain suddenly braked to a stop. A girl—a young girl dressed in a flowing white dress—was walking at the side of the road.

"'May I drive you someplace?' he asked her.

"'I'm on the way to visit my sister in Osofkee,' she told him.

"'Where does your sister live?' he asked.

"'She lives at 112 Palmetto Street,' replied the girl.

"'That's right on my way,' said Captain Anthony. 'Won't you let me drive you?' He was thinking at the time that the girl, who was young enough to be his granddaughter, had no business walking on this lonely road after dark.

"So the girl climbed into the car, but she refused to sit in the front seat with him. Instead, she insisted on sitting in the back seat. The captain didn't object, because he understood that she might be shy or frightened of him.

"They talked for a time, just general conversation about the weather and so on, but soon the conversation stopped. When she grew quiet, the captain thought that she had probably dozed off, because her voice had been getting progressively weaker as they talked.

"The captain drove until he reached Palmetto Street, and he glanced behind him, thinking he would need to awaken the young girl. Imagine his amazement when there was no one there!

"He was actually shaking when he opened the car door and looked on the floor, but there was no sign of the girl. He knew he would have known if she had jumped out anywhere along the way, and he simply couldn't understand where she might have gone.

"He went up the walk to the house at 112 Palmetto, where the girl had told him she was going, and knocked on the door. An elderly woman answered his knock and listened as the captain expressed his consternation at what had happened.

" 'Do not be alarmed,' said the lady. 'The girl is my sister Lily Ann. She died forty years ago when she was very young. You are the tenth person to give her a ride in from the country; each time she has disappeared before she reached my house. Today is her birthday.' "

When Nuala finished telling the story as related to her by Beckman, the room was silent.

And then she said, " 'Clearly William Anthony himself was no stranger to ghosts. I like to think that he returns here every night to check on his beloved inn. And if you will all follow me into the foyer, you'll have a chance to listen to him make his way down the front staircase."

She led the way, and they waited expectantly. Will came in from the kitchen and slid an arm around her waist, and then they heard the muffled crash in the attic. The clock in the study chimed eleven, and finally the plodding footsteps began.

"Just think," Will whispered very quietly so as not to disturb the enjoyment of their guests, "pretty soon it won't be just plodding footsteps on our front staircase—it'll be the pitter-patter of tiny feet as well."

Nuala grinned up at her husband. "I can only think that Captain Anthony will approve," she whispered back. "More little Anthonys can only mean that this house will remain in the family for a long, long time."

Did they imagine it, or did the cool draft sweeping down the length of the staircase suddenly turn warm as it blew across their upturned faces, as though old Captain Anthony were signifying his approval?

Readers rave about
Harlequin American Romance!

"...the best series of modern romances
I have read...great, exciting, stupendous,
wonderful."
—*S.E., Coweta, Oklahoma*

"...they are absolutely fantastic...going to be
a smash hit and hard to keep on the
bookshelves."
—*P.D., Easton, Pennsylvania*

"The American line is great. I've enjoyed
every one I've read so far."
—*W.M.K., Lansing, Illinois*

"...the best stories I have read in a long
time."
—*R.H., Northport, New York*

Names available on request.

Harlequin American Romance

COMING NEXT MONTH

185 STORMWALKER by Dallas Schulze

Sara Grant chose the wrong time to lie when she insisted that she knew all about horses and hiking. She badgered Cody Wolf into taking her on his search for the downed Cessna in the Rocky Mountains and Sara's missing nephew. Unfortunately she then had to prove she could be just as tough as her surefooted, half-Indian companion.

86 BODY AND SOUL by Anne McAllister

Her mother had always said that disasters come in threes, and now Susan Rivers could attest to it. First her teenaged brother was thrust upon her for the summer. Then, she was evicted. And when Susan finally found another apartment in southern California, the unspeakable happened: Miles Cavanaugh moved in next door.

187 ROUGE'S BARGAIN by Cathy Gillen Thacker

Only a scoundrel like Ben McCauley would have promised Lindsey Halloran three weeks of work on the idyllic island of Maui and then asked her to play a starring role in a high-stakes vendetta against a business rival. Pretending to go along with Ben's elaborate scheme, she plotted to beat the master at his own game. But what she didn't plan on was Ben's irresistible manly charm.

188 A MATTER OF TIME by Noreen Brownlie

Jennifer Bradford thought that stress was an acceptable hazard of her job as a magazine editor in Los Angeles—that is until Dr. Julian Caldicott diagnosed her severe "type A" behavior. Although she resisted the efforts of the enticing doctor to defuse her, what should have been a simple procedure turned into a battle of wits and wills . . . and much more.